SCALES

AMITY GREEN

Petrichor Press

BOOK 1 OF THE FATE AND FIRE SERIES
AMITY GREEN

Reprint. Original publication Black Bed Sheet Books 2013

Printed in the United States

Published by Petrichor Press

❀ Created with Vellum

For my brother. Eris semper in corde meo.

ACKNOWLEDGMENTS

Gratitude to the CSFWG for their faith and counsel. Special thanks to Mike Reid, Hollie Snider, and Henry Snider. Thanks and love to my beautiful, patient children.

FATE AND FIRE

Change is Fate's little sister. Fate and I shared a long, hateful history, where Change and I were virtual strangers. Change can make you or break you, just like Fate. I've let them do both. The trick is to embrace what they bring.

I was nineteen the first time I killed another person. Blood dripped from my claws, and I just stared as he went. I stood over him, watching his paling face while sight left his eyes, breath left his lungs and his soul went straight to hell.

There'd been a time when I didn't even like to watch such scenes play out in a movie.

Change played time like a fiddle while Fate watched me dance.

I hated to love my new life. Most nights I raged inside. Some nights I remembered the girl I was in another lifetime—a pastel-tinted, musical, lonely life in the sunshine. Those times were a few short months ago that felt like decades on the day. Sometimes I wondered if my new way of life was also my own, personal brand of mourning for the girl I used to be. . .

And then I was set free.

CHAPTER 1

I should have known my first trip out of Austin would turn my life upside down and nearly get me killed twice in the first year. I didn't have one of those cushy lives some kids did, where the biggest worry was whether they'd get into their dream college, so why should the rest of my life be easy?

The sourest lemons can make the sweetest lemonade. The time wasn't all bad even if I spent most of it looking over my shoulder. I'll be hypervigilant for eternity. Outrunning Fate will do that to a girl. The problem is, Fate is fast and stealthy, and fights dirtier than death. I adapted and grew, learning to face wonder with a true smile and death with a steely, locked jaw. I could never return to Austin, but when I first left, I couldn't wait to get out. Looking back, I'd still choose to leave, despite near death. I should have expected it to be a train wreck. I should have known.

The first thought I had when the jumbo jet's engines whined and we took off from Austin was that I wanted to spray the guy next to me with Febreze. I fidgeted, wondering if someone in the plane might want to switch seats. Every seat was full. The middle aged wannabe hipster guy next to me smelled like armpit and moth balls, which gave my stomach one more reason to get all knotted up. I thought he was going to get chatty when he first claimed his seat but he'd caught my uninterested vibe quickly and zonked out hard instead. The only thing lively about him was the stench. Calm, cool breaths didn't do their job when they were laced with body odor.

A flight to London from Austin, Texas is a long one. That kind of time allows the mind to travel as far as the body. I didn't have a window seat and my stomach didn't do well if I tried to read for long so I watched across the aisle as clouds overtook the view and there was nothing left to see. The sole of my shoe popped softly as I fidgeted, rubbing my feet together. The older lady who sat on the other side of my seat glanced at my shoes when the popping sounded again. I took my hair out of the ponytail and put my seat back to try and relax.

I was grateful for the time to reflect on the events of my last few days in the United States, although thinking about it stung like I'd been bitten by a fire ant. I'd left for good reasons. They were hard memories I'd done my best to make smaller and smaller, but like the tiny ants in the South, sometimes the little things packed the biggest punch. I just wanted to get the hell out of Austin and far away from the past eighteen years of my life. Seeing how I was almost nineteen, I was ready for new experiences.

As long as I could remember, I'd overheated when my emotions got the best of me so true to form, I was melting from the inside out. My hair grew damp so I twisted it all up into a bun to get it off my neck. I kept catching my jaw locking up, and sweat beaded down the valley of my chest, soaking my bra. I hated that.

A brochure about Beautiful Scotland hung out of the seat pocket so I snatched it up and fanned myself. Moving the air did wonders, both cooling my soaked face and pushing putrid air off Mr. Hipster and out into the aisle instead of up my nose.

"A little motion sickness?" An attendant pushed a strand of grey hair behind an ear and thrust a can of ginger ale into my hand, sans little cup of ice. She didn't wait for an answer, just reached across me and turned a nozzle above us. Chilled, canned air blasted right onto my drenched forehead.

"Thank you. I don't know why I didn't think of that." I really knew why. I'd never been on a plane before. She didn't need that information, though, because I planned to hold the appearance of a cool, well-traveled young lady for the duration of my trip to study in England.

The attendant smiled with red, stained lips, like she didn't believe a word of it and bustled away. I closed my eyes and concentrated on calming down and cooling off.

The hipster yawned, smacked his lips and adjusted in his seat, leaving his greasy head full of shaggy curls resting on my shoulder and his mouth wide open.

"Hell no, buddy," I said. I shrugged hard, jolting him awake.

He sat up, looking at me like I had two heads while he straightened his black framed glasses. Considering how I'd nearly snapped, he was pretty lucky I didn't slug him. I took in a cold, calming breath.

"I'm fighting motion sickness here and I need some space, so please, just . . . stay over there." I didn't wait for a response, just closed my eyes again and fanned away, trying to control my temper.

Everything was going to be okay. I had my shot at making a change in my life. I was breaking away, one sweaty mile at a time. I had to be cool until I landed at Heathrow, then the classes and tours through the play houses and museums would begin. I'd be immersed in the things I loved most.

Finally, I cooled down some and got comfortable with one of the flimsy pillows they handed out. I fell asleep and dreamed about getting lost in the UK.

* * *

THE LONDON THEATRE WAS WONDERFUL. The workshops, grueling. No complaints from me, though. Weeks before in Austin I'd been elated to get a message from my beloved Professor Douglas. When my laptop had chimed into the quiet of my Saturday morning, a simple email from my British Literature teacher changed my life profoundly. The wonderful man wanted to send me to England, and he'd done it. Since arriving in London, my writing load was over-the-top huge but I loved my time on Tottenham Court Road. The museums were my favorite part of the trip, but they were considered a "tour" rather than a workshop or a class. I was liberated despite the tight schedule, and it felt *great*.

I did my homework in the commons in order to stay out of the confines of my dorm room. The large hall was furnished with old armchairs and a threadbare couch, with numerous long tables and metal chairs. The thin carpeting smelled like mildew. A snack machine was bolted to the wall over by the metal, double doors and the thing started buzzing like a chainsaw running out of gas every twenty-five minutes. I studied there happily despite those things. My whole life was lived in a cage. I'd been given the golden opportunity to leave Saint Vincent de Paul's Home for Girls in Austin. The place really was just a glorified orphanage that had a good school and a pushy gaggle of nuns. There I got three meals a day, the opportunity to take early college English classes, and a dry place to sleep every night. The fact that I felt smothered like a flame fighting for oxygen was an obstacle. Some nights at the Home I struggled against the urge to explode and do something radical to retaliate against my surroundings. I wondered if I would lose it, like, start random conversations with myself in public, and end up in a mental institution. The thought of returning to the Home kept me on edge, no matter how hard I tried redirecting my focus. Those times were far away since I changed my outlook.

I wanted to experience as much student life in London as I could, so I wasn't at the dorm much. And besides, my room smelled like stale cheese and I only had two scented travel candles my best friend, Brea, gave me before I left Austin.

Aside from school, the nuns did their best to ignore me. They'd taught me to speak well, which day-lighted as both a blessing and a curse. I stood out from other kids for that reason, too. Social issues aside, sounding intelligent when speaking wasn't much to complain about. I knew no other existence, and it had been my life for as long as I could remember. So I rolled with it.

Student life in London was a huge improvement. English breakfast was served daily in the cafeteria below the dorms starting at seven, but I'd grown into the habit of grabbing an apple or a banana off the buffet line and taking off for a brisk, morning walk. The dozen or so other kids studying there got the vibe and left me alone. I didn't know a single one of their names. I never went out with them, just took off by myself. Being outside in Great Britain sparked a sense of wonder in my soul. I was ready to explore every mile.

A shop on a corner close by had the best Earl Grey and I stopped there a lot and checked my email or Skyped with Brea back in Austin. She seemed too far away, although it had only been about a week since I'd left. I'd see her at the end of the summer when the program was over.

I wanted to go back to the States, but not back to the orphanage. After helping myself to a trip through the records department I had a new perspective on the Home. The door was open so I allowed myself a look at my intake files and regretted it that instant.

The fact that I'd been lied to by nuns, of all people, wasn't lost on me. Nothing was that pure. The contents of the files with my name held typical junk, except for one. The *lack* of contents inside was spooky. No birth certificate. Two photographs of a towhead blonde toddler with coppery-brown, tell-tale sad eyes. Case-worker evaluations for the last two years. Medical records from each time I had a fever, which numbered so many that I didn't bother to count.

"You were spawned by aliens and left at Zilker Park to be raised by swans," Brea once told me. We'd busted up laughing about that. But despite her joking assertions, the questions tortured me. I hadn't been stirred together in a petri dish. Everyone had parents.

I'd dealt with fevers my whole life and they got worse when I was upset. It was like I'd go thermal when I thought about it all too much. Was I destined to become one of the people who simply broke down one day, doing something crazy? Did I feel like someone who was pushed too far, becoming a menace to society instead of just a cast-off child?

I hated going there so I changed focus by allowing myself to consider Tottenham Court my new home—a process that created determination in me like I'd never known. I would do everything I could to avoid returning to St. Vincent's. I was no longer an orphan. I was an independent young woman who needed no one, and nothing.

Wednesday greeted me with another gorgeous morning in downtown London. I had my tea and fruit and was on my way back to the dorm to meet with the class for the day, window shopping and daydreaming.

When I turned to walk to the next building, I hadn't fully pulled my gaze away from the last one because I smacked right into a guy who was coming from the other direction. My backpack fell to the sidewalk and my water bottle hit right on the bottom, erupting like a mini geyser, splattering both of us with an explosive spray of water.

"I am so sorry!" I didn't know if I should help him dry off or die of embarrassment first.

The man I'd just soaked swatted water from a soft looking button down shirt. He used one hand to wipe a streaming drop from his cheek. He was smiling, thank goodness.

"I've already had a shower this morning, love." He had a fascinating accent. The long O's and the rolling R's of his brogue were from farther north, someplace in Scotland maybe.

"I'm truly sorry. I've always been a noodle." I wiped at my own clothes.

"You're cup's run dry," he said, handing me my backpack. "Would you care to join me for a drink? We can't have you wandering the street, crashing into random strangers, dry."

Tempting. Dark brown eyes set in a fan of thick lashes watched me for an answer. His streaked blond hair was tied back at the nape, hanging in a corn silk fall over one broad shoulder. Natural bronze skin that belonged in morning sunlight shone from under the rolled cuffs of his shirt, giving me a peek of his muscular forearms. He smiled easily at me; the kind of smile that made little crinkles around his eyes. He was beautiful and charming in a way I'd never encountered.

"I'd better not." Reluctance mixed with fear in my words, but I knew it was for the best. "Sorry to soak you and run off, but I have class today so I'd better get going."

"Ah, studying abroad. I should have known by the accent. Well enjoy your day. I'm Kai."

"Tessa." I took the hand he offered and we shook our greeting quickly.

"It's a pleasure, Tessa."

I could listen to him say my name all day, staring as the S flowed over his tongue with a little burst of air for the A. He thought I had an accent. *Cute.* I pulled my hand away.

"Take care." He smiled again and walked away.

I took a deep breath and forced myself to keep my sight facing forward so I didn't stare at him walking away like some love-struck girl-nerd.

I don't know where the urge came from, but I whirled around. "Kai?"

"Yes?" He turned half way and peered over a shoulder.

"Do you drink tea in the mornings?" I mentally slugged myself. That was easily one of the dumbest things I'd ever said.

"Well, yes, most days." He grinned.

"Sorry, I mean . . . we're in England, after all, right?" I laughed a little, sounding completely awkward. "So, would you like to meet me for tea in the morning? I go to that café on the corner, there." I pointed back the way I'd come.

"That would be delightful, Tessa."

"Would seven work? I have to meet my class at nine." That gave me about two hours to spend with a real-life hot guy. Happy day.

"Seven is perfect."

"Great. See you in the morning, then." *Yay, for Nerd Girl!* I triumphed.

"See you in the morning."

"Okay," I said, trying not to sound overly enthusiastic. I turned toward the dorms so he wouldn't see me grinning like an idiot.

I was a little soaked from my water-bottle explosion and probably on the verge of being behind to meet my class. Normally, I would have been frantic at the thought of being a minute late. But I couldn't stop smiling.

* * *

BREAKFAST WITH KAI went a little too perfectly. I worked to ignore the feeling that something was up. Fun romances with guys like Kai didn't happen in my life. I really wanted the chance to be happy and get the guy for once so I went with it, all in, thinking maybe I was paranoid.

I'd worked a little harder on my hair and make-up that morning, curling my long tresses into spirals that hung down my back. I wore my favorite white miniskirt with an amethyst baby-doll top and I was thankful I looked good because he was dressed in low riding jeans, a white button-up shirt and just the right amount of sexy.

When it was time for me to get back to the dorms for morning classes, he walked me to my building. He leaned close, which I'll admit, caused me to panic, briefly. But then he placed a soft kiss on my cheek that lasted a perfectly comfortable amount of time. His breath warmed my face. My senses filled with the scent of him. I closed my eyes and committed the feeling to memory. When I opened them, he'd picked up a strand of my hair, letting it fall through his fingers.

"Like honey in the sun and shade," he said, lowering his hand. "Beautiful."

"Thank you." I'd never been referred to as "beautiful" before, even if he was only talking about my hair. "I'd better get going."

Perhaps, life was going to shift in my favor for once. I mentally flipped Fate the big ol' bird and entered my first class of the day smiling like a dope, Kai's kiss tingling on my cheek.

CHAPTER 2

*T*he summer course session in London would come to a close in two days' time and I was pissy. I'd found a new reason to want to stay in London. As if I needed another. Kai and I had met several times over the last two weeks. We kept conversation fairly light, not getting too deeply into each other's lives, knowing I was leaving. A rogue wave of reality crashed the dreamlike state of my amazing, yet short-lived, life in in London, dragging my spirits into the black undertow of my impending return to St. Vincent's.

Being free from the Home fostered my spirit to grow. Upon returning, I'd get my business together and leave the place, pronto. I was out of high school. Not that big of a deal since I'd been emancipating myself in little ways for years. I didn't know where I came from or where I was headed. I'd grown into a good-hearted, fairly pretty, intelligent girl. I was *now*-eighteen-year-old Tessa Marie Conley. The last time I'd been in any kind of trouble was when I was busted watching the Silva/Emerson Mixed Martial Arts fight in the media room. The nuns had *loved* that.

I arranged my schedule perfectly, preparing for my last two

days. My essays were written and emailed to Professor Douglas,—
I'd be *danged* if I would blow my 4.0 grade point average so I could
have a couple days of indulgence. I included a cheery explanation
that I would finally, *blessedly* be taking the last weekend of the trip
to myself. Sunday, I would take the Tube to the Covent Gardens
stop and go in search of Cecil Court.

Kai agreed to meet me for the last of our nearly ritual breakfast dates, but he hadn't sounded too happy about my heading
back and I didn't love the idea of telling him goodbye. Maybe we
could keep in touch. I really hoped I could visit him again
someday or even talk him into coming to Austin for a while.

* * *

"Don't go back."

I stared blankly for a moment. "I have to go back," I said,
sipping my vanilla tea.

"No, you don't. You just feel safe saying that." Kai leaned back
in his chair, stretching his long legs out and crossing them at the
ankle. He folded his hands behind his head, to add the finishing
touch to a completely kicked-back, comfortable look. His flaxen
hair hung down past the back of his chair.

He was partially correct in his assumption. "That's an interesting thing to say." I tried not to sound judgmental. Sometimes it
could be hard to understand if someone was trying to be a little
mean, or merely stating their opinion, no offence intended. His
tone told me he was being a little mean. He wasn't smiling, which
was a new element in our conversations.

"I have to go back. Austin's where I live my life." Not that I was
too enthusiastic about returning. The new atmosphere had done
good things for my soul.

"Well thanks a lot." He reached for his tea.

"I didn't mean it like I hadn't been enjoying life here, Kai. I just have to go home now. School's over and next semester will start soon. I need to get back and look for a job, too."

He had to understand, for simplicity's sake. I didn't feel I should give my life story to someone I'd only known for a couple weeks. Maybe if we kept in touch like I hoped, we could share more personal details sometime.

"We should keep in touch," I offered. "Do you Skype?"

He gave a look of amazement. "Skype?" He snorted. "No, I do *not* do Skype." He looked at me like he expected me to say something.

I picked at my breakfast.

"So that's it then? I suggest you stay and you're going to go back to the US anyway?" "Of course I'm going back. I can't just up and stay here out of the blue like that. I would need to get back home and plan things out first. Be sure it's really what's best for me." The conversation was staggering on the edge of going bad between us.

"So much for spontaneity." He sneered.

That last little retort was all it took to end the staggering and send it plummeting over the edge for the worse.

"Are you being real right now? I mean, I can't believe you'd think I'd stay only because you suggested it." I sighed. "I have a bunch of things I want to do today since it's my last weekend here. I'd better get going." I dug in my change purse for Pound coins to help pay for breakfast, feeling terrible. And I was sure that's how he was trying to make me feel.

"I'll get it, Tessa," he said, setting down a bill.

I left the coins I'd already put on the check and stood.

"Let's not end on such a note."

"It's cool, Kai. I didn't want to miss you anyway." *Ouch.* But I didn't need to allow anyone to make me feel that way. I headed for the door.

He was there to open it for me. I looked away and kept walking toward the dorms.

"I didn't mean to get you all worked up, Tessa. I guess—" He pulled me to a stop by an elbow. "I guess," he continued, "I just really don't want you to go." He tilted my face up so I had to look at him. He gave that smile that I loved so much. The playful, bright one that made his eyes sparkle.

Nice try. "Well I'm going home and I'm sorry you don't like it. Think what you want about me." I was feeling like Orphan Tessa. Not Only Girl in the Room Tessa, like he'd made me feel before. He'd ruined it.

"We'll keep in touch then. Maybe I can change your mind, get you to come back for a visit. I'll look at starting up a Skype thing, if you'd like that."

"Don't worry about it. I really have to go, Kai." It was for the best, less to lose later.

He let my arm fall. I'd delivered a brush off and we both realized that. I had to wonder if I was going with the flow of my feelings a little too easily.

No matter if I was angry or not, I would always miss Kai. He'd been the first guy who'd ever made me feel like I belonged. *Anywhere.*

"Well take care of yourself, then."

"You too. Goodbye, Kai," I said quietly.

He was already walking away.

I started for my dorm room so I could begin packing for the trip home. People window shopped, chatted on benches, and rushed to meet the Tube. A family passed, too close for comfort. Two wide eyed, grinning, blond toddlers chased around me, shrieking and giggling.

I flinched. The Home's intake picture of me as a toddler trembled in my mind's eye, but in the other photo I'd found, I was standing with a similarly featured little boy. We both stood close, one tiny hand grasping that of the other. The boy was possibly five years old, maybe a little older. The resemblance between the two children left no doubt, just like the message on the back of the picture.

Robbie and Tessa Conley

Thanks for everything. Emma and Ben Thomlinson.

Eleven scrawled words would never say as much again.

I'd been lied to. The photo of smiling white-blonde baby Tessa and Robbie taunted me in rhythm to the tiny feet on the sidewalk as the children played. The only family I had, a brother, was adopted without me.

The brilliant thing was, I had to return to that life. My jaw set in a scowl. The mother grasped her kids' hands and led them away as the beginning of a fever burned in my chest.

Looking through the records room was an idiot move. That was the day I'd stepped right across the line of demarcation that was, Change. There it was, life shaken, not stirred. No one saw or met my parents when I was brought in, there was no extended family to contact. That caused lots of problems with the adoption process. Everyone wanted to adopt a baby. Some wanted to adopt a toddler. Few wanted to adopt a five-to-ten-year old. No one wanted to adopt a teenager. Throw the freak fevers in the mix and I was at a loss. Some of us were unadoptable. That was me. I was defective. The symptoms slowed as I'd grown. Years went by since anyone saw my temperature climb over 105 degrees. Maybe I was healed.

I forced my feet into motion.

The timing of two life-changing events was bittersweet. The fact I'd missed out on having a brother ruled me and I didn't know if I'd ever forgive the administration at the Home. Despite the way my soul trembled inside my body, I had to concentrate on the future. When I returned to Austin I could attend UT—good grades and grant money made me a shoo-in—and get my English degree. I could get a night job. Maybe at a Steak and Shake or a WhataBurger. The Home was a thing of the past, one way or another. My place in the world was unclear, but it wasn't amongst liars in nun's habits.

I'd taken it too far. The names on the photo had enabled me to search them out before I left for London. The perfect adoptive family had been shattered by tragedy before I found them. I'd never meet Robbie. I was still an orphan. A survivor. *Gotta love the constants in life.* At least I knew where I stood.

The resolve steeled me. I was renewed. My life would have new direction. I wouldn't think of the Thomlinsons and I'd develop a warm place in my heart for my brother rather than harboring the feeling I'd been cheated. Eighteen-year-olds had to be resilient creatures. Still, life in Austin had been tainted. A whole new level of teen angst would accompany me back to the Home.

* * *

THE FORTY-EIGHT-HOUR COUNTDOWN until I met the airport shuttle commenced and I decided to get out for one last run down Tottenham Court Road that evening. I'd grown to love running that busy street, and learned early on to mind what the street lights said when they announced "walk" or "don't walk." That was serious business. If a person was still in the intersection when the lights changed, the oncoming traffic wouldn't slow down. Rather, the cabs would barrel into the road and blare their stuffy, snooty-sounding, little horns to announce they would soon smash me flat. *No big. It's your fault for not obeying the walking signals.*

I immersed myself in the experience because I knew it would be my last run in London, which also made me a little sad. Dusk settled quickly, and I knew I shouldn't be out much longer. The evening air was brisk and my feet felt lighter than usual as I ran along the sidewalk. There weren't many people out anymore. Mist-filled fog crept in from the bruised sky. Vendors packed their wares away for the night and shopkeepers pulled in awnings and flipped signs. Watching it all made it easy to lose track of time.

A figure leaned against the dark bricks on the opposite side of the street. As I got closer, details formed. I coasted to a stop right before I got to the next corner. Definitely male, he was tall and well-built with broad shoulders and muscular thighs that showed through the dark pants he wore. His hands were thrust into the front pockets of a black hoodie.

The air around me changed somehow. The sweetness of the cool, yet dampened afternoon I'd been enjoying melted away with the swift chill of nightfall. Sweat cooled on my skin. I shivered.

The man looked right at me. He inclined his head in a brief nod that allowed hazy light from the street lamps to illuminate his face, revealing a lower lip surrounded by short outgrowth of a beard. He reminded me of Kai. They shared height and build, but from where I stood in the growing darkness it was hard to see clear facial details.

"Kai?" I called. My voice echoed briefly, but was struck down in the dense fog.

No answer.

The longer I looked the creepier the situation became. He sulked, wearing his pullover like a cowl. I didn't know him. Kai would've answered me, even if he was ticked off about our conversation earlier.

I pulled my gaze away, slightly disturbed at my ability to stare at someone in such a way. Sure, I had been sheltered a bit during my childhood, but *come on.*

I broke into a run once more and didn't look behind me to see if he still stood there. Fighting the feeling that someone was following me, I considered turning around to check, but I didn't. Although, I *really* wanted to. Not because I actually thought someone watched me, but because I was a little scared.

Nightfall took over before I ran up the stairs in the dorm. I locked my door and chained it. The screensaver on my laptop cast dancing light around my room like a sick disco ball. I hit the light switch beside me, panting.

Nearly an hour passed before I felt better. Not so freaked out. And I still didn't understand why I'd gotten that way in the first place.

CHAPTER 3

$\mathcal{T}$he next day was the last Sunday of the trip and my afternoon to wander London on my own. Despite a lack of sleep, I wanted the day to be perfect and I didn't want to think about packing up to go back to the States. Even thinking about enrolling in courses for the next semester seemed daunting. I did my best to shake it off, concentrating on enjoying the rest of my day. Thinking about checking out shops all afternoon was much more fun.

I dressed in one of my favorite outfits, gathered my hair into a pony tail, and clasped it with a barrette. I pulled on a sweater, grabbed my backpack and headed out, making sure to lock the door behind me. I would act as though I didn't have to leave, for one beautiful afternoon. Clicking neatly down the hall in my favorite peep-toe, sling backed heels helped. The last of my time in London had arrived and I figured I might as well dress up a little.

Stepping from the Leicester Square Tube stop to the cloud-covered afternoon, I shouldered my pack and made my way along the bustling sidewalk. I toured little markets and took lots of pictures of the beautiful buildings. My gaze swept the sides of architecture along the way, reading placards attached to the bricks high above my head. To the left of a shadowed lane, my eyes came to rest on a plain sign fixed to the stone wall there. *Cecil Court*, the sign announced. After travelling nearly six thousand miles, I then stood at the gateway to the best mix of old bookstores and antiquities shops I could hope for.

I took a deep breath of sweet-damp air, scanned the court, and ripped the vision like a CD to my memory. Tall buildings blocked all but a few hours sunshine in the brick lane, adding a chill to the air and a dark tint to the stone paving and storefronts. Converted gas lights lined the center of the narrow walk, flickering to life in the midafternoon. Musty scents of old things swirled atop the herby fragrance of potted lavender. Shingles hung on ornate, wrought-iron brackets anchored in stone and brick. Not many people strolled the quiet cobbles, so I meandered freely.

I'm really *here. I want to remember it, just like this, forever.*

History called to me from door to door. The court was a small place of thrilling but murky history, the buildings there each lending stories of seedy barber shops, unhealthy eateries, and houses of ill-repute to London's colorful past.

The next shop I encountered had an especially long sign that didn't match the rest. Rather than the typical brackets, a huge, crouching gargoyle held the sign, one arm extending two-thirds the length along the bottom of the wooden plank, the creature's chin resting on the top corner in an oddly human way. The thing's skin shone like a muted oil-slick in the fading light of the narrow alley.

Old English lettering announced the name of the store below as *Librorum Taberna*, and I quickly translated the words from my small knowledge of Latin as "small shop of books," or something closely related. The elongated plank was darkened across the bottom portion, matching the upper half of the wooden storefront perfectly; both somehow winning the battle against the damaging effects of time, flame, and weather.

Only a few intact facings remained after the trend of arson amongst the residents of Georgian and Victorian London. A similar facing hung at the Victoria and Albert Museum, where I spent hours on end reading descriptions, writing in my journal, and filling memory cards with photos of Gothic architecture. The one before me remained in remarkable shape for its age, all the way to the top of the two-story building where tell-tale burn marks licked at the right side. Modern gutters were installed atop the building beside security lights.

I smoothed a hand over the age and soot darkened wood. Ornate carving twisted throughout the thick facing. Two craggy faces were carved on either side of the gargantuan double doors. Darkened to pits by time and weather, their sightless eyes stared at the dwindling patrons of Cecil Court.

Such a shop could take hours to thoroughly enjoy, and it would be dark far too soon for me to stay. The sign said it was still open.

A defiant grin tugged at my dimples as I walked inside. A delicate set of replica bard's bells hung by the door, tinkling their Faery song into the room as I arrived.

The heavy door clicked shut after I stepped through, taking with it a portion of the light in the place. I had to wait a moment while my sight adjusted to the dim lighting and my senses burst to life. Aromas of aged wood and leather blended sweetly behind a top note of Earl Grey steeped with a hint of nutmeg. The only sound that greeted me was the gentle hum of a dehumidifier. I sucked in an exhilarating breath in anticipation of touching the wonders shelved inside.

The store yawned before me like a cavern. Darkness swallowed towering shelf-lined walls leading beyond my sight, so tall that wheeled ladders rested at the junctions of rows. Occasional, gilded wall sconces added dusty light in delicate beams, casting perfect spots on labels to announce the names of writers and playwrights. I walked the aisles, perusing authors, neck craned slightly to the right as I read title after title from leather bound spines on shelves so impeccably organized, any librarian would feel envious. *Librorum Taberna* not only offered books, but also stored a mixture of trinkets, like letter openers, bookmarks with sad angels that would rest atop the pages of a read, and a variety of clunky bookends.

I rounded an ornate, bullnose corner to encounter a nook harboring two leather reading chairs and a small writing desk with a lamp. A solitary case stood against the back wall. I read the illuminated sign on the top of the bookcase. *The Works of Mr. Christopher Marlow.*

"Aw, you had to, didn't ya?" I told the empty room. I skirted the desk and centered myself in front of a sealed glass case that held my favorite closet play— Dr. Faustus. A replica sat on a shelf beside it. The banter of Faust and Mephistopheles called to me from between the tome's leather covers. I scanned the pages, reading my favorite monologues. I began walking in search of the cash registers, happy I'd found something cool to take home.

A leathery, scraping sound, then a loud *slap* popped through the darkened store. I listened hard. Raspy, scratching sounds floated across the tops of the bookcases. An odd sense that I'd read a lot longer than I should have worried me when I looked back toward the front of the store to see it was nearly full dark out.

"Hello?" My call resonated. I wondered if anyone had seen me come in. Maybe the shop owner locked up, not realizing I sat in the nook reading for so long.

Scraping. Tapping. Someone should have answered me.

I followed sounds through the darkened store to an alcove far in the back. I drew in a breath to call out, but a voice from the darkness beat me to it.

"For tonight's feature entertainment, Jack and Jill shall go up a hill . . . ," the voice trailed off, huffing with sarcasm.

Whoever recited the nursery rhyme had a seriously bad set of teeth from the sound of things. Creeping forward, I allowed only enough of my face to clear the side of the thick wooden bookshelf so that one eye could focus on who was there.

A gargoyle lay sprawled on the floor on its back, scale-like skin glistening in the dim light. *It moved.* One leg stretched long with a heel resting on a low shelf, clawed toes thoughtlessly flicking a hardback to and fro against a row of books.

Canine in shape, its head rested on a pillow formed by two folded, segmented wings. Currently silent, the thing touched one talon of a four-digit hand to a forked tongue, moistening the pad to flip the page of the book propped open on its chest. A long tail twitched, then snaked forward to scratch at the flap of a leathery, bat-like ear. The idle leg made rapid scratching motions against the shelf, almost toppling rows of dust-coated books. Relaxing once more, it settled back into its read, lyrical, boyish brogue rhyming out a cadence.

". . . to fetch a pail of water, Jack fell down and broke his bloody crown, and an idiot came tumbling after," the thing huffed again.

"Pssssscht." A reptilian palm slapped a furrowed brow as it sighed with gusto. "I'm so tired of this rubbish." Clapping the volume shut, it sent the rejected book spinning on the hardwood, the scarred leather spine coming to a sliding stop against the wall.

I found myself mid scream. I didn't realize I'd moved at all, but I stood in full view, having stepped from behind the cover of shelving.

The gargoyle shot to its feet in an instant, whirling on me. "Stop!" it snarled.

My scream diminished into a noncommittal, airy, "aaahhh."

"What the bloody hell is wrong with you?" the thing spat. Chest heaving, it lowered its arms, wings folding at its shoulders. Bright, silver-grey eyes narrowed on me. "Never, ever, do that again." After a beat to catch a breath, it stepped away from the wall. "I'm Peter. Pleased to make your acquaintance." The thing bowed in a flourish of spread wings and sweeping tail.

Wobbling, I unwillingly accepted the fact that I suffered from brain overload. I was shutting down, losing it. *I'm going to faint, this thing is going to eat me, and there isn't a freaking thing I can do about it.* I gave an ironic snort before I collapsed in my own flourish of pink and blonde on the wood floor.

CHAPTER 4

"Well, I for one, like her."

The sound of the man's voice startled me awake. My fingers felt soft fabric beneath me. The smell told me I remained in the store. Holding still to keep my breathing even, I listened.

"She's a *woman!*" a familiar voice said.

"I think she'll make the perfect addition. She adds contrast to this place."

"Ezra, can you picture her—"

"Would you rather be a downspout?" the new voice cut in.

"No. I never imagined you'd bring in a female and, well she's all . . . soft and fluffy . . . and . . . and *pink.*" The words "soft" and "pink" were audibly accompanied by a fresh spray of spittle. Peter snorted his disenchantment with the situation.

"You seemed charmed enough when you introduced yourself to her. And you have to admit she will liven things up around the store, Peter."

"Oh yes, she's a real live one." Sarcasm dripped from Peter's words, adding a hiss to the "yes" when it drew out long over his forked tongue. "I didn't know you planned to keep her."

I felt their eyes on me. I held my breath, feeling heat building in my chest as I struggled for calm.

"She belongs with us," the other voice stated. "I've a feeling about her."

"Seems unlikely, to me." Peter sounded unconvinced.

Very unlikely. I couldn't have agreed more. Sweat drew cold air against my forehead.

"You'll learn to appreciate these things. Softness, and pink," the voice called Ezra stated. "It may be time for you to start reading something other than children's books."

"That would be a most welcomed change. How the bloody hell do you expect me to retain sanity when you insist on ruining every book I try to read? There's not much to do here at night, Ezra."

One of my shoes fell to the floor with a loud thump. *Crap.* I could tell they both stared at me again.

"Again, I would reconsider keeping her here."

"It is done."

I didn't like the finality in that statement.

Papers rustled and a single set of footfalls sounded, leading away, followed by the solid click of a door shutting. I chanced a look, but with only one eye open a slit. The gargoyle slouched in an oversized armchair nearby, resting its chin on a fist in an all-too-human posture.

"I know you're awake over there."

I kept still.

"You're soon to wish you'd kept walking."

The door clicked shut once more. He'd left.

I rolled upright, checking myself quickly. My clothes were all present, save for the one pump which I hastily retrieved. I'd become puffy or something while I slept. The shoe was tight and hard to slide onto my foot but after a couple quick little stomps it was back in place. I stood wavering, lightheaded beside an ornate, cloth covered chaise in an even more ornate room. The whole area was centered around a huge, impeccably tidy, mahogany desk. A tall, rose window centered behind the workstation, candlelight glinting from its many beveled edges. Designed by a gifted craftsman, the rose was a blend of rich purple, blue and finally red at the center, where a scarlet E had been designed into the inner petals.

Ezra. The name Peter had called the other voice.

I took a shaky step toward the door but stopped short when I heard the horrible creaking my heels made when I walked. *What now?*

Swollen would be a major understatement in describing the state of my feet. Bulging toes fought against neighbors for control over the holes that were meant to show a peek of my neatly polished nails. Relief followed the removal of my shoes. I'd apparently walked a lot longer than planned. *Note to self. Wear Chuck Taylor's next time you go exploring.*

Heels in one hand, I padded to the door passing a darkened window. It was a good thing I hadn't slept the night away. I reached to twist the door handle, embedding the fingernails of my right hand in the solid wood of the door. I yanked them free, sending shards of wood darting to the floor. Enlarged knuckles burned as if my hands had been rubbed down with Icy Hot. Elongated digits were tipped with pointed nails that were foreign, save for being polished with my favorite fingernail polish. A button shot from my cardigan, ricocheting off solid wood. I squealed and ducked, covering my head with my arms. The burning sensation spread to my elbows and shoulders as the fabric of my sweater split along the collarbone, leaving bits of knit wool hanging limply from my wrists. The hook-and-eye clasps of my bra popped loudly across my back in unison to the waistband of the matching panties. My skirt slicked across my thighs, revealing a viscous grey-blue substance coating my skin.

"Ewwww!" I inhaled with a sharp snort and screamed. The only thing I could think to do was run.

After bludgeoning the door handle enough it relented, allowing access to the hall outside the study. The corridor was long, displaying huge, floor length portraits of dogs.

"Whu . . .?" I muttered, staring at the odd choice of the artist. I gimped down the hallway, my feet heavy, like walking with mud caked on my shoes. I ran a serious temperature, with too much heat burning in my chest and face. I desperately searched for a way back out of the store. I launched myself toward the next doorway in the hall, and pounded at the thick wood there. A shiny doorknob landed on the floor with a dejected thump. So much for trying to open the door.

"Please help me!" I yelled, "Somebody open the door!" Wailing again, I balled my fists and hit the door with both hands, sending it crashing open.

Silence. Not even an echo returned my pleading calls. I sniffled, head twitching with hysteric sobs, and began to run as best I could into the dim corridor.

The hall ended, offering the choice of turning either direction. Completely lost, I put trust in a snap decision and continued my flight down the hallway to my left. Incredible detail emerged, contrasting colors and shades of light popping to life, creating an echo of visible, layered dimension to my surroundings.

I slowed, lost deeper in the labyrinthine bookstore, considering the fact that I wore what I ran from. I hiccupped violently, giving in to morbid curiosity.

My hands were no longer my own. Scales covered the skin, reflecting charcoal and grey as I examined them in the lighting under a wall sconce. I trembled on elongated feet bearing claws for toenails, each tip glinting with crackled, pink polish. Muscles bulged within the plated skin of my calves, tapering to boney ankles. The fluid coating my body was drying, leaving behind glimmering, spade shaped scales that connected to form a tough interweaving of plated skin. The skirt I'd adored hung loose around my tapered waist, length abbreviated far above my knees, more of a loincloth than the previous statement of fashion and modesty. My cardigan was gone, apparently falling away completely in my frantic sprint from the study. My camisole remained, blotched with sticky fluid, clinging to a flat breast plate that replaced the curved features of my chest. A slender tail spiraled around my left leg, coming to a point on top of my foot. The tip twitched toward the ceiling.

My legs sort of gave up, sending me to my knees. Something behind me stopped my body from coming to rest on the floor. Huge, curved wings rested atop my shoulders, the boney frames jammed into the carpet behind me, holding my bottom off the floor. I grasped the base of one and pulled it free, repeating the motion on the other side. I sat back, wings stretched alongside me like a runaway kite snagged in a tree.

My hands were more like a raptor's talons, but the pads of my clawed fingers were amazingly sensitive. I touched my face. My chin jutted forward, forming an elongated jaw that rested under a stubbed nose.

"Aw, God," I said with a trembling, little girl voice. Knobby cheek bones protruded below my temples. Hair clung in spots, hanging from a ponytail with gel glopped in places. I pulled strands loose from wherever they dried to scales, some plastered to my shoulders. Some of it was stuck in my mouth and other strands were tangled across the top of my wings. When it was finally gathered in one clawed fist, I pulled it forward across a shoulder, letting it fall in a mass of swirling grey strands across my ruined camisole. Tears fell onto my folded knees. I wiped at my abbreviated excuse for a nose. It wasn't nearly as long as Peter's had looked when I'd first seen him.

I gasped.

"Peter!" I yelled. The "P" was accentuated by lips stretched across pointy canine fangs. I didn't know if Peter could help, but being lost, I had nothing else to try for. I leapt to my feet. My wings spanned wide, smacking against the walls of the hallway on either side. A wooden frame splintered when one of the dog pictures crashed to the carpet. I froze.

"Whoa," I moaned. They were like two, heavy beach umbrellas stuck to my back. Reaching back in an attempt to shove them into place I noticed that when I tucked my arms to my sides, the wings followed suit, furling together on my back with the curled ends sweeping forward to rest against the outside of my calves. My legs shook as I took a hesitant, tucked step forward, learning my stride.

Minutes seemed like days as I wandered halls of the transformed bookstore. I didn't really care about the contents of the madhouse around me at that point. I needed to find Peter, or the door. Not necessarily in that order.

I found nothing but more books, antiques, and reasons to freak out. I tucked myself against the wall in the next corner I came to.

I cracked inside, covering my face as best I could with clawed hands, and cried. Slumping down the joining walls, I gathering my knees to my chest and rocked in time to my hysterics, soft mourning sounds erupting moment to moment against my will. I tried to reason away why I'd been victimized by something I couldn't identify. If it was a bad dream, I was far ready to wake up.

Maybe I was being punished for wishing bad things for the Thomlinsons because they didn't adopt me, too. Was it against some unspoken rule to hate on a nun? Fate and Change teamed up, working together at their finest.

Peter cleared his throat gently but still managed to startle me. I gazed up at his blurry figure through thickened eyelids and pools of unshed tears. Snot ran down my lip. I scrubbed at my face like my hands were erasers. He stepped forward, an otherworldly, winged shadow eclipsing my trembling form.

"What's happening to me?"

"You're becoming," he said, just above a whisper.

"Becoming what?" I snapped tensely at his cryptic response.

"You have to ask that?" Peter held out his claws, gesturing at himself with
sarcasm.

"I don't understand," I said, averting my face. "I feel like I could throw up."

"That will pass." He pulled up close and squatted on his haunches next to me. "You'll grow accustomed to it." he offered. It was odd seeing such a beastly body use human gestures to emit calmness.

"I don't want to!" I yelled back. "Look at me! I'm disgusting. This . . . slime . . . ," I spat as I held out a sticky arm.

"It's already drying," he said. "Then you'll just have . . . ."

"What?" I snapped. "Scales?"

"Scales," he said, at the same time.

"Nooooo," I moaned. He sounded too sure of what was going to happen. "I've been . . . disfigured." I refused to accept the finality in his tone. "This isn't real. It can't be."

"You'll adapt quickly." He sighed when his words accomplished nothing more than sending me into a fresh bout of hiccupping sobs. I elbowed the wall.

"Try to stop," he whispered. Peter crept close beside me and extended an arm over my shoulders and a wing over mine, hugging me tightly beside him.

I grieved openly against his rough shoulder, shaking my head.

Peter held me close, looking down at scales—snakeskin—peeking from beneath the remaining pink fluff I'd worn into the store. His expression kind, understanding shone in his eyes, setting them off against an ethereal visage. I hated to think there was an added amount of pity mixed in.

"Unbelievable," he mused. "I wouldn't think Ezra capable of seeing this in you." He shook his head. I knew he wasn't really talking to me with expectation of holding a conversation. And I didn't answer because I was clueless. My brain was fried and I couldn't stop shaking. I scooted closer to the comforting feel of another person, a stranger that had the world in common with me.

My mind was in replay mode. I fought against it for a long time, twitching as I tried to get the images to stay gone. If I kept watching myself struggling, being tormented and transformed, I might go stark-raving crazy and never recover. Was I already there? I welcomed the lulling effect of Peter's chest rising and falling, holding out hope that I would wake up in my dorm room, and never remember the nightmare I'd suffered. My last cognizant thought was that I was fairly sure gargoyles didn't eat their own. At least I hoped not.

CHAPTER 5

*S*unlight warmed my face. A smile tugged at my features. Sunshine was a rarity in London. *And that's where I am . . . my favorite place on the planet . . . the museums . . . theatre . . . bookstores—*

"Crap!" I screamed, shooting to my feet.

Peter's head clunked against the wall. "Damn," he growled. He rubbed his temple, blinking in the morning light, grey eyes focusing on me. "Come away from the window, please."

"Huh." I patted down my back-to-human hips as I walked toward him. I looked over my shoulder, and then doubled over, looking under my skirt. *No tail!* My sweater was gone and my heels were still missing, but I was too happy to be myself to care.

"What on earth are you doing?" A man sat against the wall where Peter the Gargoyle had been, an elbow resting on his knee, watching me frisk myself.

"I had the craziest, far out dream I've ever had." I rested my rump against the wall, bending forward with my hands on my knees while my heartbeat thumped wildly in my chest. "I dreamed I turned into a gargoyle!" I giggled, out of breath. I let my head fall limply forward. After a moment, I glanced at the guy on the floor next to me. He was quiet, surveying me.

"Peter," he said. "Pleased to make your acquaintance," he deadpanned.

I was silent, slowly coming to a standing position against the wall. "But you *were* a gargoyle," I stated. The voice matched the mannerisms from the night before. I crossed my arms over my chest matter-of-factly despite the nagging thought I wasn't getting it.

Peter rose to his feet and moved to stand in front of me. "I, most certainly, am a gargoyle." He nodded solemnly. "And so are you." There was a no-nonsense tone in his voice.

I squinted at him. Familiar silvery eyes were lined with thick, dark lashes. Boyish, yet strong features met my gaze. A full, pouty lower lip curled slightly with a small grin. His thick, black hair was pulled from his face in a long tail, part of which fell over a bare, muscular shoulder. A linen vest was the sole piece of clothing on his torso, hanging open across his wide chest. Soot smudged, ratty, calf length trousers hung off his hips, displaying two ropes of tapered muscle descending below the waistband there.

I gulped, audibly.

He smiled, making me feel like a perv for checking him out. "Don't worry, Ezra will likely hand you a big book of something childish, like nursery rhymes, to keep your mind where he wants it," he said. Without taking his eyes from mine, he pulled a time-piece from the small pocket of his vest. "We have a couple of hours before the store opens. I'm certain Ezra has a room ready for you by now. So we should head upstairs." He turned toward the hall, disappearing around the corner.

I was plaster on the wall, feeling faint, as if I stood in a surreal place, looking down at myself from some mystical, veiled plain nearby while my body reacted to my new surroundings. Memories from the last night assailed me.

Peter rounded the corner to see me standing in the same spot he'd left me.

I didn't react to seeing him. Coming up the way I did always lent a majorly tenacious quality when I needed it, but then, try as I might, I was unable to draw on the strength of that virtue. I blinked, trying to clear the feeling that my vision was narrowing.

"I'm a gargoyle?" There was no way a thing like that could be happening in the first place. The fact that it was happening to *me*, was the kicker. I'd felt disoriented like that before. Once on the playground I was hit in the face with a soccer ball. I remembered that brief feeling of confusion as my mind struggled to process what had happened. I felt the same way then. My mind struggled, and I attempted to block the ball.

"Yes." Peter's voice cut through the fog in my mind. "More of a gargoyle at night." He reached for a hand and pulled me along toward the stairs.

After being dragged through the hall for a moment, I caught up and walked beside him, keeping a hold of his hand. His skin was warm and his grip was tender. Maybe it was the human quality of his touch that helped to keep my mind grounded a bit as I cased each window we passed for a possible escape. We traversed the store and made it back to Ezra's study. Peter deposited me on the chaise from the previous night.

"I'll be back in just a moment, all right?"

"Okay."

"You stay put, yes?" He looked at me with distrust, knowing I was ready to bolt.

Very perceptive. "Okay," I glanced around the study, wondering which way the front door was. He turned to leave the room.

"Who's holding the sign?" I asked. I hated that I'd said anything. It didn't matter because I'd be gone soon.

"I'm sorry, what?" He stepped toward me.

"I don't get it. If you're here, who's out there? Who is holding the sign for the bookstore?" The whole deal was BS and I was ready to hear him talk his way out of that one.

"It's not a *who*, it's a *what*, rather. It's my gargoyle holding the sign during the daylight hours."

It figured he'd have an answer. I looked at him with exaggerated doubt. "Really? That's all you've got?"

"Look," he sighed, gathering an explanation. "This defies the rational thought you're accustomed to. I'd wager *yours* is out there too," he offered. "It will be at all times now. You won't realize it, or even feel it, at all. The gargoyles hold a space to mark the transformation from being mortal," he said, gesturing through the wall to the sign. "They don't move. They're more of a representation, really. When a gargoyle is created from the life of a human, a place-holder in time is formed. *Created.* They're mere depictions of what we are now."

"Did you say 'from' being mortal?"

"Yes. Brilliant. That's it." He seemed relieved. "When the transformation took away our mortality, the statues out there were formed to take up the space the mortality consumed. The ability to pass from life to life can't be removed. That would create an emptiness in time here. Those," he said, gestured again, "fill the void otherwise created by the change."

I considered the information quietly.

Peter watched me. "You're quick." He smiled.

"You don't die." I stated.

"*We* don't die. I've been here a *very* long damned time."

There was a silence between us as we let the conversation sink in. I shook my head, not wanting him to think I was that gullible, but at the same time, I realized it made sense.

"Ezra will likely do a better job explaining. If he's in the mood. If it's cloudy I'll take you out for a moment to look for yourself."

"Okay." I went back to studying my whereabouts, bare feet hanging from the chaise.

An elderly man appeared in the doorway. My heart was in my

throat and I was on my feet like the chaise was laced with electricity. He hadn't made a sound.

"Take her upstairs, Peter. She'll have a good look from there," he said. He clomped past in a pair of thick-soled black boots, seating himself behind the huge desk. After placing wired spectacles over cataract-greyed eyes, he began examining a short stack of unopened post.

I eyed the gaunt, elderly man. *So this is Ezra.*

"I'd rather see from the sidewalk, if you'd show me out." I had a plane to catch.

"Perhaps another time, dear," the old man said, and opened an envelope.

"I think just now is perfect." I held my breath and bit down on the inside of my cheek. Tears welled up again, a show of emotion which was really starting to grate on me, and my face grew warm as I fought the urge to run. I wouldn't stop until my butt was firmly planted on a jet back to the familiarity of the States, if I could only make it out the door. I hid my shaking hands, clasping them behind my back. "People will worry about me. They'll start searching. Call Scotland Yard." I hoped that was the case, wondering if they really did that in London.

"You needn't worry about getting word to your Professor. A cheeky postcard was dropped at your campus to stave off any alarm at your absence. He knows you're fine, well, and bushy-tailed." Ezra continued to shuffle mail, so nonchalant I wanted to shred it for him. "And going out is not a possibility today. It's quite sunny outside." He set his mail aside and looked over the rim of his glasses at Peter briefly, then turned his attention my way. "We wouldn't want any mishaps, dear girl."

"My name is Tessa. I am not your *dear girl*," I said, in an exaggeration of a formal British accent. His accent sounded somewhat British, but there was something puzzling, something more to his lilt, the brogue far too deep to be the typical accent of the people in London. "And I love sunshine." I looked over at Peter, who remained beside the chaise. "Please show me out."

Peter shook his head. "Best not right now."

"I'm leaving. Now." I glared at Peter. "And if you don't lead me to the door, I'll find a way to bust my way outside." I'd toss one of Ezra's cocky, little baubles right through his pretty stained glass. I eyed a fat, squatty candle. I'd finish what someone had tried ages ago and burn the store down.

"Tessa." Ezra smiled up at me. "Tessa, I like that. So fitting for one with such . . . spark, you know." The old man winked as if we shared an inside joke. "You can't go outside today."

"Why?" I cried. Hot tears fell. I wiped at them hard, angry at my break down when the guy was only smiling at me. The last twenty-four hours had transformed me into an emotional train-wreck and I loathed the loss of control.

"Why what?" he asked.

"Why can't I leave?" I yelled. "Why am I even here? I mean, why *me*? I'll find a way out of this place." I waved a trembling hand in a quick arc indicating his study. I dropped my hand when I noticed it shaking horribly. "You see this?" I pointed a thumb at my face. "This is what 'nothing to lose' looks like!"

"Why, you ask?" Ezra stepped from behind his desk. "Well, it's simple, Tessa," he hissed my name slowly. The man stood quietly in front of us, ridged, lips drawn tight. "Everything happens for a reason."

No one moved. I examined his misleadingly feeble appearance. There was no doubt in my mind of his ability to keep order. What I'd mistaken for cataracts was a complete lack of pupils. I wasn't surprised to see something so completely peculiar at that point. The extreme white of his eyes accentuated the yellowed quality of his uncombed hair and crazy eyebrows. Oddly, he seemed physically well but weathered, his clothes perfectly pressed, right down to his thick-soled boots. Silence claimed the room. I shuddered.

Ezra's perky demeanor took over like someone had changed

his battery. He tugged at the thick cuffs of his starched, linen shirt and straightened his vest. He smiled at me as though he was my long lost grandfather.

I gulped. *He could use a couple hours of practice grinning at himself in a mirror before he takes that one on the road.*

"'Why' is very simple," he said. "Boygoyle," he gestured at Peter with a thin, dry-skinned hand. "And girlgoyle." He whirled toward me, smiling like the deranged at an asylum for nut-jobs of equal caliber.

Peter groaned and closed his eyes for a moment.

I huffed. Ezra seemed pleased as punch. Peter's reaction echoed mine. Eyes closed, he rubbed his brow with his fingers, snorted softly with half a laugh, and shook his head slightly.

"Well no one asked me!" I yelled. "This is . . . you're . . . freaking crazy!" I jabbed a finger at Ezra. "I feel like a science project . . . like a lab rat. Change me back, right this instant!" My voice was high pitched, squawking. I panted a little.

"Now dear girl, we can't always get what we want," he said, glancing sidelong in Peter's direction. "Now off with you both. We have a business to run here. I'll see you both at nine, sharp, ready to work." He looked straight at me. "Smiling," he said, without one of his own. He tugged a silver watch from the left-hand pocket of his vest, checked the time, and shot a meaningful glance at Peter.

Peter caught my elbow and gestured toward the door. I turned to follow him out, but wheeled around to face Ezra once more, ready to tell him off. Words evaporated on my tongue.

The freak was dancing at his desk. There was no music, but clearly some imaginary band in his head was rocking out.

He bobbed his head and tapped his fingers in metronome timing, grinning right at me.

"That's quite helpful, Ezra," Peter growled. He took my elbow, a little firmer, obviously sensing a possible blow up. "Time to go."

Moving would concede defeat. Conflicted, I opened my mouth to say something but words wouldn't come. My whole life, I'd been yanked around, and studying abroad was supposed to enrich my life enough that I found a way out from under other people's thumbs. Coming to London had only turned up another cage.

Peter pulled me toward the door, Ezra banging out the beat on his desk, long stained silver hair flopping against his weathered cheeks.

He looked at us like *we* were the crazy ones. "It's that Rolling Stones' song." He smiled a little, as if one of us would get it and be like, "oh, yeah. That one."

"You've gotta be kidding me," I shook my head.

"Yeah," Ezra answered from inside his study. "But I'm not."

I was simply too stunned at his audacity to say another word on my way out. That statement was completely inarguable.

CHAPTER 6

"*He*," I said, pointing a finger downstairs, "Is a first class mental case!" I paced a tight line on the hall carpet.

Peter watched me carefully. "Yes, I can't argue that. He thrives on irony. In his defense, he's had a fairly tragic life. But he has an extensive knowledge of every book in this place." Peter opened the door he'd led me to. "He really is quite brilliant." He swung the door open and strode across plush carpeting to an oversized window seat, built into the wall around a double pane of aged glass. Sunshine shone through, casting a bright wedge onto the royal blue pad on the bench below the window. "There, you see? We are both out there doing our duty, holding the sign," he said, beckoning me to stand beside him.

I strode past a station that held a mini fridge, microwave oven and a coffee pot to a four-poster bed to my right. The thick comforter was quilted in rich beige and pink satin. Matching throw pillows were arranged in an inviting, over-stuffed looking wedge that ran up the cream colored wall behind the headboard. A small, dark wood table stood beside the bed, complete with a reading lamp and a thick, leather bound book. I averted my gaze from the unwanted comforts and peered out the second-story window to the sign below.

The same, dark gargoyle version of Peter that held the sign the day before rested there, long arm stretched across the bottom of the wood, nearly to the other side of the plank closest to the storefront. Where nothing had been yesterday, a smaller gargoyle crouched against the wall of the shop, sunshine glinting from an outstretched arm holding the other end of the sign under the word "*Taberna*."

The surreal had taken place. I wasn't able to deal with such a substantial event. I couldn't imagine myself looking like the stone-faced, scaled representation that rested, dormant outside the window.

"And why couldn't we see this from the sidewalk?" I said, continuing to stare at the gargoyles.

Peter didn't answer. I traced his gaze to my forearm where it rested against the window pane.

Warm sunlight washed across the skin of my hand and arm, clear to my shoulder. A network of blackened veins spider-webbed its way across my flesh, growing darker in shade against translucent muscle. I rotated my arm in amazement, eyes widening at the sight of bright, clean bone peeking through sinewy, pale grey tendons and charcoal ligaments in my wrist. I flexed a shaking hand, bringing it close to my face. Once out of direct sunlight, the skin there returned to peachy flesh that covered the inner workings of my hand.

I wobbled slightly. "What the heck has that freak done to me?"

Putting his hands on my shoulders, Peter gently lowered me to the cushioned window seat, being careful to keep me from the sun's rays. He reached above us and released a blind to cover the window.

"Ezra has a sense about people. And fate."

Amazing. Peter said the one thing that I felt in touch with. Fate had it in for me. She had a way of sneaking in to deal low blows when I let my guard down. I could buy Peter's excuse about how the flighty, bipolar codger downstairs might have seen something in my future that didn't bode well for me. Stranger things had happened in just the previous night.

"And now you see," Peter continued, sitting beside me, "while the sun is up, we look just like we did before." He searched my face for understanding. I nodded, biting down on my lip to keep it from quivering. He continued. "We work at *Librorum Taberna* during business hours, helping Ezra with the patrons." He rose and strode to the small table, retrieving the large book. "At night, we are free to wander this place as our gargoyles. This building is huge, by the way."

He approached, handing me the book. "I'll wager this is a big book of fluffy nursery rhymes. Ezra is in control of what the pages of every book in this place contain."

"I was reading a bit yesterday and nothing was different in the books I looked through." I shrugged. Sure, I'd seen some crazy things in the last few days, but I struggled to buy that the whole bookstore, all the historical writing, was gone and replaced by Mother Goose. All that wonderful literature being removed was a sin on any day.

"It will be different now, trust me."

I took the book and flipped the cover.

"This is Mary Shelley's 'Frankenstein'. It's rather thought provoking for the current state of things, don't ya think?"

"You're joking," he said, and reached for the book.

I let him take it. He opened the cover, slapped it shut and handed it right back.

"What?" I looked from him to the leather cover.

"He must have done that just for me. I asked him to, ages ago."

"Asked him what? To change what the books are about?"

"Yes. I went through a time when I thought I'd lose my wits. I was lonely, and going insane, truth be told. I asked him to change the books. I thought it would help. Mayhap keep me calm. I was young. It was a bad idea."

I set the book aside. We could talk about literature some other time. I was beginning to count on Peter to keep me grounded, to try to stay afloat in the torrent of the last day and night. I needed him to stay in the moment long enough to show me the door.

Apparently, he agreed. He stood and turned to a row of wooden cabinets opposite the bed. Opening the first set of doors wide for me to see inside, he displayed a vanity table with lighted mirrors and a plush stool. The next opened on a student desk with outlets and a lamp to study by. "Go, Vannah," I said.

Peter gave me a half-confused look. "What?"

"Forget it."

He continued and the next set of doors revealed a clothes armoire where hung two collared shirts. Peter pulled one off the closet rod and held it out for me.

I snorted. "I am *not* wearing that." Embroidered letters spelled out *"Librorum Taberna"* high on the left breast. The shirt was, of course, pink.

"Why not? Mine are plain white," he said.

"You can have the pink ones, too."

Peter ignored me and continued flipping open doors. On a low shelf sat my backpack.

"Hey! My bag." I walked to the cabinet and greedily snatched my pack. "I'd forgotten all about it."

Peter checked his watch. "The store opens in about forty-five minutes. There is a full bath and toilet at the end of the hall," he said as he opened the last cabinet door.

"Wow," I admitted. "He thought of everything didn't he? How did he get all this out of my dorm room?"

"He has odd means of making things go in his favor. Best not ask."

I sifted through hangers of my clothes from the dorm. All my shoes were neatly arranged on a cedar rack. My shower bag rested atop a stack of towels and facial cloths. A quick inspection of a small set of drawers within turned up my underwear and sweats, along with my stash of tampons.

Peter stared my neatly folded bras and panties. He pulled his eyes away and looked at me. Something a little different sparked in his eyes. "I'll be back in half hour to get you." He tossed the words over his shoulder on the way to the door. When he heard no response, he turned toward me.

Facing being alone in my room was scary. Without Peter with me, reality would strike and I'd lose it. "So, this is it? I . . . am just *here* now?" I asked, praying for a last admission that he knew a way out. I bit down on my cheek to stop my chin from quivering. I'd become a complete, emotional marshmallow.

He gave a stern nod.

"I need to get word to my professor that I'm okay. He's got to be worried sick about me by now."

"Ezra sent a very persuasive postcard."

"I want to send my own." If someone was going to lie to my professor about my well-being, it was going to be me.

"Write a letter and I'll post it for you. Ezra has envelopes in his study so include the postal address on your note. Don't try to seal it up. Ezra will want to read it or it won't make it out of the store." He gave a nod to punctuate the importance of his words. "And keep it brief. No details about where you are. Just tell your professor that you're okay and will write more later. A 'not to worry' type of thing, yes?"

"I get it, Peter." Of course Ezra would want to read my letter. But it was better than not contacting Professor Douglas at all. The thought of possibly never seeing him put me over the emotional edge. I was losing what little grip I had on my life to the bookstore's vice-like grasp. I had to take charge. Had to get out and find normalcy.

"What about what I want? How will I ever do the things I want to do? I mean I have no one waiting for me in the States, no family, and it sucked and all, but . . . ," I clamped my mouth shut. It was a bit of a lie, omitting Brea like that, but I wasn't sure I wanted anyone to know about her, considering recent events. I missed her painfully. And besides, I'd developed a plan for my life. "I want to be a British Literature teacher!"

"I know how you feel," he offered, trying to calm me.

"How can you say that?" I asked through tears. "You can't possibly know how terrible I feel right now."

"Well, Miss British Literature Teacher Wannabe," he sneered. "You're not the only one with a tragic past, you know. My first word was 'sweep'. You must be familiar with the works of our poets, since you're willing to attempt to make a living teaching about London's history."

I eyed him doubtfully. "Now you're telling me you've been alive since the early eighteen-hundreds?"

"Born in seventeen-eighty-nine, sold in seventeen-ninety-two," he stated flatly.

Peter being alive for a couple centuries seemed to fit the theme of unbelievable happenings around the bookstore. My studies and discussions with Professor Douglas taught me about the horrible life of a child born into labor in England's Industrial Age. If he was telling the truth, Peter was lucky to be alive.

"I'm sorry, Peter," I said quietly. I didn't know if I wanted to apologize more for my anger earlier, for my disbelief, or for the torment he might have endured as a child. "I really am." I was an idiot. He'd been so calm, trying to console me and I'd repaid the favor by yelling at him. "Please, please help me out of here," I begged.

"Stop this. Now." His words were ice.

I sniffled and forced myself to get a grip.

"Be ready in half hour," he said, and shut the door firmly behind him.

I had no intentions to.

Waiting for time to go by tortured me but I did it by shoving all the most important belongings I could into my backpack. There was no one in the hall when I opened the door five painful minutes later, wearing jeans and my running shoes. Anxiety made sneaking through the halls difficult, but I somehow made it to the sales floor, turned the deadbolts and opened the door. The bard's bells chimed like a siren, setting me off. I burst onto the sidewalk, empowered, owning my right to be outside the realm of the bookstore. Ready to test the theory that *Librorum Taberna* was the source of my transformation, I peered up at the gargoyles holding the sign as I crossed beneath the plank. I would outrun the old man. If Peter ran me down, it was going to get loud and messy.

Sunshine, warmth, the sounds of nearby traffic and the aroma of blossoming flower boxes greeted me as I cleared the storefront. Two steps into liberty, so did Ezra.

"Stay back," I warned. "I'll scream and draw a crowd." Everyone would think him a freakish, dirty old man. Not the case, but I wasn't the one who started dealing low-blows.

"You want people here?" he asked, gesturing behind me. "There comes a couple, just now. We'll do this together, you and I," he said nodding. "Let us see if they like a skinless girl. Show them what you're made of." He narrowed his eyes.

I glanced over my shoulder, looking past long strands of my grey hair. A pair of ladies took their time window shopping but came our direction, and behind them more shoppers approached. The shops inside the Court would open within minutes, calling in droves from the outer streets.

Turning back to Ezra, I cringed inwardly as more people appeared down the sidewalk behind him. Tendons and sinew flexed in my hands as I tightened my grip on the shoulder straps of my backpack.

Ezra stepped aside, gesturing with his head toward Charing Cross Road. A mom with a toddler in tow poked at a cell phone with the thumb of one hand. Baby blue eyes peered up at me, growing wide as the couple neared. I panicked.

"The Tube Stop is not quite two blocks down in the Square, just past all these people." Ezra said, barely above a whisper.

Two seconds spanned incredibly while scenarios ran in my mind. The tiny child was too young to speak, just learning to walk. He wobbled nearer on novice feet, continuing to stare, eyes taking in my monstrous appearance. His mom would look up and shriek any moment. I glanced at the impossible distance between me and the end of the court. Leicester Square bustled lively beyond. I drew in a shaky breath, bracing myself for the scream headed my way as the woman took the remaining steps toward the terror waiting when she saw me.

The little boy stopped, gazing at me. His mommy looked down at him, cell phone still propped at eye level.

My heart lurched. A selfish act would cause such everlasting harm. I would change lives for the worst, starting with the two approaching. Then others that followed. I would scar them.

I gave up my freedom with a shaky sigh. My life was officially trashed for good, owned by Fate, and there was no way I could scare people that badly. I'd likely be caught and dissected in a lab somewhere if I did try to run.

"Step into the nook, child." Ezra nodded toward the shaded alcove in front of the bookstore. I walked to the safety of shadow, sunlight giving way to humanity, just in time.

The mother bent, scooping up the little boy. She placed a quick kiss on his cheek, nuzzling a giggle from his neck. He smiled at me with blind trust in the innate good in people, skinless and see-through, or flesh tone like he and his mommy, alike. I smiled at him, strangling a sob. Ezra pulled the door open and I ducked inside.

"You did this to me." My words sounded lifeless, like an echo from my heart. I turned on him. "Change me back," I demanded.

"I can't."

"I don't believe you," I said through grit teeth.

"Even if I could I wouldn't. I've made my choice."

"I'll get you back for this," I vowed. Raw hatred dripped from my words.

"I hope one day you shall." Ezra wasn't smiling, either.

I scoffed, glaring.

"What's going on?" Peter called from the stairs. "I was just by your room."

"Tessa will be back up shortly," Ezra said, keeping his white eyes on me.

I glanced at Peter. He looked at the bag on my shoulder, down at my running shoes and right back up to my face. There was betrayal in his eyes. He didn't look away, his gaze saying many things like, *"Idiot, you could've been seen,"* or even more guilt inducing, *"You were leaving me, too."*

Humiliation aside, at least I'd proven I wouldn't cow down. Neither of the guys should expect me to just hang out, to stand by and be victimized. Pride blended with defeat. I focused on the stairs and didn't take my eyes off them, even when I felt my shoulder glance off Peter's arm as I went by.

* * *

TESSA'S JOURNAL-JULY 1— This has been the longest two days of my life, easily. I never knew it would be possible to feel more alone. I am trapped. I can't leave. I am trapped. I can't leave . . . I am trapped. I can't leave . . . .

Fate still owns me and does with me what she pleases. It's compounded by what happened in Austin. I wanted my brother so badly. I'd wanted freedom. I feel like I've done a lot of growing up.

I have to find some little piece of good in life right now so I've been thinking a lot about it. My mind always returns to Peter. I feel like an ass for saying what I did. And an idiot for trying to leave when he warned me. He tried to be nice and offer friendship and I screwed it up.

He seems like a decent person, but I can't shake the feeling that this all just isn't right, and he's a part of that.

I'm still struggling to wrap my head around the fact that he's been alive for centuries. It's odd how recent events have inspired me to believe such things are possible.

Side note— that means Ezra's been around at least that long.

CHAPTER 7

$\mathcal{I}$ was in no hurry to go to work at their store when I put down my only salvaged pen and journal. But I didn't know what else to do with myself. I'd earn Ezra's trust and I *would* find a way out. I had to go along with my new lot in life for the time being. The thought was oddly calming. I saw it for the blessing it was.

Spirits slightly bolstered by a hot shower, I emerged from my room wearing the collared shirt I'd been given, my favorite jeans, and my running shoes since I was sure I would be on my feet all day.

Talking with the store's patrons helped to keep me on an even keel, and I quickly began to enjoy watching Peter interact with them. He was quick to smile, and despite the fact that he was only allowed to read what Ezra decided was safe, Peter was proficient with the reads in the shop. Best of all was the way he allowed boyish charm to radiate throughout whatever task he worked at. As nice as it was to talk with people and work with Peter, I found myself dreading nightfall each time I checked the clock.

Ezra showed up that afternoon, meeting us with a smile. He handed over my iHome (a gift Brea and her family gave me as a graduation present), three spiral-bound notebooks and a new package of pens.

"Thank you," I said, tentatively.

"You're welcome, dear girl."

I bit back the urge to lash out at him for attempting to endear me. "Ezra, my laptop is missing from my bag. Do you know where it is?"

"I have it." He pulled a set of keys from his vest pocket. "The notebooks will have to do, for now. Once you've done things to earn my trust, and it will be a long time from today, we'll talk about your use of the Internet here at the store. It's secured so you won't find any on the iPod."

I swallowed the urge to protest, realizing his offering of my music and the writing utensils were likely Ezra's version of a peace offering. He was trying, at least, to make me feel better. Or to continue to keep me. I nodded my response and handed over my letter to Professor Douglas.

Ezra read the scant lines I'd written. "I'll get this on the way in the morning," he said, and strode toward the back stairwell.

I guessed that meant he approved and was sure I wasn't calling out for reinforcements or staging a coo. "What, no 'goodnight, dear girl?'" I taunted, hating my ability to sound friendly. I needed to gain his trust, then I was out of there at the soonest opportunity.

Peter snorted a small, sarcastic laugh.

Ezra glanced over a shoulder with a smile. "You and I are going to get on just fine." He winked and continued on his way.

I doubted that. He'd done unforgivable things to me. And even more grating was the fact that he acted like what he'd done *was* forgivable somehow. I didn't know if I was capable of that.

"Shall we close it up for the day?" Peter asked.

I followed him to the entrance. As Peter flipped the "Open Please Come In" window card to read "Please Call Again at 9," I gazed out to the wooden sign above the sidewalk in my beloved Cecil Court. I'd never look at it the same again.

Our gargoyles were statuesque in the gloaming.

"What do you think?" Peter asked. He nodded toward the gothic things grasping the plank.

I couldn't tell him what I really thought. I fought the urge to bolt out the door each time it opened, and take my chances in the elements. Whether he wanted to talk about gargoyles or rainbows, that wasn't going to change. I considered his gesture for a moment. Maybe focusing on one element in a series of unwanted changes hid some genius. Fostered some sanity, perhaps.

I sighed loudly. "Better to hold a sign than be a downspout, huh?" I answered, and made an "O" with my lips.

He laughed, and made his lips round, as well. "No . . . this just isn't me either," he said, bending the words as he kept his lips in an imitation spout.

I stared at him in wonder, a little jealous of his ability to balance horror with humor. We stared out the window in silence for a moment, taking in the beauty of the London evening through a thick pane of glass.

"It's about time to change for the night," he said.

"I'm going to my room." I pulled my gaze from the beauty of cobbles and flower boxes at twilight. "I just need some time to let this all gel, ya know?" The feeling of my flesh morphing while I waited to become something foreign would never set right with me. I harbored the hope it wouldn't happen again, somehow knowing I would be disappointed.

Peter nodded. His gaze rendered understanding, making part of me want to drag him along with me, to have him to cry against. To comfort me as I came apart.

I held it together and walked away. I'd dealt with disappointment by finding resilience in myself in the past, and I wasn't going to quit trying then.

CHAPTER 8

$\mathcal{T}$he day my flight left Austin-Bergstrom International Airport, I'd spent the morning at Brea's house, having breakfast with her family. We joked about me meeting a nice English boy and never returning to Austin. Although Brea smiled when she told me she was happy for me, she choked back tears. We hugged like sisters.

I'd have given anything to go back.

I awaited nightfall, a murderer without pardon.

Part of me still didn't believe it was really going to happen, but I changed into a gargoyle again like I expected. There had been a place in my heart that held out hope I would be saved at the last moment, some part of the universe stepping up and admitting it was just messing with me. That I was still human and would never look like that again.

Darkness took the day. The change began. Just like deranged clockwork.

I turned out the light in my room while my body mutated. The severity of the transformation was too excruciating to watch and feel at the same time. It took a while before I got up the courage to turn on the light.

I examined my serpentine countenance in the large vanity mirror. The surreal feeling was back. Sadness gazed at me from receded eyes that were the only visible part of my body remaining unchanged. Thankfully, seeing familiarity there reminded me of *me*. But the rest of the reflection was a complete 180 degree flip.

I tried to think up one word that would sum up my appearance as a gargoyle. *Demonic?* I tilted my head in the mirror. *No, not evil,* I decided. I was too "puppy-dog" like for that. I opened my puggish snout to display pointed fangs shining white against the dark purplish smoothness inside my mouth. *But absolutely* wicked, *for sure.* I wiggled my upturned nose.

I trying for some semblance of normalcy in my freak show of a new life. I lit one of the travel candles I packed for the trip to London so the light aroma of sweet jasmine scented my new bedroom. Lorde's "Tennis Court" thrummed low from my iHome's speakers. I found my mini fridge stocked with fresh fruit and snacks, and after a considerable amount of crumbled failure was able to set a portion of a raspberry tea biscuit inside my mouth, chew, and swallow. I stuck out my forked tongue in the reflection, moving the two tines separately. There were dark similarities between that and the fork in my life's road. The thought pulled at my heart, my chest growing tight. What the heck did I have to return to, anyway?

Professor Douglas was still there. He'd been so great helping me get ready for the trip. I'd been scared I wouldn't be able to go. I loved remembering the day I'd gone into his office to talk to him about studying abroad. He was sitting at his desk when I burst through his door. I'd plopped into the oversized armchair adjacent to him and he'd spun in his chair with the usual, warm, paternal smile I was accustomed to.

"Sorry." I'd smiled back. I had to. I loved the man. "Did you get my email?" I'd asked him.

"Sure did." He turned at his desk to dig into the attached, side file cabinet. "Not to worry, Tessa." He slid a blue passport across the desk toward me with a grin.

I snatched it and inspected the first two pages. There was a photo of me on one page and the other held my vital info. "How did you do this? I couldn't find my birth certificate." I pursed my lips. Admitting to snooping through my files in front of a faculty member wasn't one of my brainier moves. *Nice.*

"Let's not question the good things when they come along, shall we?" He winked.

"We shan't." I beamed at him.

"We leave a week from Sunday. Your scholarship has been approved." He pushed a green folder toward me.

"That was like, lightning speed." I perused the few signed forms inside the file.

"I've got a source," he teased.

I stacked my passport neatly on top of the folder and stood to leave, an incredible sense of relief gracing me. "Thank you."

"You're very welcome, young lady." He leaned back in his chair. "Keep that somewhere safe so it doesn't get lost."

"I won't lose it." There was no way. I was like Charlie and my passport was my Golden Ticket to the Chocolate Factory. A tempting urge baited me to sprint through the halls hooting at the top of my lungs, with the little blue book held high above my head as I ran.

We said quick goodbyes and I'd gone back to my dorm room to stash my passport safely away in my underwear drawer after enclosing the photo of my brother and me inside the little blue folder. That was one of the happiest days of my life, and it was all because Professor Douglas went the extra mile to make sure an orphan got to go to London. That made him one of a kind in my book.

A light knock sounded at my door, jolting me from my memories. I really hoped it was Peter, not Ezra. I pulled it open.

"Come on in," I said, relieved. I closed the door after Peter entered. "Look at you, all . . . gargoyle-ly."

"I just wanted to see how you fared against the transformation."

"It was quick," I walked to the mirror, checking for any remnants of the viscous fluid that remained from the change. "It seemed to dry faster this time, and the burning feeling wasn't as intense as last night." I gestured down at the stained skirt and camisole I'd worn the night before. "I put these on just in case, and I'm glad I did." I pulled at the skirt, attempting to get it to hang straight across the span of my thighs. I'd given up on the thin, satin cami and it rested uneventfully against my plated chest. My body was slender and sinewy, but bulging and muscular in places like my thighs and shoulders, very reptilian in nature. I huffed and crossed my arms over my chest.

"I kind of hate this." My voice cracked. "I can't help feeling that any second, I'm going to just, like, *wake up*."

His expression was a mixture of understanding, remembrance and a new look, one that hinted that it was time to quit whining. I didn't know if I was ready for that from Peter.

"You need to switch focus. Get out of the bookstore. You shouldn't continue to stare in the looking glass. It's not going to stop."

"We can't leave the bookstore, Peter. At least, *I* can't. Ezra would lay a golden egg or something." I dropped onto the bed, causing the frame under the mattress to squeak in protest. "Sweet of you to offer though."

"Were you planning to tell him?" He didn't wait for me to answer, just pulled me up by an arm and tugged me toward the door.

"Peter, I—"

"Quiet."

I did my best to walk in silence and keep up, concentrating on keeping my wings tucked in. The dark hallways reminded me of being lost, the vastness of the store seeming endless again. We made our way up a long staircase that led to the store's rooftop. I sucked in an amazed breath as I stepped into a bath of silver moonlight in the clear chill of the night. Shingled rooftops reflected dark metal hues below our perch atop the monstrous *Librorum Taberna*, which confirmed the misleading look of the modestly small storefront. Clearly, the building that housed the bookstore was enormous beyond the façade on Cecil Court. I spun, taking in the full beauty of the London night. It seemed like forever since I'd been outside in fresh air.

"Thank you, Peter." I gazed at the sleepy city I loved, and stepped to the ledge to get a better view, hunching down. My wings furled together at my shoulders and it was such a bizarre feeling, I shuddered. Peter squatted next to me, naturally gothic in his pose.

"We aren't there yet," he said, taking my clawed hand in his. He pulled me to standing beside him. "You have to be silent when we do this, yes?"

"Do what?" I looked down. Surely he didn't want to jump off the roof or something crazy. I'd had enough crazy to last me a lifetime.

"I thought we could go for a little flight over the city. I mean, unless you're scared or something," he teased.

I looked from the street below to Peter's face, testing him for sincerity. "You're messing with me."

"I would never." He winked.

I jerked slightly as a series of gentle *pops* sounded behind me. Peter unfurled his wings to an impressive span along the length of the rooftop.

"What do you think these are for?" He shot me a look that said, *"Get on the boat kid."*

"I don't know, balance?" I said, trying to step back from the ledge.

"Scared?" His grin had an evil twist. "But that's expected. I mean you are a *girl*, after all. Wouldn't want to break a nail or muss up your hair."

I rolled my eyes, successfully prodded. I'd never been afraid of much, and painted nails had nothing to do with it, but he was right. I was scared.

He launched with silent grace from where we stood, staying level with the rooftop, gliding in a slow arc atop the crisp, night air. I watched with amazement. He flew close and pumped his wings to gain altitude above me, sending two bursts of cool air to buffet my hair. I spun around as he landed lightly on the roof. My mouth hung open a bit. I clapped it shut with a sharp snap of my teeth.

"Ready?" He strode toward me.

"I don't know if I can. I mean, I can't even swim," I admitted, sending Peter into a brief bout of laughter.

"Where's the water?" he managed. He snorted, fighting the urge to burst out laughing again. "You're something else."

"I mean, I don't float," I snapped. "I really don't see what's so freaking funny here."

He cleared his throat. "It has nothing to do with floating. But let's go anyway." He held out a claw. "There's no room to be timid when you're a gargoyle." The carefully chosen words called me out.

I looked from his waiting talons to his face, unsure if I was a fan of Peter's personal brand of tough love. I'd never been one to look for an excuse to back down, but that didn't mean I had become one to trust easily either. "Promise not to let go?"

"Promise," he stated. "Unless you tell me to."

Peter's human face flashed through my mind with his voice. "Deal." I latched onto his claw and he led me to the ledge. He took two paces back. I followed suit without questioning the actions, determined to overcome fear.

"Best to get a bit of a run at first, so we'll take two running steps then jump on three," he nodded for emphasis.

"Let's just do this thingy before I change my mind, okay?" My voice shook. I put a foot down on my tail to keep it from twitching.

"Deal." He squeezed my claw. "Look out there." He motioned to the open air beside the rooftop.

"Okay." *This is nuts, nuts, nuts. What if I pee?* I glanced to the street below, apologetically looking for pedestrians that may receive an unlikely shower.

Peter leaned forward, so I did the same, despite the shaking in my legs. He announced the first step with a stern sounding "One." I matched his pace with my right, then my left foot, and on his count of "Three" I slammed my eyes shut, diving forward. "Crap, oh, crap . . . ," I said between clenched teeth. Cool air pushed hard at every inch of my body.

"Pssst," he hissed. "Open your eyes."

I peeked. My feet hung above the lane below, making it eerily small. My stomach lurched as my eyes flew wide. I inhaled with a loud snort for a scream that resounded shrill around us. I fought through the air to grasp at Peter with my other claw and one leg, inadvertently pumping my wings, sending us both spiraling forward.

"No . . . oh, bloody hell!" Peter yelled.

He pulled my head into the crook of his shoulder to protect me as we slammed hard into stone, fracturing the wall of a building adjacent to the bookstore. Shards of limestone shot into the air, peppering the cobblestone sidewalk below. We bounced into a free fall. Peter spun out flat in the air, grasping my flailing form with a large, taloned claw. He caught my arm, dragging me through the air as he pumped his wings, towing me along until I regained a soaring position beside him and quit squawking.

"So much for quiet."

"Sorry," I yelled. A frantic feeling still owned me and I shook my head to clear the ringing that persisted from our impact. I didn't feel like I'd been hurt. Our plated, gargoyle forms made us pretty tough. I caught balance on the air, using my tail to maintain a spot next to Peter. "I think I got this," I yelled.

"No need to shout," he said.

"I think you can let go."

"You sure?"

"Yep." I gave his claw a little squeeze for emphasis.

Peter released me, dropping back so I was in his line of sight. After a few moments, he pumped his wings hard. He circled silently above me, but remained close to the bookstore.

I watched Peter as he eclipsed the moon with a wing. Moonglow shone through the membranous film spanning between the boney segments, creating a glittery halo in the sky. His body gleamed dark metallic in the night, majestic on the wind. I pumped my wings once, trembling midflight from the massive lift obtained from the stroke. One more beat against the air sent me back to his side. I smiled over at him. "Thank you."

"You're welcome," he said. "Tessa?"

"Yeah?" I said, still a bit too loud. I made breast-stroke motions beside him in the air.

"I wouldn't advise running away again."

"I don't know where else I'd go," I replied after a moment. "I mean, look at this." I gestured at my scaly body. "I can't go anywhere. And besides, I feel like I've lost . . . me." I looked away. That sounded a little lame.

"Well, I've found you."

Despite his pushing me to get past dwelling on what I'd lost, his words were a huge help. His carefully chosen statement inspired conflict in me. I yearned for comfort and he had to know it, but I was also being assimilated into his world against my will. I still fought that. Judging from his shift in demeanor, he didn't like that.

We soared a bit longer until Peter led me back toward the bookstore, where I impressed myself by not piling up on the rooftop. We rushed down the long staircase where we burst through the door, encountering Ezra on the other side.

I hunched beside Peter. Judging from Ezra's state of agitation, he'd been waiting for us to return for some time. He'd probably heard me scream.

My heart sank when I saw the way Ezra glared at Peter with his colorless, frigid eyes.

"Go to your room, Tessa." Ezra didn't take his eyes from Peter.

"Did someone see us?" I asked.

"No," Peter answered. "The shroud hid us, being that close to the store."

"Now, Tessa!" Ezra thundered.

"Go easy," Peter growled.

I gave Peter one, last, resigned glance. He looked stoic, as if he'd dealt with similar outbursts from Ezra many times. Guilt pricked at me. If he was accustomed to Ezra's temper in the past, that was different. This time, he'd taken me out of my room knowing Ezra would flip out, but he'd done it anyway.

I paced toward my room. The conversation between the two followed me down the hallway.

"You're going to pay for the damage to that building."

"Of course, I will. But you can't expect to keep her locked up inside the store."

"Don't presume to tell me what to expect."

"She isn't a child—"

"I know that, Peter."

"—and neither am I. I rescind my wishes to be treated as such with your damned books."

* * *

LATER WHEN I answered the knock, Peter was there, leaning against the wall. I let the door hang open so he could follow me inside.

"I'm sorry you got in trouble," I said, walking to my mirror. Adjusting to my new reflection was taking some patience. "And I'll find a way to help you pay for the damage we caused. I mean, it was my fault we hit the building."

"Ezra will be fine. He's angry about many things that have to do with much more that our venturing out." He watched me stare myself down in the reflection. "I've already given Ezra enough to pay for the damage, along with a note of apology to deliver in the morning." .He leaned, continuing to watch me. "I think I'll give up reading until he calms."

I picked up my brush and began pulling through knotted, windblown hair. Turned out, flying was hard on the tresses. "I just can't wait to hear what he says to me," I replied.

"I have something for you here," Peter said. I noticed he didn't add to my statement about what sort of punishment I might be in for. "It's not much but I hope you'll like it." Something pink rested in his dark claw. It looked completely unnatural to see pastel against armored grey.

"What, you pay for something I did and then you give me a gift?" I smiled, shaking my head. "You don't have to do that."

"I know that. I was going to give it to you earlier," he stated.

"Okay."

He held out a length of shell pink ribbon. "I was just remembering what you said earlier. About losing yourself. You don't have to give up everything. You're still you inside." Circling behind, he stepped over my tail and tied the ribbon around my neck. "You're beautiful, Tessa," he said over my shoulder, locking our gazes in the mirror. A dainty letter "T" dangled from the ribbon, glinting silver against my scaly throat.

Peter let his canine chin rest gently against my shoulder. "Welcome to the world of scales."

"Thanks." I smiled. I also didn't mean it. A welcome to madness wasn't something I could accept, even if he was the only reason I hadn't gone over the deep end. I wanted to hug him but fought the urge easily when I considered what it would feel like to touch another, scaly gargoyle like that. I could barely stand touching my own skin when I was all "garged out".

He gave my shoulders a quick squeeze and headed back to the hall.

CHAPTER 9

July 4—Independence Day. NOT!
*   I find it amazing how just weeks ago I was ready to stretch my wings and find independence. I had a plan and I was ready to give life an honest-to-goodness attempt.*

Now I really do have wings but no plan.

Ezra is bipolar. It's all I got.

Today's good news: Peter brought me a meat and cheese pasty and a caramel macchiato from Starbucks. I know he's trying to cheer me up. And I really am trying to find some happy. Thank goodness I've always been fairly resilient.

I miss Brea.

* * *

I SPENT the next few days giving a weak attempt at settling into my new routine. I'd wake up early, eat some of the food that kept appearing in my room—Thank you, Ezra—wait until I could shower as a human and go downstairs a little before it was time to open the store each day. It seemed even as a gargoyle, I was still chronically early for everything and didn't need much sleep. I'd work the day away, staying busy as I could to make the time go by faster, then I'd go back to my room, lock the door and wait for the change to happen, which was like being chastised for breathing. I existed; I was punished.

Some mornings I tested myself in the sunlight, if there was any. Most days in London, the sun didn't shine through the clouds or fog. Each time I examined my skin in the sun, however, my flesh did that eerie thing where I could see straight through it to the gleaming bone, lavender membranes and grey tendons. Whatever Ezra did to make me a gargoyle affected every cell of my existence.

I tried not to think about it. I was more upset about being taken. Would *other* people be angrier about being stolen from the life they lead? Before being changed into a gargoyle and confined to a bookstore by a nutty old wizard or whatever Ezra was? Would they be more devastated by the loss of their families and homes than I was at the loss of my mortality and human body? Peter had lived an incredibly long time so I assumed I would, too. I had no way to gauge whether what I was feeling was the way anyone else would be dealing with it. I couldn't help feeling a bit grateful that I wasn't missing a family right then. I would be even more crushed than I was if I only mourned the loss of my freedom and best friend. Lemonade, freshly squeezed.

The ability to stop brooding came easier when I reminded myself to find something worthy of a smile several times each day. If I had difficulties doing that, I knew that generally, finding Peter and sharing in his antics with customers would do the trick. He had a wonderful sense of humor and was so quick-witted when speaking that I always found myself smiling and joining in. We made a good team, and the customers of *Librorum Taberna* were happy ones.

I found myself staring out my window into a dreary late afternoon after Peter had locked up for the night. I pulled my earbuds away and dropped my iPod on my bed and changed into a pair of comfy capri-style sweats and a Spiderman t-shirt. I headed into the hall, planning to go downstairs to try my luck at finding a good read for the night when I heard a metallic *clinking* sound coming from the direction of Peter's room.

His door was open a crack and I made quick work of dispelling any guilt induced by my curiosity when I peered inside.

The sounds were made by a weight machine. Peter lay shirtless on an incline bench, thick arms spread wide, gripping a long, heavily weighted bench-press bar. The muscles of his chest and shoulders bulged as he pushed the bar up, straightening his arms. Sweat glistened on his skin, running in rivulets down his ripped abdomen. The waistband of his pants was soaked and his long ponytail hung wet against a shoulder. His room smelled of salty sweat, but I imagined it was much better than a boys' locker room.

He counted to himself in soft grunts. When he dropped the bar into the saddle-brackets above his head, I knocked softly on his door.

He walked toward me, stopping to grab a towel on the way. I stepped back, trying not to make it seem completely obvious I'd been watching him work out.

He smiled at me through the sliver of sight between us, letting me know I'd been caught watching. "You'd have a much better vantage from inside." He pulled a t-shirt over his head and down his torso, covering all that muscle.

Sad me.

"Sorry to interrupt." I smiled and tried sincerity.

"Right." he winked, and wiped his face with the towel.

I smiled, trying to keep with the façade that I had no idea what he meant. "I just wanted to say hi. I was getting bored. Don't know how you deal with these long afternoons sometimes."

"Well, now you do." He smiled, gesturing to the large set of weights and other means of self-torture, like a jump rope and a speed bag like boxers use to work out. He continued to wipe away sweat from pumped up muscles, still breathing a little hard from his work out.

"I miss running. That's how I used to blow off steam. It sort of made me feel liberated somehow. Writing makes me feel better, too." Over his shoulder, I spotted a hallway leading beyond the room we stood in. "Hey, your room is huge. That's hardly fair."

"There's more to my presence here than just selling books." He gestured toward his bed, so I sat. Apparently I wouldn't get a grand tour.

"I've a bargain for you." The offer was laced with warning. "If you can be trusted." He looked like he wasn't so sure if opening his mouth was the greatest idea.

"That would be awesome." I was all ears. We had to start somewhere, and I'd much rather work on trust with Peter since he seemed more pliant toward accommodating my well-being. Ezra was distant, easily angered, and unapologetic. And he didn't offer any concessions.

PETER and I worked out a deal during the next week. Before closing every day, if there weren't many customers in the store when it was close to time to flip the sign, he'd lock up when business slowed in the afternoon if I would open up in the mornings. Being the early riser I was, I gladly accepted. The bargain between us allowed for extra journaling time for me, which was much easier accomplished without talons, so I tried hard to find time to add entries in my journal while human every day. It was perfect. I could find a quiet place each afternoon and tuck myself between the pages of what I wrote. I was briefly happy during those times when I detached myself from my surroundings.

I sat on the second floor of the bookstore, ensconced in one of my favorite reading nooks, scribing away in a creamy moleskin notebook with the perfect shade of green ink.

A book fell on the ground floor. I set my things aside. Peter had locked up already. I'd seen him flip the sign myself. I chilled inside, rising from my chair in an instant when I peered down through the banister to see a girl walking the aisles, innocently perusing the reads at her leisure. I could barely make out her face from my vantage point on the second floor. She'd been locked inside the store and must have knocked a book over on a shelf to cause the noise.

Holy hell.

Nightfall approached and there was a teenaged girl in the store. Not good, considering that's how *my* life got *jacked* out from under me. I needed to get downstairs and get her to leave. As far as I could tell there was no way to *unjack* my life, and it wouldn't do for someone else to suffer the same fate as me merely because they were curious and young, too.

I took the spiral stairs two at a time to get down faster and rounded the corner at a run, looking for her and trying to catch up before something horrible happened. I'd be Garging Out any second but I couldn't risk Ezra finding her, so I didn't call out to get her attention. If I could just meet up with her and convince her to leave and come back tomorrow morning, I'd save her. I ran, peering through bookcases and around corners, looking franticly.

A loud *thump* sounded ahead of me. I broke into a sprint, hating the tingling in my skin that marked the start of my nightly transformation. It seemed to be happening a little faster because I was so amped up. I stopped short in the entry to one of the store's many alcoves.

I was too late. The girl I'd been searching for had collapsed on the floor, just inside.

A gasp pulled my attention to the right of the nook.

Ezra stood motionless. He appeared a little paler than normal, if that was possible. My hands went to my temples as I digested the scene. Why couldn't I have been seconds quicker getting to her? He'd beaten me to the punch. But he just stood there. Statuesque. Even creepier than normal.

Something wasn't right. Not that anything in my new world was the way I'd pictured it. Ezra seemed to be in shock. His pure white eyes were transfixed on the young girl.

"No . . . no," Ezra moaned. He crouched beside her crumpled form.

The realization of what I was seeing hit me hard.

Unbelievable.

"You've lost control of it." I stepped through the doorway and straight to the two of them. I was changing fast, my emotional state speeding my transformation. When I tried to take a knee beside the pair of them, I went back on my haunches and rested on a splayed wing.

She wore a faded black t shirt that was so old I couldn't make out the design on the front. Dirty jeans and tired sneakers with no socks made up the rest of her outfit. Long, blackish brown hair had fallen in a mass of twisted strands across her face. Her hands were dirty and she didn't smell all that great. I wanted to cry for her.

I glanced at Ezra, who'd still said nothing.

"How long?"

"How long what?" he answered.

"When did you lose control of the magic that does . . . this!" I yelled. I couldn't help it. Seeing the unconscious girl and knowing what awaited her hit home. My temperature soared. I wanted to reach over and throttle him, but I knew better. I didn't know for sure, but something told me he could end me just as easily as he'd created me.

"I wish everything had always gone as smoothly as it did with you, but it's been a challenge at times." He reached to clear the girl's hair from her face.

"Smoothly? You call this smooth?" I hated his ability to downplay the most terrifying event in my life. I hissed at him. "Do you have any freaking idea what it's like? Just . . . ." I grit my fangs. "Don't touch her," I snapped, in a new, lower range for my voice.

"Watch your tone, Tessa. You forget yourself." He glared across her form at me. It amazed me how he managed to pull off a perfect glare with no pupils.

"What, you going to lock her in a room and let her fall to pieces while she changes? Alone?" It's what he'd allowed to happen to me, and we both knew I'd never forgive him.

Guilt covered Ezra's face, so fast it could have dripped onto the floor.

I scooped her up, careful not to scratch her with my talons.

"Keep a close eye on her."

I ignored him. She was so light in my grip, although she was rather tall. Tears stung the back of my eyes. I would do for this girl what Peter had done for me when I changed. Where he'd only been there for the end, I'd be at her side for the whole, terrifying experience. I would be there from the first instant she awoke. I stole out of the alcove with her in my arms and half ran, half flew to my room. I didn't look once to see if Ezra remained where I'd left him.

CHAPTER 10

*S*he started changing and woke up before I got her inside. Her body twitched against my chest repeatedly while I worked to open my door. She screamed at me to let her go. I laid her down as gently as I could while she thrashed. Her skin turned a deep red, almost the same shade as blood.

She shrieked at me when she saw me watching her. I tried to calm her by speaking softly. "It's okay. I can explain it all."

She stared with pain dripping from her eyes.

"The burning will pass and things will be easier soon." She had a friend to lean on. I would help her.

Her transformation seemed to pass faster than my first one had, but it could have seemed that way because I was watching it happen to someone else rather than feeling the terror and pain. I continued to try to calm her.

She glared at me from a serpentine shaped face and head. Her hair clung to her cheeks in matted strands of copper and blood red. She hissed at me, showing a long tongue between jagged rows of shark teeth.

My bed was shredded and my reading lamp crashed to the carpet with one last spark of life.

Her eyes were on me again, a beautiful shade of hazel. I reached to put a hand on her shoulder but she jerked away, slapping my forearm hard.

"Ow!" I cried. "What was that for?"

"Don't ever touch me again," she hissed. It was barely audible. The girl had major work to do in the articulation department.

"I was just trying to comfort you. I know how you're feeling," I offered.

Her head rocked back toward the ceiling and she laughed. It was the laughter of someone sick. Deranged. She stood and took a few steps away from the bed.

"You'll pay for this, if it's the last thing I do." She glared at me. I could detect a British tone to her words when she spoke a longer sentence.

"Wait, wait. Whoa. I didn't do this to you. I saw it happen and brought you up to my room here to try to comfort you as you changed, so you wouldn't be alone somewhere. I was trying to help." I stopped talking. It probably sounded unbelievable to her.

She examined me through narrowed eyes while her head rocked from side to side. I shuddered. The girl's transformation had left her more "angry monster" than the canine nature of Peter and me. She was a lot like a big snake with wings and it was freaking me out. The way she had no fear of me was alarming, because I was under the impression she'd never seen a gargoyle before. Perhaps I was wrong.

Her eyes darted around my room and came to rest on the window where I had half drawn the blinds earlier.

I was a millisecond too late trying to grab her when she ran toward the window and lunged through the glass into the night. She screamed viciously from outside. I carefully stuck my head through the jagged glass but all I saw was a long skinny tail slipping away into the dark of the cool night sky.

I sighed. I'd never find her by the time I made it outside and she wouldn't come back with me, if I was lucky enough to pick her out in the darkness. Flying must have come easier to some than others.

* * *

I POUNDED CONTINUOUSLY on Peter's door until he opened it. I stalked inside.

"Won't you please come in?" he asked dryly.

"You, my friend, are a freaking *saint*." I panted a little.

He regarded me with one raised brow. "What is going on with you now?" His tail twitched despite his obvious opinion that no matter the case, I was overreacting.

"There is a new gargoyle," I stated. I crossed my arms over my chest plate and stared up at him, tapping away at the floor with the tip of my tail. "You are a very patient and sweet person to put up with the emotional outcome of someone changing for the first time, without throttling them."

"Where is it?" He stepped toward his door. The "stop over-reacting" look evaporated from his face.

I exhaled and put a foot down to stop my tail from swishing like an agitated cat's. "There's a problem." I scratched my fore-head. He was going to lose it when I told him.

"Come on then, let's have it."

"Don't snap, Peter." I fidgeted. "She left." Might as well just put it out there.

"Left?"

"Yes. She flew out my window."

"What the bloody hell were you doing with a strange, new gargoyle in your room, Tessa?" he yelled.

"Don't yell at *me*, buddy. I was just trying to make sure she had someone with her the whole time, instead of wandering around this place not knowing what was happening to her!" One more person yelled or hissed at me and I was going to chew one of their arms clean off.

"I just remember looking for you everywhere because it seemed like finding you was the only thing that would help when I was changing. I didn't want her to feel alone." I looked down. I'd failed miserably at helping the girl at all. Peter was mad. Ezra had even warned to keep an eye on her, and I was so full of my ability to take charge that I'd paid no heed.

Peter sighed. He continued in a low, emotionless tone. "Does Ezra know?"

I perked up. "Well there's an interesting, new development with him. He didn't do this." I had the inside scoop, for once.

"Come on, you can explain that on the way to find him." He pulled me out of his room by an elbow, so fast that my wing struck the door jam.

"Ow!" I winced, reached over my shoulder, trying to rub a part of my body I was unable to touch.

Peter turned quickly when I cried out. He stopped moving and took a deep breath. "I'm sorry, Tessa. You all right?" he examined my wing with concern, pulling me around so he could check the damage.

I jostled myself free of his grip. "I'm really tired of being shoved out of the way." I rubbed the side of my wing, close as I could to the actual injury and followed him to the stairs.

"She hates me."

"Who hates you?" he said over his shoulder.

"The new gargoyle. She thinks I'm the one that made her Garg Out."

Peter stopped moving and shook his head. "Really, Tessa? *Garg Out?*"

"What?"

He continued down the hall. "Let's go talk to Ezra first. He'll know what to do."

"Well that's the thing," I began. We glided over the banister to the ground floor of the shop. "He knows already."

"That she left the store?"

"No, not that part."

"Knows what then?" The loss of his patience grew obvious.

All I could do was try to explain it, best as I could. "Because changing her into a gargoyle wasn't exactly his idea. Somehow, she was changed without him doing it."

Peter studied me as if he had a dozen unspoken questions, none of which I had the answers to. "You're telling me someone here, in the store, performed the magic to create a gargoyle, and it wasn't Ezra?"

"That's a good point. I don't know. I mean it was obvious Ezra isn't the one who did it, but it's possible it could have happened outside, before she walked in, right? Someone could have zapped her outside and then when she was in the store and it started getting dark, she changed in here?" I was reaching for answers, but it had to have happened *somehow*.

The feeling that I knew more about the situation than he did abandoned me like a bee to a fresher flower. It figured. And Ezra was going to be pissy because of the way I talked to him when I saw him last.

"I don't really want to see Ezra. He's mad at me again. Still, I mean."

"He's never going to stay mad at you for long, Tessa, trust me." His statement was stone-cold, harboring an edge of sarcasm.

"Why would you say that? He acts like he hates me."

"Well he doesn't. He calls you our 'perfect addition.'" I imagined Peter making little air quotes around the words as he spoke, to match his tone.

"That's ridiculous."

"Mph."

"Hold on there, Peter, do I sense a bit of jealousy?" I teased.

"Don't flatter yourself."

"You're jealous!" Spit flew from between my fangs with my lisp.

He shook his head.

"Well who could blame you?" I laughed. "I am pretty darned thpecial." I bounced along behind him, fluffing my wings.

"Special. Exactly," he laughed.

"It's okay, buddy. We can't all be his favorite." I giggled, poking at his shoulder with a talon.

He laughed. "Just keep telling yourself that, sweetheart."

Peter kept walking and I didn't know what else to do but to follow.

CHAPTER 11

*E*zra reacted with the couth and temperament of a spoiled three-year-old. He threw books and the lamp from his desk.

"Brilliant," he sneered. "Leave."

I did that without being told a second time. Peter stayed behind and the two men shouted and grumbled behind the closed door. I waited for Peter to emerge and broke into step beside him, but he was silent. The emotional tension eased as we walked toward my room. I'd left my door open in my haste to get to him after the other gargoyle broke out, so when we arrived the trashed out bed was in clear view.

"Well this is a fine mess." Peter glanced around. "I'm going to go get a couple things from downstairs. Take those sheets off the bed and I'll be back with fresh ones."

"Thanks." The air was cold in my room and smelled of the damp city outside. The blind was pulled down with slats broken out in the middle. I decided to make short work of the situation and picked up the mattress, shaking loose a pile of bedding.

Peter returned with a small tool box and a stack of neatly folded sheets that smelled of lavender.

"You're my hero," I told him as I took the linens. I tried to be careful, but felt a claw dig into the fabric.

"That didn't take much."

Ignoring his commentary, I replaced the bedding while he put thick plastic over my broken window, being careful to leave what glass remained hanging where it was, from outside the plastic. He was impressive with his claws, while I struggled to keep from ruining my new sheets. When my room was fixed up for the most part, we gathered up the bedding and broken glass and headed toward the back of the store to the alley. We left everything stacked neatly beside the door to go out to the rubbish bin.

New morning light paled the room around us, announcing impending dawn. We'd been up all night. It had to be close to four AM.

"If you sleep fast, you can get a nap before the store opens," Peter said, as we headed back upstairs.

I yawned, feeling my forked tongue curl at the top of my mouth. We stopped at my door.

"Good night. Or good morning," I laughed a little.

Without thinking, I leaned forward to give him a quick hug, feeling our armored chest plates click together. He wrapped his arms around me tightly.

Suddenly, the rough feeling was replaced by soft skin. I was aware of every centimeter of bare flesh pressing against his. I looked up to see Peter's human face looking down at me. We stared in unison. My breath caught in my throat and from the look of Peter, he wasn't breathing either.

He broke the embrace and stepped back, becoming his stone colored gargoyle again instantly. "Interesting." He looked at me warily, backing away, staring as if I'd done something crazy to him. Like I was responsible for what happened.

I bristled. It could have been him. I wondered if he ever considered that. My hands had become claws once more. "Yeah." I nodded.

"I'll see you in a few hours. Let's get some rest." He stepped toward his room.

"Goodnight, Peter."

I closed my door and lowered myself gently onto my freshly made bed. I examined my thick forearms and clawed hands, amazed at how quickly they'd changed form. *Definitely interesting.* I was too tired to give it thought for long. Sleep crept over me quickly, putting me out like a light.

I was startled awake what seemed like minutes later when my iHome's alarm sounded. AWOL Nation's "Sail" resonated through my room. I needed to spend some time on iTunes.

I drug my tired behind up and pulled on the same jeans I'd worn to work the day before, jerked a collared work shirt over my head and grabbed a hair tie on my way out of the door, grumbling inwardly. It was going to be a long day.

July 10—I can't get hugging Peter out of my mind. Seeing him up close and in his human form seems like an impossibility. To appear as humans to each other must take more physical contact than just holding claws or grabbing each other's arms, because we did that when he took me flying. He's held my hand and touched me before without it happening.

From the looks of him, he is completely mystified, too. He seems a little distant. Even more so than when he's in "stop over-reacting" mode. Not anything bad, but he has looked away a few times today when we're talking or whatever, and that's just not like him. I hope this doesn't do anything bad to our friendship. He is my one source of sanity around this place, besides talking and working with the shoppers in the store....

I chewed on the cap of my pen, reading what I'd written. The replica bard's bells tinkled in the entrance downstairs, announcing Peter had closed the door and was locking up for the night. By the time I set my journal aside and went to the banister to look for him, he was gone.

CHAPTER 12

*P*eter succeeded in avoiding me for the entire night. If that was his goal, he accomplished it. I stopped looking around for him close to midnight and decided to go to my room and get some sleep. I turned on some low music and kicked back, best as a gargoyle could, on my bed. I looked around my room.

My window was fixed, with new blinds. My running shoes peeked from beside my desk, sad and ignored for too long.

I missed going for my nightly runs back at the Home. I used to sneak out and cruise through the quiet halls and the grounds while the temperature was low. The feeling of being free, even temporarily, was addictive. All those times had been extremely therapeutic and taken completely for granted. My head rolled back on the pillow. Going for a run as a gargoyle was definitively out. And I worked nearly every day at the bookstore with Peter.

But I didn't have to be to work in the mornings until nine. During the summer in England, it began to get light about four-thirty AM. I had free time every morning in human form, before I opened the store. Time *outside*, as long as I stayed clear of direct sunlight. I'd be careful. Baby steps. I'd take them.

No one checked up on me to see if I was in my room during my time there, so far.

Butterflies took flight in my belly. *Freedom.* I briefly considered an important point where freedom was concerned. I could likely get pretty far in those few deserted, early morning hours before I was to report for duty at the store.

But what then? What if the sun came out and someone saw me without Ezra stalking me, ready to bail me out? What if I got lost, was caught in the sun and picked up by some paranormal, monster-chasing unit, then put on a table in some lab somewhere while they examined me? Then, that night I would deliver a big treat and Garg Out for everyone to see.

Running away was not an option. Yet. I needed to think about it more. But I could go for an early morning run as long as I was careful and didn't stay out too long.

And if Ezra found out and decided he was pissy? Well, then I guess I'd be testing Peter's theory about Ezra not staying mad at me long. I'd cross that bridge when and if I came to it. I really didn't see what could possibly go wrong if I was careful about the sun and sure to be back in time for work in the mornings.

Although I was exhausted from getting nearly no sleep the night before, I had to tamp down my excitement at the thought of getting out of the store. I reset my alarm for four, right before predawn light would begin to gray the streets outside. I could almost smell the dew covered, potted lavender and Italian coffee stands already.

The next day would be the best day I'd had in over two weeks.

I SKULKED. For the first time in my life I was afraid to see someone coming at me on the sidewalk. The sun wasn't even shining and I dodged, swerved, and sought cover, a sugar statue in an impending rainstorm.

I jogged along at a good pace at first, the fresh air bolstering my outlook, cool morning breeze adding just the right chill for a good run. Then I saw the first stranger I'd seen in days. I dove into a skinny alleyway and untied my shoe so I'd look legit tying it. I'd been damaged by the transformation. More than my physical appearance had been stolen. My sense of character had withered and I doubted my ability to be seen by another person without— . . . what?

I didn't even know what would happen if someone saw me. The way the change was supposed to work was when the sun wasn't on me, I looked like regular-girl Tessa. Pink skinned. Blondish hair. No freak show. My heart thumped too fast and I struggled to get a full breath.

Getting out of the bookstore would take practice. I wouldn't give up. I waited for a break in the passers-by and ran straight back to the bookstore.

Bottom line—I was so scared of someone seeing me that I wasn't willing to take a chance outside. That would have to change. I, myself, was so scared of what I'd become, that I receded. I felt my usual, bubbly self take a backseat to trepidation.

I would not give up. Rolling over and settling weren't me. I'd be back.

* * *

JULY 15—I went for my fourth run today and it felt great! Way better than the first day. There's hardly a soul out that early, the sun's not even close to clearing the horizon line of tall buildings yet, and I feel like I've got most of Covent Gardens to my freaking self! It's better than running the halls at the Home could ever be on its best night.

I was gone from the store today because I ran farther. And yesterday I was majorly paranoid. I made it simple, taking a long look down the lane, and staying close to a building in case the sun came out. It's been a while since I was able to work out this way so the first time I grew tired soon after I first got out. This morning I ran for just over an hour and I loved every second.

I used to be a worshiper of the sun. I am now a servant of shadow.

I'd better go get a shower. After that I need to find the laundry room so I can wash my sweats. I had to run in shorts today, which was a little cold when I first stepped out into the back alleyway, but as soon as I'd run for a couple minutes I felt fine.

I LOVE me some London in the morning!

* * *

AFTER MY SHOWER I dressed in my pink work shirt, white skinny jeans and a cute pair of fawn colored leather boots. I put on a little mascara, dangly earrings and curled the ends of my hair into long spirals that hung around my shoulders and down my back. I felt great. A little happy, even. Energy thrummed through my veins from my run and the exhilaration of being free from the bookstore, out into the city I loved on my own terms.

I started a "kicked back" alternative rock playlist on my iPod, filled my backpack with laundry, and left my room bopping merrily as Death Cab for Cutie's "Where Soul Meets Body" set the tone for an excursion into the back of the bookstore in search of laundry facilities.

Normally I would ask Peter when I needed help finding something but he'd been so distant since our short, revealing hug that I didn't feel the urge to get him out of bed just so I could wash my clothes. If he was in bed. I didn't know much about Peter, really. For all I knew he didn't sleep much, either. He wasn't chatty, or easily giving with information about the things he did when I wasn't around. He was a master of stepping into a different vibe to work in the store, but after hours, he was quiet and most times, gone.

Regardless, I could find my way. He just needed time to mull over what happened. And besides all that, it was high time I started exploring the massive, mysterious bookstore for myself. Ezra couldn't truly expect me to be locked up in there all the time and not have a look around.

I'd been charmed the first day I stepped foot through the door at *Librorum Taberna* and heard those little bards' bells chime my arrival. I still loved old bookstores and the antiques there. Before work, I'd start learning the place.

* * *

I DIDN'T FIND the laundry room. I'd gotten hung up when I turned into the west wing of the store under the sign *Trinkets*. Circular racks of picturesque bookmarks, word games, book bags, even items of décor such as small, stained glass art was the stuff of "trinkets".

Some of the objects made their way to the cash register occasionally when I'd been working, so I knew the fun items were displayed somewhere. I dropped my bag and shopped, forgetting about the need for clean clothes.

Before long, I'd blown my extra hour and a half before work. I had to sprint up the stairs to drop my bag of dirty laundry inside my room and run back down just in time to open up the store.

Peter met me at the door, eyeing me as I leapt in front of him to perform my duty as the store's designated morning sign flipper, per our bargain. I clicked open the heavy locks and swung the door wide.

"Gorgeous out this morning, huh?" A wedge of sunlight made one of my eyes squint, dissected my face, chest and one arm, turning my body into half a "*Body Works*" display right in the entryway. I beamed up at him, ignoring how I must've looked skinless and gruesome.

Peter pulled me deeper inside. "It's bright out today. Best keep back from the windows, yes?" He was smiling. His eyes traced over my glossed lips, styled hair, and the cute boots. "You look . . . perky. What's the occasion?"

"What, can't a girl express herself around this place?" I felt myself preening a bit, and stuffed my hands into my pockets to quit fluffing in front of him. "I'm just in a great mood. Let's roll with it, okay?"

Peter laughed, throwing his head back a little. His grey eyes sparkled with a brilliant silver lining against black lashes. His hair was loose, brushing the shoulders of his white, collared shirt. He wore jeans and a pair of athletic shoes. When he moved past me the air smelled of musk and spice. He was semi addictive to be around when he was in a good mood. Watching Peter laugh was quickly becoming one of my favorite pastimes. I followed him to the check stand and manned my post behind the register beside him, craving interaction with someone other than my Garged Out reflection.

"Well I'm glad you're in good spirits." He pulled a delightfully buttery smelling carton from beside the register and opened it up to display two of the most delectable looking almond croissants I'd ever seen. Confectioner's sugar powdered the bronzed tops, mixing deliciously with sprinkled, thinly sliced, roasted almonds. My mouth watered.

"Oh, those are beautiful." I breathed in the aroma of amaretto and warm butter.

"Help yourself," he said and began counting bills and coins from a zipper pouch into the till.

"I'll wait until you're done. A thing of such beauty should be enjoyed together," I gushed.

When he had taken all the money from the pouch he pulled two envelopes free and handed over one marked with my name. Inside were a bunch of crisp, fifty pound notes. It was payday at the bookstore. I hadn't given it much thought. But I did work there. It made sense to get paid, but what the heck was I supposed to do with all that money? Rat hole it for a rainy day? I wasn't allowed outside on the sidewalk, much less a trip to Harrod's. No one knew about my morning ventures out.

Peter watched me examine the contents of my envelope. "You won't be confined to the store forever. You need to prove to Ezra that you won't wander off and get hurt or do anything equally . . . dangerous."

"Yeah, that's what you were thinking." I knew he meant that I shouldn't consider flat out running away.

He looked back to the till.

"Today just keeps getting better and better." I'd indirectly landed my first job. Bye-Bye Steak and Shake and WhataBurger. I grinned. There wasn't enough money in the envelope to cover the cost of me Garging Out for the rest of my life, however. The opportunity for some range of freedom in the near future was the icing.

"Why is today so special?" Peter asked. "You've been all smiles since I saw you at the door. Which you were nearly late to open up, might I add." He bit into his croissant, leaving a trace of powdered sugar on his bottom lip.

I involuntarily licked my lip, watching. "I don't know, just woke up in a good mood." It wasn't a complete lie, just a half-truth. I wasn't sure about sharing the fact that I'd been leaving the store. I took a huge, unladylike bite of my croissant.

Peter smiled while he chewed, watching me. "I'll get tea." He placed his partially eaten breakfast back in the carton and headed to the back of the store.

The bells at the door tinkled so I put my croissant in the carton with his, wiping at my mouth to be sure I didn't have white powdered lips when greeting a customer. I slid the till closed and went to greet the day's first patron.

"Good morning," I said brightly. "Welcome to *Librorum Taberna*." A man had his back to me and was looking through magazines.

My smile faded slightly. The left over taste of almond croissant soured on my tongue.

Kai smiled down at me. Silver-blond hair was held out of his face by a pair of sunglasses resting on the crown of his head. Eyes so brown they were nearly black locked with mine. A gold and silver twisted torc cuffed his neck. Kai looked more intense, like he'd taken a step into a primal side I'd missed seeing before. It had been over a month, and he was shopping periodicals where I worked and lived. *Holy hell.*

"Good morning." His Scottish accent was so thick it was almost a purr. He smiled easily, but something about him was off. I couldn't quite put a finger on it. Thankfully, I didn't feel as charmed as I did before, more tentative, but I was sure it was because of the way we'd left things. I didn't like him being in the store.

I chewed the inside of my cheek.

"Glad to see you again." It slid from my tongue like an automated response. *Lie.* I caught the scent of something herby on him, not quite a spice, but something natural.

"You look different when you're not out running. Or soaking me. Or blowing me off."

"Likewise." Then I caught myself. He'd seen me out running. "Not that you were running, I mean. Or soaking me . . . you just look better close up." I pursed my lips to keep from embarrassing myself any more. It was nice to see my ability to shove a foot in my mouth had followed me to the UK.

He laughed. "Likewise."

"So, I'm going to go back over here now," I gestured over my shoulder to the register stand. "If there is anything you need help finding, or can think of another way I could thoroughly embarrass myself—"

"—or if I need a shower—"

"—don't hesitate to come find me," I said. "Witty one, aren't you?"

He grinned. "Glad you found a way to extend your visit."

"Got a job." I didn't want to discuss the real reasons I remained in London. He'd think I'd lost it. And although I could be pretty happy staring at the guy all day, I was still on edge being around him. The hair on the back of my neck pulled tight, standing on end.

He picked up a copy of "Mojo" magazine. "I've found what I came in for."

We walked to the register. Peter still hadn't returned from his excursion to get the tea. *Crap! Did he have to go pick the freaking tea leaves or what?*

I rung up the music mag for him, slid the book into a slender media sleeve and handed it over. "Have a great day," I said with a smile. I wondered if it was obvious I was trying really hard to act like it was no big deal that he freaked me out a little.

"You, as well, Tessa." He smiled again, taking a little too long looking at me. He pulled his sunglasses onto his nose and turned for the door. *Finally.* The bells sounded his departure.

"About now you're hoping you didn't eat my croissant." Peter appeared, joking like I wasn't about to blow a gasket.

I breathed a gusty sigh.

He set down two mugs and plopped flat a potholder, onto which he placed a fat tea pot. Steam twisted into the air from the spout.

"Sweet," I said. "Let's dig in." I was desperate to get my wonderful, light hearted, mood back.

Peter took a tea towel from across his forearm and poured a mug of tea. He handed it to me and said in his best, stuffy British waiter voice, "How many lumps, mum?" He bowed slightly, reminding me of the first time I'd met him all Garged Out, short weeks that seemed like a year ago. My perception of him had changed so much. I loved when he was in a good mood.

I laughed. "Two lumps, if you please." I surprised myself by sounding equally stuffy.

"Very good." He dropped two cubes of sugar in my mug. I added a healthy dollop of milk from a small pitcher, stirred, and sipped my tea with relish.

"This is great."

"It's mere garden variety Earl Grey." He winked.

I decided it was probably a good thing Kai had left before Peter returned. They really didn't need to know about each other. Maybe things hadn't worked out so badly after all. I grinned.

* * *

A CHANCE ENCOUNTER with an Iranian postcard dealer made my next morning outing the most liberating of the fog-laden days I went out running. He balanced a large box between a hip and the brick exterior, and was reaching around the enormous carton trying to open the shop door. Being the polite young lady the nuns raised me to be, I stopped and pulled the door open for him, at which point a handful of scenic postcards drifted from the top of the box, landing with a smattering of light smacks onto the threshold of his front entryway. I'd passed many of those short, squatty red post boxes, and the front glass of the man's store was strung with signs advertising postcards and other wares for tourists. One black and white placard close to the door held a lone, magical word: Postage.

Those stray postcards were given to me for free. That day's Starbucks money was easily reallocated to the communication section of my mental budget. I bought stamps from his shop right then and ferreted the stationery away to my underwear drawer for after work, which went by a little slower since I was so excited to get some correspondence on the way, by my terms this time.

Realizing my delusion didn't take long. True enough, I could fill out the cards and mail them all by myself, but the things I wrote skirted issues and glorified white lies. I wrote to Professor Douglas but I left out anything that would worry him, so there really wasn't much to say. The card I'd chosen was a twilit view of St. Paul's Cathedral from the Thames side of the river. He would love that. I missed him terribly and thought of how I'd taken his council for granted. I would have given a lot to spend some time with him.

Writing to Brea reduced me to tears. I had to be untruthful to her. If she knew what had happened to me, big-sister-mode would kick in and she'd come looking for me. I couldn't bear thinking of her going through what I had, if she got stuck in the bookstore and Ezra zapped her with his mojo. I made the note as cheery as possible, telling her I'd write more later. Not to worry.

Before work the next morning, I slowed briefly, dropped the cards in a postbox, and kept running.

July 31—What kind of a life do I live when I am virtually kidnapped, forced to live and work in a bookstore (which really is probably the best way I could be kidnapped), and I only miss two people from my pre gargoyle life? And one of those people is my English teacher?? Now that I'm settling in here, I think this requires some examination. Who else do I miss? My life was completely unsatisfying. There is a whole, shiny endless world outside of Austin, Texas. I'm here in London now, and although I'm trapped at the bookstore, a huge part of me has been freed. I'm so conflicted. I'm a free prisoner. Being kidnapped liberated me. Ugh.

I remembered old Mr. Thomlinson and the photos of the boy who'd been my brother. I continued through a film of tears.

If Robbie had become "real" to me, what then? And if I had a family? Would we all be heartbroken at missing the sound of each other's voices? The feel of warm hugs and kisses on the forehead at bedtime? Midnight phone calls when we can't sleep and dozens of emails from college, or basic training, in the case of the brother I never got to know? And what about Brea? I miss her more than anything—

"You all right?"

I was so engrossed in my journal I hadn't heard Peter

approach. "No." A sob escaped. I slapped the arm of the leather chair I sat in. I sounded like an overgrown five-year-old.

He pulled me to my feet. My journal and pen thumped lightly to the floor, but I didn't care as he wrapped his arms around my shoulders. Thankful for the comfort, I was determined to enjoy it, no matter how briefly it lasted.

"You've been doing so well lately." His words said one thing but the gesture was lost in the delivery. The tone wasn't giving. I wanted him to concede, to allow me a breakdown without his usual rub-some-dirt-on-it mentality. I could just hear his thoughts saying *Suck it up. Gargoyles don't cry.* Judging Peter based on his actions was a tough call. He'd become hardened, as if he was preparing me for something, urging me to strengthen the walls that were already in place around my heart. As things stood, the protective barrier was a little perforated, the occasional show of emotion allowed through. Peter wanted more brick and mortar.

Being made from stone wasn't that easy for me. "I'm homesick for a home I never had," I held my breath against his shoulder to quit crying. "I know that makes absolutely no sense."

"You have no idea how much sense that *does* make." He rested his chin on the top of my head. I thought I heard a little un-Peter-like sigh of sentimentality. It was short-lived. He felt himself slip up too because he broke the embrace.

I stepped back, wiping away evidence of emotion as if I'd been caught stealing.

Peter replaced the brief encounter with his human side, displaying practiced stoicism. "You're going to be okay."

"Yes." I nodded up at him. "I'm going to be great."

CHAPTER 13

*T*he morning was cooler than normal as I ran down Charing Cross Road. I loved that road in particular because of all the flower boxes and gas lights. The tall buildings provided a shadowed safety zone. My morning route was extended to include my favorite parts of SoHo. I'd run through sleepy Covent Garden, slumbering St. Martin's Lane to Trafalgar Square if it was cloudy. Trafalgar Square sprawled an expanse of flat, open concrete and fountains with nearly no cover, so I had to be especially careful on the days I was bold enough to run around the statues and the big ship-in-a-bottle.

I took breaks sitting on the bases of the multiple, artsy elephant statues that decorated the lanes. My heart soared on those mornings. I inhaled the liberty of open space like fresh, morning air. Gorged on freedom like manna from the universe itself.

I was running back toward Cecil Court, with the Dropkick Murpheys' "Shipping up to Boston" driving my feet forward in a rhythmic cadence, when Kai stepped out of a cafe and into view just ahead. He vanished around the corner before I made it much closer.

"Kai!" I tugged my earbuds free. Maybe talking to him a little would get rid of the odd feeling between us. My little chunk of London needed to be free of awkwardness. I rounded the corner, intent on chatting with him for a bit before I had to open the store for the day.

Brilliant sunlight hit me like a perpetual strike of lightning when I turned onto Irving Street. Reflex and shock made my eyes slam closed. Weeks had passed since I'd been in direct sunshine. I stumbled. My skin tingled and my pulse raced. I spun in a lopsided one-eighty, hoping for one eye to open a slit to find my way into some cover. It didn't work. I panicked, being temporarily blinded and scared that someone could see me as a monster in the sun.

Someone yanked my arm hard. I inhaled to scream, but a hand covered my mouth. My breath was coming so hard that getting enough air into my lungs through my nose was an impossibility. My body was thrown over a shoulder like a sack of potatoes. I dangled upside down well above the sidewalk, my ponytailed hair and the hood from my running jacket blocking out what little I might be able to see if my eyes would adjust to the light. Bile rose, fell rather, in my throat. Whoever had me began running, beating my guts in loping jolts with each long stride.

"Please put me down." My voice was a mere notch above a whisper.

We stopped. I was deposited next to a wall on trembling legs. My head spun but cool air surrounded me, rather than searing sunshine. My rescuer stood so close my nose touched his thick chest, buried in the musky scent of a black hoodie. My eyes were slits, but at least they fought to see. I peered up into Kai's hooded face, grateful for being saved, a little angry because he didn't answer when I called, and mortified at being helpless.

"What the hell, Kai?" I shoved at him, creating a buffer between us. He fell back a step into the glare. He'd seen me in the sun and that was far from a good thing. My heart continued to pound viciously. Vomit remained at the back of my throat, coating the root of my tongue with acidic bile.

He jerked his hood down. Tendons linked behind the thinned skin of his face, showing dark jawbone and sinew. Light shades of pale and sick grey twisted at his neck where a pulse beat inside his throat around his gold torc. A hand pushed a strand of white hair behind an ear made of blackened cartilage.

I slapped a hand over my mouth and retched.

"Thanks," he said dryly. "You're not looking so hot yourself."

What little I'd eaten so far that day, mainly water, splattered the concrete. I'd never been an easy puker. Lots of elements combined and attacked me and seeing Kai was a morbid cherry on top. The kicker had to be the sun. If it could make my skin see-through, it could probably make me vomit. Kai sure didn't seem to have a problem standing in it, however.

"Get back." I leaned back on the wall, wiping my mouth with the sleeve of my hoodie.

"I rescued you from the light." His eyes narrowed on me. "Why did you follow me?"

Good point, I guess. "I just wanted to say hi," I said around a thick tongue. "Maybe chat for a sec before I have to go to work. And that's not a good reason to snatch me up and take off running like that!" I glowered at him. "I feel like crap."

"That's more likely from the sun, than from me carrying you. And you're welcome. You looked like you were going to fall to the ground. Would have been great to vomit from that position." He crossed his arms matter-of-factly.

Somehow I didn't feel like thanking him for the rescue. "You're a gargoyle!"

"Shhhhh!"

His hand was over my mouth again. I pried at his fingers and blew clear snot over his hand. It served him right.

"Yes. Thanks to that old idiot at your store and his tendency to

95

play with magic he doesn't fully understand," he whispered. He dropped his hand.

"Ezra changed you, too?" I panted, stomach reloaded and at the ready with a fresh batch of vomit. I doubled over, bottom firmly against the brick and hands on my knees.

"Ezra is a fool. He knows he can't control it." He stepped away from me and looked in the direction of Cecil Court. "Some things are locked away for a damn good reason."

"I have to get to the store." I peeled myself from the wall, woozy and staggering a little, trying to stay in the thin rail of shade that remained beside the building.

"Why?" He asked.

"Why what?" I hoped I sounded as irritated as I felt. My face flushed and my chest started to burn inside. Finding and talking with Kai had not accomplished what I'd been after. Instead my temper was barely held in check and I was more uncomfortable with him than before. A healthy dislike had developed in me and he did nothing to stop it, but so much to foster it along.

"Ever ask yourself if you truly have to stay in that store? You've been fairly adventurous lately. Looks like you didn't 'have to get back' to the States at all."

Insinuating I'd lied to him pushed the button. "I'm fine, thank you. I have a job there." Between him and me, since he'd made me feel helpless, the job was a big deal. Employment was a form of independence.

He laughed when I said that.

I felt myself growing more ticked off by the second. I pulled my hood up and traced a path in the narrow line of shade toward Cecil Court. Our conversation was over. I'd chalk it up to a learning experience.

He pulled me around to face him again. He'd replaced his hood. "Don't you question the things you feel inside? That heat inside you," he shook his head slowly, eyeing me. "I'll take care of you, Tessa. Out here," he gestured wide to the freedom of downtown London. "You could go where you please when you feel like it. Within reason, of course. We are bound to our forms. But that would be all. You'd be free with me."

I jerked my arm loose. "Stop acting like you know me. And don't you *ever* touch me again." The offer for freedom was squashed by the way Kai insisted on manhandling me. I locked eyes with him to punctuate my statement. "Leave me alone. I mean it." There was no need to wait for his response. I made it back to the bookstore by sprinting down Charing Cross Road in the shadows, in the sunlight, I didn't care. By the time I made it through a shower and downstairs to open up the store at nine, I knocked the bard's bells off their hook above the door when I jerked it open.

It was going to be a long, long day.

CHAPTER 14

*P*eter crossed his arms, leaning back against a metal folding table in the laundry room. His leathery wings stuck out to the sides centering his stony form inside a dark arch against a yellowed wall. The table creaked, straining back with his weight. The scent of herby, lavender detergent hung on the air, which was a little muggy from the driers. The machines hummed, doing their duty without argument as we hung out, waiting for our work clothes to finish.

He'd shown me the way down to the maintenance area after the day I failed at finding the facilities on my own. We chatted comfortably, keeping it light, and attempting to entertain one another by seeing who could line up more M&Ms on our forked tongues without dropping them, choking on them or eating them. He was winning. I gobbled mine up. He seemed to be in a good mood, so I figured I'd try picking his brain for some information.

"Can I ask you a question? It's going to sound odd so try not to look at me like I've lost my mind."

"Of course you can ask a question. But I'm not going to make any promises about the looks you receive," he said, and began placing candy on his tongue to continue the game.

Here goes. "Do you know if there are any other gargoyles running around London?"

He crunched through the candy he'd begun to line up. "Why do you ask?"

"Because I've seen one. In addition to the girl who took off from the store the night she changed."

He gazed at me silently for a long moment. I squirmed.

"I wondered if you might run into one." He pulled away from the table, tail twitching briefly, but coming to a quick stop.

It was my turn to be silent. I looked at him for a moment, mentally shrugging. He knew I'd left the store. It was what it was. I had to have some room in my life.

"How many are there?" I asked.

"It's hard to be certain," he said. "Did you get a name?"

"Kai."

His eyes widened. "You met a gargoyle named Kai?" His voice was elevated enough to shake me up.

"Yeah." I nearly groaned out loud. Peter knew Kai. Perfect.

"Why didn't you tell me you knew Kai earlier?"

Because I didn't want him to know I'd dated someone in London. It was so clear and easy in my mind, but complicated to talk to him about. And since that someone wasn't just any-old-body, it was uber-complicated. "I met him weeks ago. He sort of freaked out a little when it was time for me to go back to Austin after the program was over. We parted on awkward terms and I didn't want to feel bad each time I saw him."

Peter raised his brows.

I chewed my lip. "I just found out he'd been turned into a gargoyle. I wish Ezra would never have made him. He gives me the creeps."

"Ezra didn't make Kai into anything. Did Kai tell you that?"

"No, but he didn't exactly deny it. He's a gargoyle. I saw him in the sunlight yesterday."

"You were in the sun? With Kai? What the bloody hell were

you thinking, Tessa?" He tossed the bag of M&Ms on the table, scattering wayward, colored chocolates with a loud clatter.

"Well it wasn't my idea. I went out for a run and saw him so I thought I'd say hi and talk to him to try to get over this weird feeling I get when I see him. I followed him into the sun by accident." I decided to omit the part where Kai had thrown me over his shoulder and ran into the alleyway.

"You'll likely never get past feeling odd around him, *friendship* aside."

I ignored his jab about my admitted "friendship" with Kai. Technically it wasn't his beeswax. "Well I feel worse about him now than I ever did before. I never want to see him again."

"That's good because Kai is not a good . . . man, Tessa." He paused, shaking his head. "And this thing with him being a gargoyle . . . ."

"I saw it."

"I'm not arguing that."

"Good idea."

"Don't push it."

I rolled my eyes.

"He is a monster, ancient as the world is old. He's angry at Ezra, because Ezra was given the Book of the Ancients. It happened in Scotland centuries ago, but I don't have each detail. That's how Ezra was able to make me. Then you."

That was a lot to wrap my head around. "Aren't you angry with Ezra?" I'd be thrilled never to see him again. And it had been a while. Maybe he'd moved to Guam.

"When he made you, he was probably just trying to make up for something that happened years ago." Once again, Peter had neatly avoided talking about how he felt, putting the spotlight on me. He was good at that.

"What do you mean?"

"I know you heard some of our conversation that night in his study. Ezra has regarded me as a "son" of sorts. He's carried guilt because I've been here alone for so long. We'd talked about him finding another to work with me here. Maybe someone who was on a bad road in life, like I'd been. I was thinking about a friend. Ezra apparently looked a little deeper, and made you."

Ezra's words waltzed ironically back into my mind. "Boygoyle and girlgoyle."

"Exactly."

"You tried to talk him out of keeping me."

"You tried to run off," he countered. He didn't respond with *I was wrong,* or even *I didn't know you then.*

I would not accept the assumption that he didn't want me there. Peter had done too much

to show me the contrary. I was there. Time for ticker tape and cotton candy.

The laundry machines hummed a discordant conversation, sloshing and tumbling.

"The thing with Kai . . . ." He sighed. "He's just one of the reasons you were told to stay in the store."

"Well it's not exactly that easy, Peter," I snapped. "I feel so confined here. I need to run and think. I love London and I'm finally here. Of course I want to get out of the store sometimes. And I met him before all these things happened to me." I sighed and rubbed my rough forehead.

Peter stepped toward me. I backed up and he kept coming. My wings slapped flat on the wall. Our bodies met, triggering our human forms to be seen, his soft skin a contradiction to the hardened force driving him. His grey eyes sparked. "Let's get one thing lined out." Our faces were centimeters away, hot breath pouring across my skin. One of his hands cupped my jaw, tilting it upward. I focused slowly on his eyes, then his lips. He crushed me close and more sensitive skin collided. I held my breath.

"You will not see Kai. Not even if you are on fire, will you ask his assistance." He tilted his head, lining us up perfectly, searching my face. Anticipation jumped in my stomach.

The buzzer on Ezra's dryer sent an electrified alarm through the confines of the laundry room so loud I jumped, feeling the top of my head bump against Peter's nose. It was the most nerve-wracking sound I've ever been subjected to.

"Oh my gosh! I am so sorry, Peter!" I grabbed both sides of his head so I could examine his face. "Are you okay?"

The separation of our bodies triggered our gargoyle forms. Peter's tail twitched on the floor and I bounced on my haunches, still gripping his head. He was bent over so far he might fall on top of me.

"I'm fine," he said, rubbing his snout. "Let go of my head," he growled.

"Sorry." I released my grip and walked to a dryer that was stopped. I jerked the door open a little too hard. Our work shirts spilled to the floor before I could catch them with my tail, knees and one hand. The boney tips of my wings cracked down against the tile floor. "Crap."

"You need to come to me when you need to get out of here."

I didn't look at him.

"I'll take you out for a little flight as soon as we're done with our clothes."

"That would be great." I had to admit, it was the best change of subject I'd ever heard. "Good. Mayhap we won't fly into any buildings this time."

"Mayhap, indeed."

* * *

WE SOARED for hours above London. We played tag. We held clawed hands and did loops in the sky under a cloud-covered moon. The playful demeanor I loved about him remained, but it was held in check underneath a new, regal dimension. When he flew, Peter owned the sky. I barely had to pump my wings when we held on to one another. He flew with such strength he pulled me with him effortlessly. He tugged me into spiraling summer-saults that made me giggle and scream with excitement. He pulled me close, and flew with me mere inches below him, staring into my eyes as we glided on the heavy, wet air. I longed to be closer to him but I knew if our bodies even touched a little bit, we'd return to human form and plummet. Scaly as it was, at least we could hold hands and still have wings. A light drizzle began to fall, coating us with moisture. I drifted below him, shielded from gentle rain by the massive umbrella of his charcoal wings.

Peter gleamed as if he was made of polished onyx in the damp atmosphere of night. He was sleek and powerful when he flew. An obsidian demigod of the night sky. I was charmed beyond my comprehension. He became everything to me in our world above the city.

CHAPTER 15

I slowed at the red post box, dropped two more postcards and kept running, almost without missing a beat. I been mailing the cards ritually for the last two weeks. It was a connection I could have with Brea and Professor Douglas. I considered using one of the matching red phone booths to call but the thought of lying to either of them via post *and* verbally put a quick stop to the idea. I could be a coward and tell a big fib indirectly. So the postcards were going out more frequently. It wasn't so bad. I found the most amazing shots of London on those cards. The beautiful images outweighed the ugly little white lies I told on the backs. Or so I continued to tell myself.

I ran more during the mornings than I ever had at night at the Home, and I could tell from the way my clothes fit. I used to have a little extra curve here and there, especially along my hips. The remaining, slightly chubby, youthful appearance was leaving me. My human body had become lean and toned. My feet felt light and I ran faster every day. My expanded route covered more ground.

Ezra was waiting for me at the back door when I came through the alley. It had been weeks since I'd seen him, the last time being when the new gargoyle ran away. Deep down I'd known he was aware I left the store. It was time to pay the figurative piper for my dance of freedom.

Oddly enough, he didn't look mad.

"How was your outing?" He opened the door for me and we went inside.

"It was good." I worked hard not to betray the anxiety in my stomach. Ezra would always make me nervous. He was a thief that smiled while he stole me blind. "Where have you been?" Switching the spotlight to him probably wasn't going to work, but I might as well have tried.

"Business," he said.

I didn't question that at all. Ezra straddling a broomstick, flying off into the night briefcase in hand, silhouetted against a yellow moon flashed through my mind. I gave an unwilling snort.

He gave me a quizzical look.

I ignored it.

The stairs to my room beckoned from out of reach, maybe 15 feet away that may as well have been a mile. The urge to bolt was held in check by my well-instilled manners. It wasn't the first time I'd been in trouble. But Ezra was no nun. Not even as easy-going as one of the most cantankerous ones at the Home.

"I just want to go to my room, shower and come down to work for the day." Despite the cool air, a coat of sweat glistened on my skin. I didn't smell all that great.

"You've been doing a great job here, dear girl. Peter has told me good things."

"You've talked with Peter?" Peter hadn't mentioned it. He didn't feel a need to check in with me, apparently.

"We chat weekly, if not more frequently. He keeps charge well in my absence."

"Oh." I hadn't thought of Peter as being in charge. I offered nothing, lest I say something the two hadn't discussed, and the conversation was pushing me further into isolation. I stepped toward the stairs.

He followed. "Have you had anymore contact with Kai, Tessa?"

"Not since the last time I saw him in the alley. It's been a couple weeks." I wondered if he knew *everything* I told Peter. It figured.

"Good. There is something you need to be aware of. The mornings are getting shorter, I'm sure you've noticed."

"Yeah, I've noticed. I set an alarm on my iPod while I run to give myself time to get back here and get a shower."

"You're a good girl. Very responsible."

"Have you found that girl that changed and ran off?" *Speaking of responsibility . . . .*

"Not a trace of her. But not to worry yourself over her. You just keep up the good work around the store." He stopped walking. We'd made it to the stairwell.

"Will you be around the store later?" I took the first step, hoping he would leave the store and take the nervous edge off my day.

"I've got to run, I'm afraid. Duty calls. Be well, Tessa. And stay close to the store. The morning outings are fine and expected. But please stay close to Peter."

"Of course, Ezra."

"And far, far away from Kai."

I stopped midstride to look at him when he said that last request. He was already walking away. Kai must have done something seriously wrong to make both Peter and Ezra warn me about him. I thought jealously motivated Peter, but Ezra was a different matter entirely. Kai made my skin crawl. He was beautiful, true, but the nastiness in him outweighed his physical appearance and made me see him in a different light. Neither Peter nor Ezra needed to worry about me looking to hang out with him.

Only a few minutes of my shower time remained but I was

relieved the conversation with Ezra went smoothly. Our first encounter in weeks could have gone much, much worse.

I was so thankful Ezra didn't know Peter took my flying.

* * *

"I'VE DECIDED it isn't fair that I get to read whatever I want and you don't," I said and dropped *"The Importance of Being Earnest"* onto the leather couch beside Peter. It was early afternoon and I'd decided he could use some humor. Business was slow at the store. Peter would lock up in a few minutes. We could Garg Out and we could read some trivially ridiculous comedy for a while. It sounded like a pretty good way to spend a Friday night to me. I plopped onto the couch and opened my journal to write for a bit while he closed the store.

Peter grinned down at me with a smile that made my tummy flip a little. In the beginning, I'd managed to ignore how attractive he was. It seemed I was reminded every time we were together for the last few days.

"How thoughtful of you to rescue me." He eyed the book warily.

"Yeah?"

"Yeah." He tried to imitate my accent. "I'd better go turn the sign."

"I'd better go turn the sign," I bantered back, in my best British.

He laughed and got up as I opened my notebook and began jotting down my thoughts.

September 2—Happy birthday to me. I don't feel 19, and am not sure exactly what that's supposed to feel like. I'm not a typical teen. I don't want to celebrate a birthday anyway, not that anyone knows about it. Or in the case of Brea, anyone who can do anything about it. I'm going to celebrate my inner nerd by sinking into some Willie Shakes with Peter.

It's been getting pretty chilly around here in the afternoons. I'm curious to see what winter will be like. I'll bet it snows a ton.

* * *

PETER WAS BACK UP RIGHT after the bells sounded at the door. The night was officially ours. I'd started a fire in the gas fireplace in front of the couch and warmth radiated cozily from the faux logs into to the room.

Only a few of the nooks in the store had fireplaces or old, coal-burning stoves. I liked the alcove I chose to journal in daily for the homey feel of a hearth, and also because it was close to the entrance of the store so I could hear Peter lock up every day. Knowing I wasn't alone in the store comforted me. It was what it was.

Peter took a seat on the couch, spreading his arms across the top of the cushions. He gave a half smile as I pulled the book from beside me and opened the cover, peeling pages.

I snapped the book shut and dropped it onto the carpet. The pages were blank.

"Frustrating, isn't it? We could read nursery rhymes, if you like," he said with a wink.

"I thought you told him to change them back now."

"I did. He thought better of it and I can't blame him for his concern." Peter looked to the vast, towering shelves that ran from the ground floor and reached even higher than the second story where we sat. "I know these volumes so very well. For a time, I was lost in the darkest of tales here, and craved the most pained story." He pulled his eyes from the shelves and locked his charcoal gaze with mine as I tried not to tear up.

"One final night I continued to obsess with adding my own to the best and worst of tragedies. That's when I went to Ezra. He changed the books and only after that did he share the fact that I wouldn't have been able to take my own life."

"He would have stopped you?" I'd listened to him talk, fighting the urge to grab his hand or hug him close.

"He wouldn't have had to. We gargoyles can never fall to our own hand. At any rate, he saw the books as the problem and followed through." He smiled. "And I've never had anyone try to read to me before. I thought it might work, although I'm certain I'm the problem, not you." He got up from the couch. "I'll be right back."

I was too shocked to do anything but nod. Peter seemed so together. I'd never pictured him fighting inner darkness that way.

I got up to shake it off. I'd go bonkers if I couldn't read so I didn't know how he could stand it. It was one of the perks of working in a bookstore. I wondered if it would do any good to talk to Ezra. I doubted it.

Peter returned with a MP3 player and a small speaker dock, which he plugged in and set playing low. I'd never heard the music that he selected, but I liked it. Only instrumental, it was slow, with a resonating, hypnotic rhythm.

He held out a hand. "May I?"

I hesitated for about a millisecond. Dancing slow, the way he proposed, was something I'd never done. I stepped into his arms like I was crossing a stream by way of a few, staggered, slippery rocks. We swayed slowly while I concentrated on not stomping on his feet.

"Shouldn't let our nice fire go to waste, yes?" His voice was deep, resounding against my chest when he spoke. Goosebumps streaked down my spine.

"No, we shouldn't. This is nice." I realized my arms were up and hoped my deodorant would last the rest of the day.

One song led into another and we didn't stop dancing for the brief silence in between. He caressed my back and pulled his fingers through strands of my hair. I held onto him, hypnotized by the physical contact of our bodies touching.

"Happy birthday, Tessa Conley."

"How did you know it's my birthday?" I was stunned.

"You left your student identification card on your desk the night I helped you clean up your room."

I sighed and hugged him close. "Thank you."

He kissed the crown of my head. It was getting late out and I snuggled in tightly. When I let go of him I'd be a gargoyle and I wanted to make the comfort of his embrace last as long as I could. We danced away the time into darkness, not needing a single word between us.

Glass shattered at the storefront, followed by a crash. Someone, or something, screeched like an angry cat. A really big one. Our separation made us gargoyles in an instant and I faltered, smacking a wing against the flat of the couch. I tripped, unceremoniously lunging toward the stairs with my legs pumping to try to catch up.

Peter leapt over the banister, gliding toward the floor below. I reacted fast, sailing over the handrail, pumping my wings twice and flew past him before he touched down. He landed half a second after me, looking at me a little oddly. I shrugged, not knowing what to say about my burst of speed, but impressed all the same.

Broken glass and shards of wood peppered the front room. A chipped piece of a statue that I recognized as part of a decorative elephant from around London had come to a stop at the foot of a tall bookcase.

"Bloody hell," Peter said, under his breath.

"Holy crap," I mumbled. "It's her." The runaway gargoyle stood in the broken out doorway, chest heaving. She screamed and hurled two more pieces of elephant statue into the store. I dodged them easily, moving fast to stand by Peter.

Human eyes in a snake's face squinted on him. She took a couple steps inside, gaze still locked, and sat back on her haunches, wings spread in a horned fan behind her, tail whipping back and forth in the debris. She continued to stare intently at Peter, who seemed shocked, gazing back at her.

I reached for the nearest piece of broken, stone elephant and whipped it at her. She ducked the missile and hissed at me.

"Get the hell out of here," I commanded, the Texan in me tainting my words with a heavily pronounced drawl. I don't know where my audacity came from, but she'd chosen to do two things that she shouldn't have. First, she trashed my home, aka the bookstore, and second, she'd gotten a real long look at my very good friend, Peter, who was oh, so very far off limits. The destruction at the front of the store marred the entire entryway. Sounds from the London night echoed softly through the broken storefront, cool, damp air following on its heels, heavily laden with humidity and frost.

I was a second away from exploding at her. "Are you deaf or just plain stupid?" I took a step forward. I don't know exactly what I planned to do, but it was going to be substantial. My proper-Southern-girl alter ego was terribly unladylike in my gargoyle form, and it felt *great*. Heat rushed through my blood. I hissed back, mocking her. My wings beat slowly, lifting my heels from the floor.

Peter grabbed my arm. "Really, Tessa, that's quite plenty," he growled, giving my arm a hard squeeze.

"I'll be back for you," she said. After one last glance in Peter's direction, she turned away, fluid in the backdrop of night, and was gone in an instant.

I turned to the destructed front end. "What a mess." Books were destroyed, as was the glass from the front window on the right. The thick, wooden door hung split, the hinges still fastened to the frame but holding only a slender strip of what had been a regal entryway. Plaster dust and colorful pieces of elephant statue lay around the room. Cold air gusted hard from outside, allowing a fresh burst of damp wind to buffet us. Shards of busted glass and cracked paint chips mixed with small hunks of wood in the breeze, scooting around as if in search of each other. We watched from behind a book station, careful to stay out of sight in case someone walked by in the sleepy court.

"Ezra will be livid." Peter kicked at a piece of splintered wood. "This store is really all he has."

"Well, he can't be too angry about it." I stated.

"Why is that?"

"Indirectly, this is his fault."

Peter just shook his head.

CHAPTER 16

*P*eter drug two sheets of plywood from somewhere in the back while I swept and we boarded up the front of the store hastily, to try to avoid drawing attention. Ezra arrived about two hours after the incident and was frantic as he tried to find someone who would repair and restore his antique storefront to its previous state. *Librorum Taberna* would be closed for repairs the next couple days. He grilled Peter and me about the girl's possible whereabouts. When we'd done as much sweeping and cleaning as we could, I slipped upstairs to get some sleep. Not long after I made it to my room, I heard Peter's door shut across the hall.

Predawn colors streaked the sky outside my window. I curled up inside my wings, exhausted, watching dawn break through lowered lids. No reason remained to fight sleep.

* * *

Too short a time later, I was jostled awake by a sharp, clicking sound. My body still buzzed with the dizzy feeling that accompanies a lack of sleep. I didn't open my eyes, I waited to see if it would go away, dozing off.

The sounds pecked a merry good morning on the thick glass of my window, getting louder and more forceful with each new blast. I'd never heard pebbles being tossed at glass before and I wasn't a fan. Sleep-soaked thoughts quickly gave way to confusion. Who the heck would be out there?

Daylight pushed bright lines onto the walls and floor of my room. My iHome told me it was eight minutes past ten. I sat up in bed, not happy.

The tapping sounded again as I walked on shaky, tired legs to put on pajamas. I drew up the blinds and look down to the alley below. Someone was going to get a big piece of my mind, or a good look at my middle finger.

No—

Brea stood on the concrete below, hands bound behind her back. A thick line of silver tape was over her mouth. Mascara traced dark circles around her eyes and down her cheeks. Two hooded figures stood behind her, one tall and one slender, obviously female.

I knew before he dropped his hood it was Kai. And he wasn't reacting to sunlight anymore. It was another trick. No wonder Peter sounded perplexed when I told him Kai was a gargoyle. Kai had never been one to begin with.

What I didn't expect was the other figure to be the girl I tried to help when she changed into a gargoyle. She smiled up at me with a sinewy, toothy face. I shivered. Getting used to my own skinless face was hard enough and seeing a new one would never stop freaking me out.

Kai shook Brea hard by an elbow. She cried out angrily against the makeshift gag. Her pajama bottoms and a lacey sleeveless t shirt were rumpled and her feet were pink from the chilled pavers. Brea did her best to scream through the tape covering her mouth when she saw me. Long strands of her brown hair were stuck in the adhesive. Her eyes were wide and glassy, a side effect of terror I'd seen on my face, too.

Instantly incensed. I yanked open my bedroom door and ran to the back of the store on bare feet and didn't slow until I sprinted into the alley, disregarding the sun in the midmorning sky. I moved faster than I expected, clearing the store fast. Momentum gave way to an unenthusiastic stop where they'd been standing moments ago.

They were gone. *Brea* was gone.

My gaze was drawn immediately to something that looked like a photograph lying ahead in the alley. When I picked it up, I began to shake.

One of the cards I'd mailed to Brea trembled in my grasp. It wasn't postmarked.

I'd inadvertently given Kai my best friend's address in the States.

I flipped the card over. A message had been scrawled in black ink over my purple writing.

Be at this spot at daybreak tomorrow, packed and ready to leave. Speak of this to no one. Fail to do this and I will end your friend's life. Make a wise choice. I do like her so. ~Kai

HOW COULD I have missed seeing the psycho for what he was? I knew I'd never really hated anyone until that moment. Even considering what the administration at the Home had done when they hid my brother from me, I still didn't hate them. I could safely say I hated Kai. I wasn't feeling too fond of myself, either.

Tentative steps took me inside, numb from seeing my best friend tied, gagged and terrified. Crying. I released the door handle slowly to deaden the sound of the latch. Waking Peter would create another problem. I couldn't let him know what I was about to do.

There was no telling where I'd end up a day later. I may never see Peter again, and that thought jabbed me in the stomach. Leaving with Kai to save Brea was a new imperative. Kai was winning the psychotic game he played with my friend's life, maneuvering his pawns into place, preparing to call a check-mate if I made the wrong move. Brea's postcard hung in my hand, her address in Austin calling a reminder in bleeding ink. I'd given him advantage, the best player on his team.

Finally, Peter's door opened and smacked closed down the hall.

I rubbed my eyes to make them appear pink from sleeping and swung my door open to look for him. The time was past noon. He looked about like I felt.

"Good morning, sunshine," I said with my best, sleepy smile.

"Good morning, yourself." His eyes traced across my messed up hair, the sleeveless t-shirt and Grinch pajama pants, coming to rest on my polished toes. He half smiled at me with narrow, sexy, sleepy grey eyes, pulling a hoodie over his head.

"Mind if I tag along this time?"

"Not at all," he said, leaning a thick shoulder against the wall by my door.

"Cool, give me a sec." I ran inside to throw on sweats, pulled on socks and shoes, and grabbed some loose change off my nightstand.

We walked toward the smell of coffee and baked goods, keeping an eye on the overcast sky in case the sun decided to push through. Neither of us spoke. I shook inside, thinking about what was to come the next morning but I did my best to hide it.

I ordered two Grande caramel macchiatos and handed one over to Peter.

"I thought you might like a change from your usual."

He sipped a small taste, barely masking a grimace. "Not a good replacement for strong tea but thank you." He smiled, at least.

His smile made the long morning of waiting for him to wake up worth it. The possibility that I'd never see him again loomed, and that ate at me, making me determined to spend my remaining time with him. Maybe since we didn't have to work at the store I could act a little lost for something to do without it seeming odd to him.

We walked toward the bookstore, window shopping and dodging traffic. Victorian flower gardens caught my eye as we passed and he watched me gawk, smiling from under his hood. We finished our coffee and looked for what seemed like hours for one of London's illusive rubbish bins.

Peter grasped my hand, pulling me after him, downstairs to the Charing Cross Tube Stop. He bought two passes and we boarded the Northern Line. We found seats together, slightly away from others, which was pretty lucky riding the normally crowded Tube downtown. Enjoying the safety of being underground, we dropped our hoods.

I forced Brea's scared, tear-streaked face from my mind and managed a smile.

Peter responded by turning my chin his way with a finger, and placing a soft, magical kiss on my lips. I was caught off-guard and gulped, loudly. He drew back slightly, looking at me to gauge my reaction.

One small peck wasn't enough. I wrapped my hand in the fabric of his hoodie and gave two quick little tugs. I was out of time.

The hint wasn't lost on him. He cupped my face with one big, gentle hand, taking what I offered with a disciplined touch. The sweet taste of whipped cream remained on his lips. I melted against him, craving any contact and the warmth of his breath. The world quieted. He filled my senses, making me want for nothing but more of him. At that moment I lived to maintain that feeling, wishing away the dark parts of my life, concentrating on each physical sensation and banishing each thought of tomorrow. Peter helped me, fueling my ability to lie to myself with his touch.

We rode the Tube in big, lazy circles as long as we could,

allowing time to get back inside the bookstore before sunset. The prerecorded voice in the train sounded with "Mind the Gap" so many times I mimicked it, dead on.

Peter walked me to my room that afternoon, holding my hand. I pulled him close for a goodbye hug. While I held onto him I leaned close to his ear, talking to him softly.

"No matter what happens I will never forget today."

"You sound like you're going to turn into a pumpkin at midnight."

I snorted at the irony. Poor guy and his fairy tales and nursery rhymes. "Ever had like . . . a foreboding?"

He tried to pull back some but I wrapped my fists in the back of his hoodie, keeping my face pressed against his chest. Tears threatened to tarnish a great day between us. I didn't want to see him turn cold, all business like he did when I let things get to me.

"You're just tired, Tessa. It will be a bright, new day on the morrow."

"Yeah, I guess you're right." I took a deep breath and bit the inside of my cheek. I gave him a quick smile I didn't feel. "Goodnight, Peter. Dream well." I turned before emotion betrayed me.

"You, as well. 'Night."

I used pillows to muffle the sound of myself crying once I was safely in the privacy of my room. The idea of never seeing Peter again added a layer to my personal hell. He would go back to his life pre-Tessa, working at the bookstore, bantering with customers and being charming. As for me, I couldn't help the feeling Kai would succeed in keeping me away. I would betray Peter, had already betrayed Brea, and would continue to let myself down for as long as I drew breath.

CHAPTER 17

The night wore me down to nervous pulp, but morning still came too fast. My stomach was too tossed to eat so I ran on sheer adrenaline. My temperature was elevated, causing sweat to glisten on my scales.

My backpack was jammed with a few necessities, keeping it light and leaving plenty of room—a thing that was contrary to my previous nature. I wished I had some sort of weapon to conceal in my bag. I looked around my room. My brilliantly colored, rainbow pen collection went into the bag with my journal. My room at *Librorum Taberna* hardly held an arsenal. Thank you, Ezra. I'd rely on fangs, claws, and a bad attitude to rescue my best friend.

I pulled on black jeans, Chuck Taylors and a black hoodie over a Tinkerbelle t-shirt. Each time I blinked it was like I'd run through a sandstorm during the night. My outfit matched my mood without much thought being put into it—dark on the outside and cinder black on the inside.

Kai was looking up at my window when I peered through the blinds to the alley, and so was his female sidekick. He smiled when he saw me. I let the blinds down, dug deep for some steel and walked outside, so tense and full of dread my jaw was locked to the point of pain.

"Say your goodbyes?" Kai said as I approached. His groupie snorted a laugh.

"You really want to play with me today?" I stared at her, half expecting a sarcastic retort, but she didn't say anything.

I approached Kai with determined steps, intentionally walking past her because she simply didn't matter. "Where's Brea?"

"We'll be taking a drive to get to her. She's safe and unharmed other than what she's done herself."

"What does that mean? She better be okay." I locked eyes with him. I didn't know what I'd do if he'd harmed her, but the way I'd felt lately, I was likely to surprise both of us.

"Or what?" said the groupie.

My temper flared. "I told you it was a bad day for this crap." Kai had threatened my best friend's life, and that made the chick's existence seem completely unsubstantial.

The cocky idiot shrugged at me.

"Petra, enough," Kai hissed.

"Petra?" I drawled. "Did your parents not like you or something?"

"At least I have parents," she sneered.

Something snapped inside me like a dry twig popping in my chest. Pent up, years'-old anger burst free. I swung hard and fast, bloodying her nose, a little shocked at myself. She reached for me and succeeded in grabbing a small handful of my hair, which snapped, sounding like static electricity. I threw my other hand hard and busted her lip. She cried out and covered her face with both hands. But I didn't stop. She wanted to push buttons about my lack of family, she'd better pack a lunch. It was the single, most hurtful issue she could poke at. I launched myself at her and took her to the ground. Air pounded from her lungs with a sick, whooshing cough as I straddled her chest to pin her arms. I grabbed her hair at a temple to measure her out and landed another of my fists against her mouth. Heat surged through my veins. All I could think was that she needed to be quiet, not dead, but silent. She could never talk about my missing family again and I would make sure she had a hard time talking shit with no teeth.

The back of my jacket yanked rigid around me as Kai pulled me off her. I barely found my feet before he let me go and grabbed Petra from the ground. Blood ran freely from her nose. The left side of her top lip was distorted and growing purple. She glared at me. I smiled, frankly a little impressed with myself. My hands stung. I may have broken a knuckle or two but I was wound tight, overheated like I hadn't been in years and indulging in some old-fashioned stress-relief. Shame crept in but was ousted by the sound of her voice playing through my head. *At least I have a family.* I triumphed inside. Chalk one up for Little Orphan Tessa.

Petra hunched over and spit blood-infused saliva. I snorted. It served her right. My body felt impossibly light. I bounced a little on the balls of me feet.

"Enough!" Kai snapped.

"Let's go," I gestured toward St. Martin's Road and picked up my backpack. "I want to see my friend. Petri dish can stay right here."

Kai and I looked at Petra in unison. She wasn't moving, still bent at the waist and spitting clotted blood.

"You need to control your groupie."

Kai glared at me.

I shrugged. "She started it." I nibbled at a string of torn skin hanging from a knuckle on my right hand.

Petra righted herself and began walking.

Kai shook his head at me, squinting.

"I warned her."

His graze traced over my messed up, ratty hair, bloodied hands and dirt-streaked jeans. I shuddered. How could someone so beautiful to look at be such a creep? It reminded me of an old song I heard once on one of Austin's Country Music stations.

Something about how everything that glitters is not gold. That was definitely the case with Kai. He was shiny on the outside, but full of nasty, rotting dead things on the inside. I looked away from his glare, feeling like a ruffian, and began to walk toward the corner, sensing him following me.

A black Aston Martin waited around the corner, complete with an attending black-clad, hooded driver. I would always trouble over why the bad guys got the good cars. To own a car and drive in London usually meant a person had some cash to play with. Everyone else always hailed those stuffy, "P.T. Cruiser" looking cabs or took the Tube.

When we'd driven for about a half hour I couldn't help but ask him a question that had been stabbing at me since earlier, when we met in the alley."Kai?" I said quietly. I didn't really want Petra in our conversation, but she was seated ahead of me in the car, beside the driver. My only option to limit how much she heard was to try to keep my voice down, and hope Kai would, too. I took a breath and scooted closer to him, ignoring the senses that screamed at me, telling me to get back on my side of the car.

"Yes," he said, leaning closer on the seat we shared.

"How did Petra know that I didn't have parents?" I whispered.

Kai sat straight on the seat, contemplating. Finally, he leaned close and gestured for me to, as well.

"I compelled Brea to talk a little bit."

"Compelled?"

"It's merely a subtle way of pushing with the mind. She wasn't harmed, I promise you."

I looked out the window. Brea knew so much about me. We'd spent nearly the last two years becoming so close we called ourselves sisters on many occasions. Kai had taken Brea captive two days ago that I knew of, possibly longer. How much talking could she have done? Enough, apparently.

Brea knew the story of my recent attempt to find my brother.

I'd gone looking and found only regret that I'd even bothered trying. It happened a couple days before I left for London. A quick Google search found a landline phone number and an address in the Lake District of Austin for the people who'd adopted Robbie. A feigned fever with a little help from my hair drier's "hot" setting to my forehead right before the Sunday school bell excused me from church for the day. When the digitized bells ceased chiming, I'd made my way off the grounds.

Google map in hand, I'd stepped from the Capitol Metro bus, my imagination whirring happily with anticipation. I drew a mental picture of Robbie. He'd be taller than me. He had my eyes. He would protect me like big brothers were supposed to. We would be closer than any pair of siblings anywhere. I would hug him so tight, and he'd never want to let me go. He would smell good, reminding me of something buried in the past I didn't know I had. He would tell me about our parents. We would cry together and then laugh because we cheated Fate. We'd vow to never be separated. My heart soared that day. My steps were light. I prevailed against life for once and loved every second.

I'd walked five, meandering, sweaty blocks southwest and knocked on the Tomlinson's lakefront mini mansion's door.

My gaze travelled over the impeccable lawn and perfectly pruned hedges while I waited for someone to answer. A magnolia tree thrust from the center of a side yard, heavily laden with cone-shaped buds. The house at 7013 Oak Shores Lane was seamlessly manicured, from the cobbled flagstone drive to the gleaming Doric marble columns mounted at either side of the sprawling, white veranda.

The posh nature of the place chafed. I couldn't help feeling cheated. Not only had I been denied an adoption, complete with parents and a real *brother*, and some sense of a normal childhood, the family was apparently wealthy. Maybe I had the wrong address. I hoped I did. These people didn't want me, and for that, they didn't deserve nice things. Tears welled, but practice helped me blink them back. I was hurt. Bone deep. Whatever the case, the couple that lived there didn't matter at all. What mattered was finding Robbie. I would be cordial enough to see him or get some information and then I'd leave.

After a series of three rings of the doorbell, each a little longer and more impatient, the thick door finally swung open. A gust of cold, conditioned air blasted me. I would never forget the tall, elderly man who stood in the doorway. Shining blue eyes gazed from a gently lined face. Thin hair stood in a military cut atop his head. He wore a long-sleeved, button-down shirt rolled back at the wrists to expose suntanned skin and shiny gold watch I imagined cost as much as a new Prius. A pair of distressed, loose fitting jeans with beige deck shoes completed his outfit just right, even at his advanced age.

I stared. The man had been extremely handsome in his day. He still was. He smiled easily at me with the smile of someone who naturally grasped sincerity. Some people just had that quality.

"How can I help you, young lady?" He continued to grin.

I had to work hard to shake off the charm. I checked myself. This man had denied me. Adopted my brother and stole him from me in the process. He could smile all he wanted while I grilled him long enough to find my brother.

If Robbie was inside the house right then, it would've been perfect. Or maybe he attended University of Texas and would be home soon. I would be reunited with my brother and this guy could go play on his boat undoubtedly tethered in a private slip in the lakefront backyard while I basked in the glory of rebuilding a precious piece of my life.

I had to be a bulldog.

"Hi, Mister Thomlinson?" I waited a split second and went on without his response. "My name is Tessa Conley. I'm looking for Robbie Conley." I flashed the photo at him. "He is my brother."

The smile faded.

I held steady, not knowing what to expect since I was actually having that conversation with the man. I bit the inside of my cheek to hold my focus. *Bulldog, remember?*

"Won't you come inside, please."

Gotta love that Southern hospitality.

His smile was replaced by practiced stoicism. Lines on his face became clearer. Deeper. I'd mistaken them for laugh lines, crow's feet from smiling in the sun. The deeper lines were etched by grief, like the faces on the cover of National Geographic when the photojournalist was working in a poor, third-world country.

A small sense of dread churned the nerves in my stomach as I stepped inside to follow him to a den in the depths of the sprawling home.

The walls were hung with tastefully matched picture frames that complemented various still shots from the days in the life of a man and his son.

"Can I offer you a cold glass of sweet tea? Looks like you were walking and, well, I know it's a hot one today." He tried a smile once more, but it lacked the radiance of the one he greeted me with.

"I'm fine, thanks. I won't take much of your time. I need to be put in touch with my brother."

A triangle shaped, military flag case caught my attention from above a fireplace mantle. I tore my gaze away quickly and looked a little closer at some portraits on the wall. A young man in a blue military uniform stared from an eight-by-ten, jaw locked, familiar copper-brown eyes intense beneath a gleaming white cover. Dread worked toward full-blown foreboding. The face in the picture held a flawless kindred nature to mine.

"You two could've passed for twins." Mr. Thomlinson splashed a drink from a decanter. "Call me Ben."

"Ben," I tried limply. The gusto that carried me there rapidly deserted me. Something was horribly wrong. I knew, deep in that place inside my heart, the place I worked so hard to protect on any other day, that I was getting ready to get hurt. *What would he think if I made a break for the door?* I would sprint to the bus stop and catch the Metro back home. Forget this whole, bad idea. He'd said "could've." Past tense. I went numb on the outside while I panicked on the inside.

"It happened in Afghanistan, last year." He downed a healthy swig from the tumbler. "The vehicle he was operating rolled over an IED. They told me it was instant." The remainder of his drink was gone and replaced in practiced routine.

"Was he a Marine?" The impeccable uniform matched those from the television commercials where the men saluted proudly, sword in white-gloved hand.

"Still is. He guards the streets of Heaven. Once a Marine, always a Marine." The pride in his statement stabbed at my heart. I glanced to a framed certificate stating Robert Donald Thomlinson was Honorably Discharged from the Department of the Navy and United States Marine Corps.

"You wanted a son, but not a daughter?" I blurted the question. My subconscious demanded action so I didn't stand still waiting for some other horrible thing to happen. I'd already started to cry. The events hadn't matched up to my expectations. The new hope was shattered, each tear a shard.

"We were introduced to both of you kids and, well, I know there was no question we'd take you both." He stepped closer to the cold fireplace. "But then you got sick with that fever and convulsions. My poor Emma, God rest her soul, well, I know she was crushed. The adoption process was stopped for you and they wouldn't hear any argument we gave. They wouldn't let us have you." He ran a fingertip lovingly across the top of a framed photo on the mantle. "Emma was broken hearted over it."

Aged fingers grazed the cheek of a bride gazing up at a young Ben Thomlinson. There was no question the woman lived for her groom. Affection glowed in her eyes and young Ben's gaze mirrored the emotion. Love like that was forever.

"We went ahead with the adoption process, but only with

Robbie. You weren't expected to pull through that coma and we were not given the go ahead to adopt you because we couldn't finish up the meetings with you. We checked in with the workers at the adoption office a lot. We made them promise to call the second there was any change in your condition."

My breath locked in my throat. "Coma?" I croaked. *Did he mean I was in a coma?*

"You were so little, really just a baby still. The Home did the right thing and called me when you'd come back from the sickness, but by that time Emma had passed." His hand dropped from the mantle, falling to his side. He tipped his glass, swallowing hard. "I was a wreck trying to console Robbie and keep up with him when she passed, along with dealing with my own grief at losing my beautiful wife, after our family had been made complete."

I flinched. *"Complete."* Their family had been whole. Without me.

"I knew there was no way I could care for a little girl." He searched my face, gazing from eye to eye. "And I could barely care for Robbie at that point. When I told him about his momma passing away, he got real quiet. The poor kid had just stopped asking to see you in the hospital about a month before Emma's accident. And well, I guess losing her and you were just too much. He quit asking, and I let him forget."

"You *let* him forget me?" I was stunned. I watched him fill his glass again. It was unforgivable. The decision that mapped my life was made by a man who'd chosen to let his emotional defeat create my loneliness. "How could you do something so thoughtless? I've been at that home ever since. It's the only place I've ever known." I clenched my teeth against heartache. I was crying hard and I couldn't stop.

"He's gone now," he said, drinking. "Imagine how hurt you'd have been when he was killed."

"I would have had you!" I yelled. "I wouldn't be alone. I would have had my brother and a father for . . . all my life until then!" I felt my soul fracture into pieces, trying to claw its way out through my chest. I hated everything. I wanted to leave and to die.

Ben's eyes held tears.

I was happy about that. Anger crept in front of sadness, helping me pull myself together. Slightly.

I'd somehow managed to apologize to Ben for his losses that day. I didn't know if I meant it. I didn't know what else to say, years after the fact, and my day had switched up so horribly. I'd been ready to meet my brother, and if that would have happened, if the "forces that were" would have allowed me one speck of grace that day, Ben could've remained a side note, and I likely would have told him how bad it hurt me to be discounted. I wanted to scream at him for hours about how my heart shattered, blow by blow as he spoke of his decision not to bring me into his life after the death of his wife. It didn't seem worth the time because I truly never wanted to see the man again. Ever.

My being there would have helped ease his suffering if nothing else, instead he'd concentrated on evading a potential burden. The icing on the figurative cake was that he admitted to allowing the only family I had on the planet to forget about me. Thinking about that changed tears of sadness to tears of anger. I wished bad things for Ben as I thought about it. I was happy he'd suffered and his heart hurt. I secretly wished he cried every day, missing his wife and my brother. And I hated that I felt justified in wanting him to have that sort of pain, when I was suffering that way, too.

I left his house without looking back at the place. While I'd been inside, a thunderstorm cast the sky in grey. Light drizzle fell, upgrading to full-blown rain drops while I walked. It was a blessing. No one would see my tears through the rain. I raged against my decision to look into the records room. Finding that photo had done nothing but get my hopes up. My body reacted to the surge of emotion by overheating even though rained soaked me as I walked. I felt like a glowing cinder, and I wanted to burn everything around me to the ground. It was the worst day of my life and I'd shared each painful detail with my best friend.

And Brea had been forced to tell my story to Kai and his minion. I glared at Kai, on the seat with me. "I disagree," I said, realizing too late I'd been staring out the window for quite a while.

"About what?" he sounded disturbed at my audacity to think on my own. His look asked, *"How dare I disagree?"*

"You harmed her by making her talk about me. She must be crushed." Sadness tugged at my features, so I turned away. Brea had to feel turmoil, she'd betrayed me on top of being kidnapped.

"You love her," he said gently.

"Like a sister."

"Stop kidding yourself, Tessa."

I looked at him sharply. "Kidding myself?"

Kai leaned in so close that I could smell the herby, spicy scent of his skin. "We all know you have not a damn clue what it feels like to have a sister. Or a brother for that matter. Saying you love that . . . person like a sister is a stretch and you know it."

His words stung with truth. No matter how much I tried to glorify my friendship with Brea, she would never really be my sister. She'd never be a replacement for a family. I loathed that he knew intimate parts of me, of my life. I bit back tears and took a breath to get past his intently cruel words, not willing to betray the way he'd affected me. I huffed, resorting to sarcasm, feeling around inside my head for some anger to play off of.

"You're not doing much to win me over to the Dark Side, there big guy."

He laughed. "Since our little 'episode' in the alley, I've decided it may take a bit more than compelling you to my side."

"Episode?" I sounded just as pissy as I felt. So far, the highlight of my day had been smacking his stoolie. The day had gone downhill from there.

"I attempted coercion with you that day, and it simply didn't work." He looked at me, curiously.

"Good." I retorted. Served him right. "Don't forget the part where you lied to me about being a gargoyle. I was wary of you before, but now, after kidnapping and hurting my best friend, and lying, I'll never trust a word you say. And I'm thrilled your little magic tricks won't work on me."

"You think so? You vomited, instead. I had to search the damned *United States* and all of Heathrow Airport to steal the only person on the planet you're fond of, push at her fluffy little mind for a few days and make her cry because you didn't succumb to my compelling you. Still good?"

"I really don't like you."

"Yet." He added.

"It won't work on me."

"We shall see."

"So, what, I'll have to stay like, hypnotized forever to be around you? That makes you the biggest creeper in the world."

He laughed again. "Hypnosis is not even in the same arena as the magic I have, Tessa. You'll not only like me, you'll love and adore me. Hang on my every word."

"Don't count on it."

He sounded so confident, his words chilled me. The possibility of my free will being taken was eerie. And how dare he discount the way I felt about my best friend?

"Talk me down all you want about the way I feel about Brea, Kai. Say what you want about me being an orphan. But know this," I leaned forward. "No matter what you do with your little magic spells, I will never, truly and willfully want to be with you. Ever." I turned back to the window.

"And Peter? Do you want to be with him?" He said, whisper elevated into a casual speaking voice. I guessed it was okay with him if Petra got to hear all about Peter. She seemed fascinated with him when she'd trashed the bookstore.

"Who's Peter?" I deadpanned. Of course he knew Peter, I just hoped there was no way he knew anything about Peter and *me*. Kai had more ammunition than he needed already. "Really, that guy's hardly my type. He's just something to keep me occupied till I can find a way to get out of here."

Petra snorted in the front seat, shaking her head. I ignored her.

He laughed again, deep and musically. I loathed him for that.

The meager solace of my window provided minimal comfort from such touchy conversation. I'd never been a hateful person. Matter of fact, I took steps, even made excuses for people, to avoid letting hate into my life. Where Kai was concerned, I welcomed the target for my anger.

We drove for hours into the English countryside. I put up my hood and tried to take up the least amount of room on the seat as possible. I couldn't wait until I didn't have to sit next to him anymore. Didn't have to smell him or hear his voice. They were too pleasant to belong to such a dirt bag. I wondered if those things were part of the "magic" he bragged about. It was like he was doing it on purpose to make me want to be close to him. Maybe I needed to get a better understanding of his power over people.

Allowing myself to hate meant I'd changed. I'd begun mourning the loss of myself, and just when I'd tried to accept living at the bookstore. At least there I was trying to be myself, as best I could given what I had to work with. I could enjoy a little bit of London. I ran a lot, read, wrote, and found something to smile about every day, despite the scales. Possibly, I'd begun to love. And Kai had taken me away from Peter, as well. I should never have let myself fall for Peter. I wouldn't have been hurting so bad thinking about losing him.

I fogged up my window with angry, hot tears.

We drove on and it seemed like forever. I watched the driver's gloved hands maintain the wheel and flawlessly shift the car for miles. I looked around the cockpit. On any other occasion I'd be thrilled to be on a long ride in such a magnificent car. Instead, I couldn't quit thinking about how lost I was.

So many hours travelling north had to put us deep into Scotland. The sun peaked through a pouting sky at times, but for the most part, the day was another typical, dreary, sometimes drizzly day in the UK. A kaleidoscope of several shades of green covered the hills, so vivid the brilliant hues shone through the dark tint of the auto glass. A monstrous bridge spanned a huge bay and as we crossed the expanse, the stealthy car's shadow bounced from blue to black wave below us.

I'd had to pee to the point of cramps for what seemed like over an hour so when we pulled into a station I got out without asking, shouldered my bag and headed inside. The air was thick and chilled, heavily laden with salt from the sea. The driver fueled the car and talked with Petra. She eyed me when I walked past. As if I'd be running away when those *people* had taken my best friend. That was genius. And I didn't know what she thought she was going to be able to do if I tried to take off. I felt we'd established an agreement. She may have been bigger than me, but I had a whole lifetime of pissed-off energy waiting for an excuse to jump, hair-trigger quick.

When I came out of the stall, Petra was examining her purple lip and swollen nose in the mirror, scrubbing dried blood away with a paper towel. Without the busted up face, she was very pretty. Her skin had a natural, suntanned quality that made her hazel eyes glow. She had one of those youthful, classic looks, like a model at Abercrombie and Fitch. Where I was *kind of* pretty, Petra was beautiful. She stood over me by at least four inches. I'd been too angry to notice those things before. I almost felt a little guilty, looking at her then. *Almost.*

She still shouldn't have poked at me earlier. The secret was out like headlines in the National Enquirer. Everyone knew I'd grown up in an orphanage. Most people would have put two and two together to figure I wasn't afraid to throw down. I didn't care if she looked like a sweet, girl-next-door. She tried to be cruel and I felt victimized. She'd brought out the worst.

Petra stepped away when I approached to use the sink.

"Looking good." I winked.

She glared.

"You have to know by now that I'm not the one that changed you, right?"

Petra looked away.

"So now that *that's* all cleared up, why do you have it in for me?" I dried my hands, watching her in the mirror. "I mean, you don't even know me."

"Think you have it all figured out then, do you?" she snapped, shaking her head. "So vain, thinking it's all about you. I'd not mind if you fell off the earth, never to be heard from. I don't want to know you." Her stuffy British lilt amplified the hate.

"Piss off." If she wanted to be snotty she could knock herself out. I pulled the door open, flipped the light switch down as if no one remained in the restroom, and went back to the Aston.

Kai stood beside the dark figure that drove us. The man tugged his head far into the hood of his jacket, his face recessed deep within the pocket of fabric. They talked quietly. As I approached, the driver went about his business fueling the car and Kai approached me.

"Just a thought, how's your car going to hold up to hauling two —" I looked in the direction of the driver—"or three gargoyles, messing with the leather and all?"

"We'll have reached our destination well before dark. Not to worry about my car." He held open the door for me, flashing a smile laced with underlying innuendo. "Sweet of you to consider, love."

"Don't call me that." I glared, but got in the door he opened for me. I jerked it out of his grip and slammed it a little too hard, chiding myself for being mean to the car.

I'd been playing at seeing how far we were from London, and

he'd given me my answer. That morning I'd left my room when the sun rose, which was five past five AM. We'd probably made it to the car by about five-fifteen. A clock inside the station said eleven-seventeen. By my math we'd all be Garging Out by one minute before eight. Wherever we were headed was around eight hours from London.

Two things bothered me about being on the road so long. The first thing was I was pretty sure we were in Scotland. The second I wasn't particularly wild about—I had no idea how I'd make it back to London, let alone Austin, once I found Brea.

CHAPTER 18

*A*round an hour later we turned off the highway, cutting down a road that weaved through tall trees, many ranges of bushes and scrub brush that were all entwined with ivy and the tiniest white, pink and yellow blossoms. I doubted the sun could've broken through the thick canopy above the lane on a cloudless day. Everything in the wooded scene appeared dew-covered and glistened in the low light. Had I not been in such a bad mood I may have said it was beautiful.

We passed through the Village of Kelty. A proud sign announced our whereabouts with dated charm. Well away from the speed and traffic of the highway, the two lane road dissected the village and became what appeared to be the main street of the small community. A Gothic town hall scowled down on age-darkened cobbles and strips of chipped pavement. Pubs and restaurants touting the best fish and chips for miles competed for patrons on the sidewalk. Shops were open for business and people walked the street, sightseeing and window-shopping. An ice cream truck drew a small crowd. Bipod signs stood in the middle of sidewalks announcing football matches and drink specials during the games. It would have been heaven to get out of the car and become lost in the scene.

Just before a right turn into a forest, we left civilization behind. An equestrian center of some sort went by on the right, with winding white fences and small herds of beautiful horses and ponies grazing beside the road.

After two more turns to the right and about three miles, the forest became thicker and the trees closer to the car. The road became a lane. A deep blue loch shone through the thick foliage. The driver navigated slowly because the tight path slithered through trees with switchbacks and dipped a lot. Sometimes, when we bottomed out on one of the slopes, the car passed through standing water. I wondered if it was runoff from the lake or just piles of water from rain. Whatever the case the air was cold enough the driver switched on the heater and the defroster.

Outside the car, the forest loomed dark with a bone-chilling cold. I shivered despite my warm seat.

"Would you like more heat?" Kai offered.

"No. I just want to see my friend." I didn't take my gaze from the window. "All I want from you is Brea."

A stone outcropping shone white through the thick brush. When we rolled past, an arrangement of moss-streaked monoliths formed from the mass of twisting vines and stems. An occasional bunch of ivy crept a ways up the side of one of the standing stones. Each enormous rock was backed by two tall trees and the interior was clear of brush. I straightened in my seat to get a better look.

The driver stopped the car at a gate set in a limestone wall so tall I couldn't see the top when I leaned down to peer up at it. As we waited for two wrought iron panels to part, I shifted to look out the windshield. Two massive, stone pillars exceeded the wall in height, each bracing the end of an elegant arching sign that read "The Grotto".

Gothic spires thrust from the east and west turrets of a manor that crouched from full view behind trees and a ruined curtain wall surrounding the house. Corner drum towers stood at differing heights in their state of crumbled erosion. The modern house had been built squarely in the inner ward of a castle's remains.

We curved to the side of the site along a low garden barrier of polished limestone. Frothy bunches of ivy thrived at the ground along a neatly kept path of multi-hued roses. Afternoon sunshine peeked through the clouds. An open flower box ran the length of the stubby wall, adding layers of colorful blooms. Breathtaking and forlorn, the beautiful garden was misplaced in such a malevolent place. We rolled toward a carriage house, the ancient bastion of the old castle walls surrounding us. The stone mansion stood in regal splendor outside my window.

Humble in size, yet stately in sprawl, the building was an architectural masterpiece against the array of blossoming gardens and courtyards, backed by the sad, crumbling castle. Ancient looking Roman fountains were inset along the cut-stone walls in places, complete with troughs at their bases. Birds flitted between baths and flowering trees.

Talk about conflicted. I was at odds admiring elegance through ruin.

The same as great cars, I wondered why the bad guys always got the cool digs. And it seemed like the other occupants of the car took such ancient beauty for granted. No one else seemed to gawk out the windows the way I did. Maybe they'd seen it countless times, but it was so gorgeous, I knew if it was me returning, I'd take a moment to count my blessings. I felt like I was a fairly good person, and I was "lucky" enough to grow up in an orphanage. Fate had a truly odd sense of humor.

We rounded the circle drive. My door was opened and by the time I stood beside the car, the driver was back behind the wheel. An automatic garage door lifted in the stone carriage house. Petra said nothing, trudging toward the house. Kai exited the car as I shouldered my bag. We all had our hoods up because the sun flung rays onto parts of the yard in quickly moving beams, as clouds and fog fought for control of the day's light. I wondered that since the others had their hoods up, if that meant there were "non-gargoyles" on the grounds. Or maybe like me, they weren't comfortable, knowing what they looked like in the sun.

The car eased into the deceivingly small appearance of the carriage house, revealing it was actually a huge, deep garage, and multiple, blanketed cars were parked inside. The door came back down before I had a chance to try identifying the makes through their covers.

"This way please, Tessa." Kai gestured toward the walk the led to the front doors of the house.

"Where's Brea?" I tried to ignore the circular herb gardens, the sweet smell of roses on the breeze, and gushing fountains. Typical to the ass he was, Kai stomped up the foot path like he waded through stinkweeds. I was ready to get to my friend. I fidgeted with the ties of my hoodie.

"She's inside." He continued to lead the way.

"You didn't like, change her, did you?"

"No." He said it like I'd asked if he'd eaten dirt or something.

"Well, good for you. And I was asking because you changed Petra, and who knows how many others," I fished.

He glanced at me sidelong as we walked. "Tread lightly with the unknown, Tessa. Ask yourself now . . . do you really want to push buttons?"

Kai quickened his pace. I'd struck a nerve.

We entered a foyer that was nearly as big as the library at the Home for Girls. I tried not to look around too much but beautiful things called to me, urging me to explore the spaces we passed.

Marbled tiles gleamed up from the floor in the low light. Several enormous windows lined the walls. The entryway opened on a great room with a huge, wide stairway that split midway, joining a round balcony at the curving sides of its ornate, wooden bannister. A domed, cut-glass skylight was set in a tall ceiling, casting refracted, grey light onto the center of the room. It added the feel that aside from dividers between the windows, we could be standing outside in the cloud sprinkled afternoon. For a guy who had gargoyles around, Kai sure did like ambient lighting.

I mentally shrugged that last tidbit off. It wasn't the only thing about Kai I didn't understand, or want to ignore. But I still couldn't help wondering exactly what he was. The word "magician" sounded too "stage" for him. I knew I wouldn't see him pull a rabbit out of a hat. He was something other. Something dark inside.

"Welcome to my home," he told me.

I shot him a look that screamed I didn't want his welcome and remained silent as we climbed stairs leading to the upper level.

"I've had a room prepared for you. I hope it's to your liking," he continued.

I stopped walking. "Look, this is not a vacation for me and you know that. You know I don't want to be here. I just want to see Brea, please."

He said nothing, but led me to a massive, half-circular room off a west wing. A similar skylight to the one in the great room downstairs lit the room brilliantly, even in the greyed out light outside. White walls were alternately lined with floor-to-ceiling bookcases and windows. A creamy, suede chase with a reading table was positioned next to a grey marble fireplace to the right. Beige tile covered the floor with the exception of a few well-placed, plush carpets. There was also a writing desk and a minibar with a fridge and microwave set up in one of the corners by two closed doors.

Wow. I was impressed despite myself.

Kai strode toward one of the doors by the kitchenette and held it open for me to walk inside. The décor of the bedroom was similar to the den outside, all white and cream colored, completely sumptuous and plush down to a gleaming bathroom.

"Yay, a suite," I said dryly. "Would you quit ignoring me and tell me where Brea is?" I was worried about her. The day Kai tossed me over his shoulder and took off into the court with me in London, he'd tried to control me with magic. I couldn't guess what else he was capable of. And since he'd obviously been after information about me, I hated thinking to what ends he'd go to, to get it from Brea. The thought terrified me. Not because I was scared for myself, but I was truly afraid of what he may have done to her by then. I was still angry at myself for sending the postcard that allowed him to find her. Not that I was aware that monsters like him existed, for real in the world, but I was still the reason she'd suffered.

"I'm sure you need to rest after the long ride," he said as he turned toward the door.

I picked up a vase from the end table nearest me and dropped it to the time, watching him stoically as glass shattered beside me.

Kai didn't even blink at the mess I'd made. "And you'll be reunited with your friend soon."

"No, Kai, I don't want to stay up here in this room," I snapped. "Take me to her, now." I glared at him and stalked toward the door before he could leave me there.

"You will stay here." He stepped toward me, grabbing my shoulders. "Do you understand? Here. In this wing. You have food, your beloved books. Things could get much worse for you." His teeth were clenched. Something flashed in his eyes as he spoke, honing my attention on his words. "Get it?"

I flinched and hated it.

"Do you understand?" he repeated, louder this time. He shook me, rattling my teeth.

"Yes, okay," I pushed at his chest. "Point taken, you dick."

"Good girl," he said softly. The grip on my shoulders relaxed into a caress. His thumbs smoothed over my biceps. "That wasn't so very difficult, now was it?"

I didn't answer him. I hated the fact that I had to play nice, when I really wanted to pound on him. My chest grew hot with heat that flushed my face.

He traced my jaw. "I know why your body overheats the way it does." The statement was clipped, ringing with surety.

I gaped. Surely there was no way he could actually know what was wrong with me. "Do tell." I pulled my cheek from his hand.

"Once a soul reaches a certain age, or has been placed in the world a certain length of time, it grows weary of controlling forces. You, Tessa, are a very old soul, to say the least. Throw your life experience on top of that, and it creates something volatile inside you. You've fought constraints all your mortal life. It's the immortal one that fights for freedom."

I never thought a madman could make sense until that day. As a child, there had been times I felt like I might catch fire inside. Kai gave a half smile as I reasoned through his words. He knew he was right.

He lifted my chin. "I can speak to you with the rapt clarity of the kindred and the ancient, Tessa."

I jerked my face away. I couldn't stand the way he always picked his words so carefully. Each syllable said so much, each word laced with double meaning. "You're such an opportunist. Just because you know about me, doesn't mean you really know me." I stepped back. "You said you'd take me to Brea."

"In time."

"You ass."

"That attitude isn't going to get you far," he warned.

"What do you want?" He confused me. I loved hating him.

"Don't play stupid. We both know you're far too intelligent."

"Forget it. I can't stand you."

Kai snarled, grabbing my shoulders hard. "It seems I'll have to find another way to keep your mind where it should be," he said, between clinched teeth. He let go fast and I almost dropped to the floor. I eyed him curiously. He acted like he'd dropped a hot pan.

He couldn't control me the way he could others and it goaded him.

We always want what we can't have.

"Spoken like a true barbarian. If it won't go of its own free will, force it." It was my turn to be right. I crossed my arms over my chest.

Kai glared, shaking his head. I'd struck another nerve.

I smiled. Maybe it was impossible for him to hurt me. It made sense, since he couldn't use magic on me, either.

He watched me, an amazed expression on his face. "So enigmatic," he said. He turned back toward the door. "You will stay here. Sneaking out will get you hurt." The door clicked solidly shut behind him, leaving me in silence.

I kicked the shards of busted vase into the corner beside the door to my room and sat on the bed weighed down by genuine worry. I was in trouble. Kai had no plan to take me to Brea. He lied to get me there, but what was I supposed to do? I felt like I was missing part of the story somehow. He had to be after way more than just "having me at his side". He knew things about me that I didn't, and that put me on edge.

But I'd fought him off, and that thought alone gave me hope.

* * *

SUNDOWN APPROACHED and I needed to get my bearings while I was human. Attempting stealth as a gargoyle was something I'd hardly mastered.

My plan was accompanied by a back-up. I would get to the garage and filch the keys to a car, along with a way to open the overhead door. I would locate Brea and we'd drive out of there. If nightfall came too fast for Plan A, then I'd implement Plan B. I'd break free of the manor and fly her back to London and the safety of Peter and the bookstore in my gargoyle form.

Unknown elements would surprise me, but I had to start

somewhere. I hoped finding Brea was easier than I thought it might be.

Kai was so angry by the time he left, there was no telling what I might find guarding the room. I couldn't imagine why he was so enamored with *me*. I was nothing special. I was not such a beauty as to inspire the kind of attention I got from a man like Kai. I was sure he wanted to use me for something, and I worried it had a lot to do with what he'd told me about being an old soul. Kindred to him, somehow. I wanted nothing to do with finding similarities between us, but was a hundred percent willing to take advantage of the fact that he didn't want me dead.

He'd hit home with the way I burned inside sometimes. When I was little, I'd thought everybody did it. Then the nuns at the home started taking extra care of me, checking my temperature a lot. I had to stay in some times when I felt good and wanted to go to school or out to play in the courtyards but they made me stay in bed because I had a fever. It happened a lot. And it got worse when I started getting my periods. Hormones intensified the bouts with high temperatures. By then, I'd learned to hide it from the staff at the Home and the other girls, for the most part, if it suited me.

I needed to clear up some uncertainties. Location didn't seem to matter much anymore. My world was a state of flux as far as location. The things that comprised my "new world" were the changes that found me, creating insecurity in who I believed I was.

I had no idea if I would be able to fight off another of Kai's advances. He'd seemed rushed so next time he might bring a bigger arsenal of mojo. My system repelled against him with bouts of nausea. I could tell him he made me sick to my stomach. Maybe I was allergic to his brand of magic. Whatever the case, waiting around to be a victim wasn't part of the plan to look for Brea.

The door opened. I was a little surprised, thinking he'd locked me in. *Holy mother of pearl —*

A familiar, dark figure leaned against the wall opposite me, black hood obscuring most of the man's face. He'd frightened me so terribly, weeks ago, as I ran down Tottenham Court Road. He inclined his chin in a familiar nod, the way he'd done on the street that night, showing the same slight outgrowth of a beard. His hands were hidden inside the long pocket of a black jacket. I stopped one step into the circular library. Up close he was huge, well over six feet tall and all muscle. The guy could bust me in half if he got his hands on me. He wasn't smiling.

I was crushed. The hall was less than twenty feet from where I stood at the ready, half inclined to bail for the door, to take my chances outrunning him. I hadn't come that far looking for my friend to be headed off by some guy, obviously using his hugeness and dark, skulking demeanor to intimidate me into giving up. I took one more step.

He came off the wall.

"Get back in there, close the door, *lock it*, and do not come out again until you're called upon." The voice matched him perfectly, deep and menacing.

Lock it, he'd said. If he wanted to get at me, he wouldn't have suggested I lock myself in. I was nothing, if not an excellent listener. There was opportunity in the details. "Or what?" My words were small, my voice too feminine.

He scoffed, shaking his head. "For your own protection." He stepped toward me.

"Not from you," I shot back.

"Get the hell back in there. Now." His voice elevated, betraying a lack of malice.

I turned my head toward the door, going for broke, calling his bluff. Breaking into a run, I stretched my legs picking up speed, and didn't look back.

He was on me quick, snatching me by the back of my jacket.

Whirling on him the best I could, I unleashed a tirade of blows, striking whatever I could reach. One landed firmly across the side of his face, rocking his head back a little despite the fact I'd struck him through the fabric of his hood rather than bare skin.

He growled, jerking me around hard until both my arms were pinned at my sides and my backpack fell to the floor. Using brute strength, which still seemed a little untapped, he picked me up by my shoulders and slammed my back against the wall. My head snapped back as my skull cracked against the plaster behind me. The world went white, a little shiny around the edges. I struggled to focus, dangling off the floor at eye level with the man I'd mistakenly thought wasn't going to hurt me.

Ice-blue eyes squinted on me. "Feel me now?" He smacked me into the wall again, his jaw set, unmasked fury scorching from his gaze.

Words wouldn't come for lack of air in my lungs. I was yanked from the wall, carried five long strides toward the bedroom, where he kicked the door the rest the way open and simply tossed me inside onto the carpet like a load of unfolded laundry. My bag followed, thumping the floor by my feet.

He glared down at me, grasping the door handle. "Lock this, and I mean it. Understand?"

I nodded from the floor. The door was slammed shut and I rolled to my hands and knees, loping forward to turn the lock on the handle. I didn't know what I was locking out, but I sure as hell didn't want another run-in with the guy guarding the door. Lungs and back aching, stomach empty, and head throbbing, I crawled onto the massive bed, sinking into the unwanted comfort of thick, down ticks under a soft duvet. The hum of forced air lulled me. I'd wait him out, looking for an opportunity. All there was to do until then was sleep.

* * *

Tingling skin woke me and I made it into the bathroom and stripped bare just before wings sprouted from my shoulder blades. My stomach rumbled a protest, so empty it felt like it rubbed a blister on my backbone. I gulped huge mouthfuls of water from the faucet at the sink, but it wasn't a big help. I needed food.

Hearing my door click and swing open didn't make the "guard" too happy. He'd Garged Out, too, and spun from the window when I stepped out. A full, yellow moon hung low having just risen above the stone circle and treetops outside, casting golden light onto scales as black as night. He leaned a broad shoulder against a wall, arms crossed over a thickly plated chest. Gleaming fangs and ice blue eyes were the only parts of his face that stood out against his jet form. Spiked, curving wings stretched high above his head, arcing to rest calf-length at his back. Scales so dark they gleamed as he moved reflected from his body in a silent echo of light. A chest-length braid fell across his shoulder. He shook his head at me, a gesture that said *"Really? You're this dumb?"*

I waived my claws at him like a white flag. "I just need something to eat. I'm freaking starving." He watched me closely as I strode to the bar and turned sideways to fit my wings behind it to get to the mini fridge. A big jar of marmalade, a butter knife, and a flat loaf of grainy bread accompanied me to the other side of the bar while he continued to stare through narrowed eyes. I imagined myself trying to carve through his chest plate with the dull blade and snorted as I stepped up to a tall backless stool and perched, digging into the bread and spreading large dollops of jelly in a thick layer of orange peel and pectin. I chewed rather ravenously, but I hadn't eaten in over eighteen hours.

The black gargoyle continued to watch me. I swallowed a huge mouthful, staring back. "Kai's pretty worried about me escaping, huh?"

He didn't answer.

"I mean he must be, making you stay here all night."

"I volunteered." He turned back to the window. "I didn't expect you to be so bloody thick."

"No need to be a prick." I turned back to the bread and coated another piece. "And how could you know what to expect? We haven't met or anything. Maybe you have the wrong girl."

"You are Tessa," he looked over a brawny shoulder. "Raised to adulthood in the South United States by nuns." He turned again, leaning a claw on the wall above his head.

The thick accent didn't account for the way he'd said my name, like it had a ZZ instead of an SS. "It's Tessa," I clarified, pronouncing my name the correct way.

He responded with a quick bark of laughter, shaking his head.

I continued, ignoring his outburst. "And everyone probably knows that about me. My best friend is being held here someplace and Kai has been making her tell him about me." I bit into my makeshift meal. "Nice try though."

He just stared into the glass.

"So why did you volunteer to stay up all night watching my door?"

"For your protection, since you won't listen and stay inside of your own accord."

"Yeah, I'm believing all that."

He turned slowly. "Watch your tongue."

"Wouldn't want to give you an excuse to throw me around some more."

"That's bloody right. And what do you expect to get for striking another?"

"You grabbed me, remember?"

He crossed his arms, considering my words. "Fair enough, but you didn't listen to me."

"You growled at me. And did you hear the part about my friend being locked up out here somewhere? She's why I'm here."

"Brea is well."

I swallowed a lump of dampened bread, looking away. He had to be playing with me, which was mean as hell, but I couldn't take the chance that he was being sincere and really knew something about her. "Where is she?" I looked back toward him, locking my gaze on his eyes in attempt to gauge whether he was lying to me.

"She is safe, don't fash yourself."

"Thanks for nothing." I slid from the stool and began replacing the food in the kitchenette.

"You must to be taught so many things, and need to remember so many more, lass."

"I don't do psychobabble."

He'd made two things clear; one was that if I tried to leave my room, he'd throttle me. Maybe he'd have a smile on his face and maybe he wouldn't. The other thing was he knew things but wasn't willing to help me out. I slammed the bedroom door shut and was sure to lock it. I was exhausted and needed a fresh mind at first light. Maybe he would be at my door in the morning. Either way, I would begin my search. I just had to get around him.

CHAPTER 19

I poked my head into the library moments after dawn, scanning the place. The room was silent. Abandoned. I didn't question the opportunity as I skirted the bar, made it through the den and walked smack into something that felt like sticky, slimy Saran Wrap at the hall entrance. I was slung back, feeling bile creep into my throat. My eyes watered. I swallowed hard, approaching again, sticking my hand out to feel my way through the air.

Slime oozed through my fingers. I gagged but kept pushing, fighting to keep images of drowning in invisible gel out of my mind. I put my other hand out. Whatever the stuff was blocking the hall was hard to push into. I had the image of one of those squishy, stress balls, like I was attempting to walk through a big, slimy one. The sensation that my arms were covered with some sort of cold, creeping, viscous fluid overwhelmed me and I stepped back again, retching as my temperature spiked. If I kept that up, little piles of puke would be scattered all over the expensive tile.

There had to be another way out. The windows opened to vent the room, but were too far above the ground to jump. Cool air beckoned, soothing me. I gazed out at the Scottish morning. The air was salty and held the sound of water moving over sand and rocks. Clouds danced in the pale sky. Gulls called. I was jealous of their freedom. I kept at the window for a couple deep breaths until my stomach felt better.

Recharged, I pulled out of my hoodie and stuffed it in my backpack, making sure the shoulder straps held the bag good and tight against my back. I tied my hair back and paced across the large room to the wall opposite the "blocked" hallway. I bounced on my toes a couple times to psych myself up and took off at a dead run, straight at the exit.

Cold gel soaked me. My mouth filled with vomit. Air left my lungs as I hit the gooey wall. There was no sound but the quick pounding of my heart. Or maybe I felt it rather than heard it. I counted beats, panicking, unable to move. One . . . two . . . three . . . . four . . . .

The next thing I knew, I stumbled outside the library. I gasped lungful's of beautiful air, and triumphed with a couple glory-filled hops, grinning. It was the little accomplishments like that one that would fuel my spirits. Maybe, by some whim of the universe, I was really going to find Brea and get us out of there.

Sunlight coated the staircase, reflecting off the tile below. I stepped lightly down the stairs, listening for anyone who might be approaching.

On the ground floor, I ran close to the wall and dropped to all fours to hide. On hands and knees, I crept beneath rows of glass, pushing my bag along in front with my sinewy hands, changing back to flesh tone in the shadows, white knuckles grasping the slick fabric. Scooting the bag quietly and fast at the same time was impossible, so I chose fast, and *ripped-clicked* along the floor with my backpack hopping over grouted gaps between tiles. Freedom approached.

My bag slid into a scuffed, brown pair of boots, inertia knocked dead along with my momentum. A startled gasp hissed past my lips. I'd never seen boots like those before. The leather was thick and the sole soft, not manufactured, but crafted. Scared to look up to see who, or what, wore them, I sat back on my heels, ready to bargain or bluster the rest of the way outside if I saw one iota of opportunity.

A gargoyle stood in a stray sunbeam. Copper faded to deep brown under thin membranes and tendons. From my angle, he seemed incredibly tall with waist length black hair. He tilted his head, regarding me. It was hard to tell with the effect from the sun, but I think he was grinning. A lot of brilliant, straight teeth were showing.

"Why make this any worse on yourself, lass? Go back up there and play nice."

Play nice, I would not. I pushed to my feet, shouldering my pack. White bone gleamed inside my hand from the corner of my eye, a stark reminder of common ground between us. Taking a breath, I prepared to question the guy. It was a long shot, but it was possible he'd seen Brea.

"I need to find a human girl named Brea. She has long brown hair and stands a little taller than me, probably wearing pajamas." My voice held a pleading note despite my best effort to be assertive and sound tough and capable. "Seen her?"

"Aye. There are more rooms on the other side of the stairs, there." He gestured behind me. "I didn't expect you to be out this early." He grinned. The guy's brogue was going to take practice to understand. His words registered just as he continued with more lilting articulation.

I stepped closer to the wall, out the line of sight from the windows. "I'm Tessa," I said. He seemed pleasant so I rolled with his demeanor, trying to be friendly. Finding someone who didn't seem like they were willing to turn me in the second I was caught was refreshing.

"Osgar. Now go back upstairs." He smiled again.

Maybe I was mistaken. "I can't do that, Osgar. I need to get to my friend and get out of here."

"That's the tactic with Kai. He holds one of our own to keep us around. We all feel that duress, and have for centuries." His words were carefully chosen. It made me think he knew more about my situation than I did. I grew tired of that happening.

"We don't belong here."

"Just where do you belong, Tessa? You appear as one of us."

"Well," I said, after some thought. "You have a point about that. But my friend isn't like us. She needs to go back to the States where she'll be safe from all this . . . stuff. And Kai isn't being honest with me. He told me I would get to see her after I came up here with him. I just want to get my friend and go back to London."

"And what makes you believe Kai won't come to London to look for you?"

"I have a couple of friends there that will help me." I knew I could count on Peter. I couldn't wait to get back to see him and I would be danged happy to see Ezra, too.

Another man walked inside to stand beside Osgar, his skin taking on a silverfish tone when he stood in the sun, the inner workings of things beneath his skin flowing like molten lead. He smiled when he saw me.

"You must be the lass from London," he said. "I'm Crispin."

"Crispin is my cousin," offered Osgar.

"I'm Tessa. And I'm not really from London. I'm from Austin, Texas. I was studying abroad in London and ran into a bit of a . . . situation."

"Aye, great word for it, *situation*." Crispin beamed. "And you'll never be mistaken as British with that accent."

Crispin was friendly and genuine on a level I hadn't expected to encounter at The Grotto. "What are you guys doing here?" They didn't seem the type that would take up with someone like

Kai. They were too nice. I didn't pick up on any of the same creepy vibes.

"It's more like 'What's Kai doing here,'" Crispin added, quickly.

Osgar leveled a warning look at the younger man. "That's not going to help at all."

Crispin shrugged. "Really, Tessa, we were here first. Have been for centuries. This is our home, not his. One of us is kept away during each moon cycle so we have to stay—"

"That's enough, Chris," Osgar snapped. "Tessa, return upstairs to keep out of trouble. Not everyone here will be as kind."

"I'm going to talk to Kai." The lie slid from my lips like a greasy snake. I regretted each syllable, but I sensed they weren't going to let me leave the house.

Osgar eyed me tentatively. "He's about the grounds." Osgar stepped aside, moving his large frame from in front of the door. "A word of advice, Tessa?"

"Sure."

"Be back in your room by nightfall."

"I'll do my best." I moved to the door. "Thank you, Osgar."

He nodded and continued into the house, heading to the stairs.

I opened the door barely enough to squeeze myself through and shut it again. Staying low, I crept between the wall of the house and the shrubbery, being careful to keep out of sight. The going was slow, but I made my way toward the courtyard wall. I intended to sneak to the carriage house in the hidden safety of the bushes against the tall masonry.

Clouds eclipsed the sun, dropping the temperature around me severely. Every bit of moisture in the air seemed to burrow into my skin, chilling muscle deep. I shuddered, wishing my bare arms were covered with long sleeves rather than bumpy gooseflesh. Men's voices drifted from the direction of the garage. I toed my way along the side of the stone wall, listening as the conversation grew louder, but still too unclear to make out words. There was laughter, but the conversation was a low murmur. Muffled words tumbled over the barrier, losing their shape as I strained to listen.

I froze when the voices stopped, just before the end of the garden wall leading into the courtyard. Remaining still, quacking like a sitting duck and waiting to get caught wasn't the way I wanted to go out. I peeked around to get a look at the men.

Kai turned in the direction of the house and started toward the walk. I hunched low against the wall, leaning into the ivy and bushes to conceal myself. Hopefully he'd walk right by me.

Being sincerely scared, holding my breath was something I didn't have to think about. I was paper thin against that wall, waiting to be caught. Luck had never been a friend to me. I was sure he'd spin and lunge at me, finding me hiding with some sort of freaky, mad wizard sense. Astounded, I watched as he continued at a fast pace, disappearing around the corner of the house. I leaned forward onto my hands to glimpse who the other man was before he left, too. Getting a look at all the players on the field seemed like a good idea.

The driver from the day before stood in the same place, hood up, face dipped low as if in deep in thought. He tipped his head back to the sky, lifted his hands, and let down his hood to reveal a familiar face.

Peter.

I pulled back out of sight, my head loll back against the cool limestone as the reality sunk into my consciousness. My heart felt like it would claw its way through my chest, shattered and screaming. I'd been cheated, again. But, this time, it was my fault for letting my guard down. I let Peter in, and I was paying the price. A major shift of focus washed over me like black paint. I lost some determination to get back to London. Peter was the biggest reason I looked forward to returning. So why bother?

Betrayal ran hand-in-hand with the times in my life I went looking for answers. When I'd poked around for answers to questions about my missing family at the Home in Austin, I'd found betrayal. And then, when I'd gone looking for answers about how to escape with my best friend, I'd found it again. Betrayal must have been another of Fate's little sisters. I swallowed a sob.

Roll with it. Rub some dirt on it. Bulldog.

One more peek around the wall revealed Peter had gone. I crouched down, gathering my bearings after the punch to my emotions. I would get to the garage, find the keys, locate my best, and apparently *only*, friend, and leave, not wasting a second thought.

I put Peter in the back recesses of my thoughts alongside Ben Thomlinson and Robbie. They stayed locked in my mind's closet, and Peter had just won himself a membership to the "Things-Tessa-doesn't-want-to-think-about-ever Club." Friend card revoked.

Friend was one of those words with different levels of meaning. It ranged from low-level friends, like acquaintances. The next step up could be friends from school, the ones kept at a distance and generally lost over the summer. Then there were true, good friends, besties, like Brea and me. Finally, there was the kind of friend I believed I'd had in Peter. I'd developed feelings for him that belonged in a new place in my heart, a place turned hollow, echoing with emptiness, but shriveling as my anger grew.

Screw it. I'm out of here as soon as I get Brea into a car. Bye-bye, bad guys.

Determination renewed with good, old-fashioned pissiness, I shouldered my bag and took a step toward the garage, face-first into a waiting, chemical-laced towel.

I pulled at the hand over my face, scratching deep into the skin there, thrashing against a thick, wall of a man I couldn't see. I tried to scream but the harsh fumes choked me up. The minute bit of distorted light peeking through the cloth left me. I tried to break free, to run. The vice-like grip around my head was relentless. A weight developed in my chest, pulling me toward the ground like a heavy chain was anchored through my sternum, each link ratcheting me lower and lower. Dizziness met nausea, dancing from the top of my head to my stomach and back up.

I hope Peter can't see me now. I hope I never see him again. . . .

I fell onto the grass as my mind dimmed out, thinking of how truly deep green it was in the shrouded sunshine.

CHAPTER 20

*T*wo years ago I lived my life on a mission to remain alone while I accepted the system, and rolled with the punches until I could spread my wings. I wanted to be freed into the wild like a feathering hawk. We'd taken a field trip to a bird sanctuary where a young golden eagle was brought in with an injured wing. It was nursed along and eventually released. That would be me.

I remember the feeling of being forced to wait. Not forced by some evil captor who cackled and poked at me from outside my cage, but held in place merely by the fear of being alone in society. Fairly natural in a child of 17.

That was a lifetime ago. Memories were vague on a new level. Did I even remember what it felt like to trust that good remained, veiled and hidden, waiting for the day when I was rewarded for putting up with the crappy hand I'd been dealt? Was that youthful blunder at its finest or what? There was no good. I could think of none. Except Brea, but she was a lifetime away from me.

Consciousness courted me, but I pushed it away, content to listen to thoughts swim through the crashing waves in my mind, beckoning me to fade back to oblivion. I took the easy road and slept.

A stream splashed over rocks nearby. A breeze mixed with the scents of honeysuckle and warm amber. I was the most detached from my body I'd ever been. But I was warm and felt oddly comfortable and at ease.

I opened my eyes to see the greenest canopy of leaves above my head. Multicolored birds flitted from branches, singing in long coos and tweets. Sunshine peeked through, streaming onto thick grass beside me. I moved my fingers in the light. They were slender, peachy and polished with my favorite shade of pink. My body rested flat. I crossed my ankles, staring at the beautiful trees.

I didn't wonder where I was. Nor did I worry about when I would leave. I smiled when the breeze urged the trees into motion and sunlight caressed my face. I closed my eyes and just breathed, belonging.

Footsteps approached, swishing in the grass, and rather than becoming alarmed, I welcomed whoever came to join me. It was a man, gold and silver from time, deeply etched with knowledge and kindness. He wore a long wrap of light cloth which hung from his frame nearly to the ground. When he came to his knees beside me, his tarnished-copper beard grazed the grass, flowing with bronze and silver. A talisman of amethyst and shining grey and white feathers was shaped into the like-ness of an owl and hung to his chest, holding his beard flat against him. Brilliant green eyes watched me knowingly with kindred regard. He smiled easily at me, bowing his head when I turned his way. He was entirely familiar, somehow. I'd spent a lifetime knowing him.

"Bandia na Tessa," he said. His smile radiated warmth. His voice was low and soothing. I didn't care that I didn't understand what he told me. At least he knew my name. He inclined his face to the sky, chin tilted high. He breathed deeply, feathered talisman rising and falling gently, tumbled amethyst glinting in eager sunshine.

His act was serene, utterly pleasing, when he knelt beside me. I sat up in the grass, looking to see what held his attention, but finding only the beautiful canopy of trees and birds.

"What is it?" *I asked.*

He didn't answer, but inhaled shakily instead. He lowered his chin to glance at me with blackened eyes. Even the whites were solid and dark. He began to weep. I slid back on the grass when a tuft of white smoke appeared above him. His face grew reddened, and more smoke billowed around his long robe as it turned charred and brown. His jaw opened impossibly wide, giving me a view of flame licking the back of his throat. He screamed, high and loud, crying. Mourning.

I covered my ears and stumbled to my feet.

The skin of his face and hands began to blacken and stretch, melting away in places to reveal bone that gleamed white as heat consumed him. The feculent smell of burning hair and flesh impregnated every breath I took. His mouth worked with no other sound as his hands clawed at his face, pulling away more charred, bloodied flesh. His entire body huffed into flame like he'd been soaked in accelerant.

Screaming, backing away across the turf, I fell backward and my body submerged in cool water. I stilled with the sound of the rushing stream, floating and crying, watching black and grey smoke twist into the air, smudging the beauty of the canopy. Birds fell from the branches and sky, drowning beside me without struggling for life. Paralyzed, I watched one after the other plummet, listening to them die. I continued to cry for days.

* * *

PAIN STOMPED AROUND in my head. My mind struggled to clear, fighting the urge to fall back into painless sleep. I focused on trying wake up. One of my eyes was submerged. I lay on my side in a slow eddy of water that had no temperature.

I opened my eyes to near darkness, and distant, throbbing music. Everything was made of water, the walls, the ceiling, it all moved with streaming currents. A woman looked into my face, brushing hair from my eye with a gentle touch. Her entire being was a transparency of moving fluid with silver flashes refracting through it. We lay on our sides, staring at each other. Her smile injected light deep within my soul, making me want to cry in the face of tranquility. I'd never known such profound peace before. She was beautiful and unreal, like a fairy, or a sprite molded in prismic shades of silver.

"Breathe now, old one," she said.

I smiled back at her. Or I think I did. "All this has been a dream, hasn't it?" I was relieved, ready to wake up in my bed back at the Home.

"Life is a mere, endless dream, sweet. We all remain trapped, in one way or another." Her light, musical voice rang in my mind, urging me on. At once she leaned close, becoming liquid, rushing over me as if I stood under a gentle waterfall.

I gasped from the feeling of being submerged and instantly wished I hadn't.

Breath caught in my throat as I curled up, coughing up river water. A trickle ran from my nose. Spitting hurt, but I expelled more, even after I thought I was done. My nose was raw inside. The metallic taste of old pennies coated my mouth.

I rolled to my knees in about three inches of clear water. Blood dripped from my chin, churning in the current. The water was crystalline, showing pebbles of varied hues beside my hands where blood swirled crimson before being washed away. When I shifted my weight, my muscles retaliated with pain. My body protested movement, unresponsive to my urges at first. Hysterical, I was overjoyed that parts of me lacked feeling altogether.

The concept of time lay beyond my grasp. I felt like I'd inhabited the same place for days, but that couldn't have been right. My fingertips were pruned to the point of deep crevasses, devoid of sensation when I tried to touch my throbbing temple. My forehead lacked no gusto in the lightning strike of pain that shot through my skull when I probed a wound there.

Blood-laced water continued to build up in my mouth so I kept spitting. My throat ached all the way to my lungs. When I exhaled, a sick gurgling noise rumbled deep in my chest. My hair

When we stepped close to any of the pools, the air warmed with damp heat radiating from hot springs. Stone created natural bridges over flowing water as it emerged from the floor in several places across the yawning cavern, only to disappear below the floor.

Rhythmic, low music resonated through the rock. Ambient lighting flooded a small area of the room, casting rays from above through a grate-covered hole in the ceiling. The illuminated area below was smooth, likely a dance floor. Electric sconces lit the dark corners of the place to perfection. Overstuffed leather furniture created an air of leisure, arranged in separate areas of the large, open room for places of intimate semi-privacy or open conversation.

"Do you like my grotto, Tessa?" Kai asked.

His voice resonated into my ear from deep within his chest, jarring me. I pulled my head from where it rested against his body, suddenly too aware of my ability to relax any part of my body touching him.

"No," I rasped. I needed water, not a grand tour of an egotist's wadey pool. Even though, it was a *really* great wadey pool. I coughed, which hurt like crazy from spewing inhaled water.

We passed the curving staircase carved into the wall. Jagged stairs were measured perfectly and knapped into stone. I felt the lump on my head with shaking fingertips. Dried blood clumped in my hair there. My elbow hurt when I straightened it and my right knee felt like it had bent in the wrong direction as it dangled from Kai's arm. I pictured my unconscious body being flung down those stairs, tumbling over step after rocky step. I shivered, glancing up at Kai. It was the only explanation I had for the injuries that spanned my body. Someone had tossed me down the stairs like I was a ragdoll.

There were dark corners in Kai's grotto I couldn't see into. I had no idea who else was down there with us. Or *what* else. If there was one thing I'd learned in my short time in the UK, it was how strange things happened when the sun went down. The Unknown could be as powerful as Hindsight. Even more so, in a case like that.

Kai dropped my feet to the ground with a heavy *clomp*. I wasn't ready for him to release half my body so I landed awkwardly. It hurt. He pushed me backward onto a large armchair and I glared up at him.

"Maybe you'll use your pretty head and stay put this time."

I nodded. He walked toward the bar we'd passed. Darkened figures frolicked in the heated pools around me.

I inventoried my situation quickly. My body was poisoned and injured to the point I couldn't run away. Someone had thrown me down a deadly set of stairs, I assumed, with no other rational excuse for my condition. Kai could've been the one who tossed me into the cavern, but something about that didn't make sense. The trip down the stairs could have easily killed me. Kai might be mean to me and hurt me, but he'd made it clear he had a use for me somehow, which meant I would be kept alive. I still had not seen Brea, which was the only reason I got in Kai's car in the first place. Although I had been forced not to involve Peter, he was my one "ally" in the mix and had turned out to be one of the bad guys. I was pretty much screwed.

The events didn't bode well for me finding Brea, escaping, and saving the day.

But I still had tenacity. I rolled with things. This was easily the worst situation I'd been in so far, but I'd be damned if I was going to give up on finding Brea.

Weighing my choices for an ally was a quick process. Petra was out for two reasons, the first and biggest being she'd had it in for me since the first time we'd met. The other reason was that I was sure she was looking for the right time to get back at me. I couldn't blame her. If someone had busted my lip, I'd swing back at the first given opportunity.

My second choice was Peter, but the thought of him seared my heart like a bloody steak on a grill. He was a special breed. I would never understand how someone could be so tender but so quick to deceive. The day we rode the subway, kissing and holding each other while we traveled for miles beneath the city was one of the best of my life, and it hadn't meant a thing to him. He wouldn't get the chance to betray me again.

As much as I loathed the thought, I would need to rely on Kai. The idea gave me the creeps. There were many dark things I didn't know about him. I was certain he could pull off things that would undo me. The emotional battering I'd endured over the last couple of months had been excruciatingly painful, much worse than the pain in my body.

I couldn't remember how young I was when I made the connection that emotional pain could actually make my chest ache, deep inside. It was a familiar sensation that made me feel weak, victimized, in a way. Tears welled in my eyes and sweat beaded on my fevered skin as fire ignited around my heart. A small, waning bit of confusion tagged along every time I heated up that way, but given my circumstances, that time it made a little sense.

Life's events had created a monster in me long ago. The "fevers" were my monster raging. I'd been angry as long as I'd been alive. I must have been a complete trip to the nuns at the Home. They probably thought I was possessed by a demon. Maybe they were onto something. A hysterical laugh barked from my chest, echoing. A few "swimmers" glanced my way briefly.

The heat inside me became invigorating. I sat up on the chair, ignoring the hurt in my body, feeling oddly empowered at being able to shelve such pain. I knew myself better at that one moment than I ever had before, which wasn't saying a lot. Given my circumstances though, I'd take the perks when they came my way. When I'd heated up at other times in the past, I'd always felt a little frightened. Out of control. It was the Unknown. I greeted it with open arms for the first time ever.

I could work with it. Use it.

Vertigo tipped my balance slightly but I managed to stay upright. Kai must have been watching me because he was beside me a moment after I came off the chair.

All my efforts got me stuffed back down onto my bottom. "Why do you always have to put your damn hands on me?"

"Don't try to move. You won't get far in your condition, and it will serve to piss me off."

"We wouldn't want that," I shot back as he walked away. My head rested against the arm of the chair, relieving the throbbing at my temples. He could've been right about the part where I wouldn't get far.

Something clammy stuck to my face where it contacted the upholstery. My clothes were wet and I soaked the chaise with warm, dirt-and-blood streaked water. The comfy bedroom Kai had given me sounded pretty inviting. I'd start with a hot shower to clean out my wounds, then nurse my system back to runaway condition by snacking at the kitchenette.

Kai returned with two bottles of water and an apple. He dropped my backpack on the floor beside us and sat on the foot of a nearby chaise. I drank one of the bottles without coming up for air and ate a few bites of the fruit like a ravenous grasshopper, handing it back to him. I desperately needed to brush my teeth. Bits of dried blood streaked the uneaten meat of the apple.

"Where were you trying to go?"

"I was looking for Brea." It was odd how lying could come so easily. I wasn't going to tell him I planned to steal one of his cars before I went looking for her. I didn't bat an eye.

"In the courtyard by my coach house?" he said, watching me carefully. "You think I have your friend stashed in one of my automobiles?"

"Had to start somewhere." I opened the other bottle of water, grimacing against pain in my wrist. "Did you throw me down the stairs over there?"

"No. How long have you known Peter?" He gave an answer and expected one in return.

"I don't know Peter at all. How long was I out?" I tossed back. *Lie, lie, and lie.* If hell truly existed, I'd be a guest really soon at the rate I was going.

"Two days. You were looking for Brea, nothing else?"

"You left me down here, knocked out, for two freaking days?" No wonder I felt like crap. And Ezra probably thought Peter and I had run away, being gone for so long. Had Peter even realized I'd disappeared, for two damned days?

"Answer my question."

"What else would I have been looking for?" He was probing to see if I knew Peter was there, too. "I can't believe you left me sprawled in the water for days. I could have drowned— ow." Yelling made my head scream back at me. I slammed my eyes shut, caressing the temple that didn't have a goose egg on it. I might have been having a big epiphany about rage being my new friend, but I was still beat up.

"You were told to stay in your room." He gritted the words at me with a locked jaw. "If anything, you should have listened for your own protection. This," he waved a hand at my disheveled condition, "serves you right."

"You punished me by leaving me lying in the water back there?" I gestured toward the corner where I'd laid in the stream, inhaling water. I'd been unconscious, out of view of the people who recreated in the pools. "You bastard. I could have laid there and died."

"You're lucky I'm not the one who found you skulking in my courtyard. You'd be feeling entirely. . . ." He searched my bruised face. "Differently." He stood. "I'll warn you once more about angering me. This is all you get, so you'd better learn quickly." He offered a hand. "Let's get you back to your room."

We headed for the stairs. I insisted on walking myself, concentrating on putting one foot in front of the other, counting my steps.

I stopped, looking back at the water for a glimpse of the water lady who'd helped me.

"What is it?" He narrowed his eyes on me, watching me closely.

"Nothing." I turned to take the next stair.

"What were you looking for?" He grabbed my arm above the elbow.

"Ow!" I snarled, drawing my arm back quickly. "Stop grabbing me!" I took a breath to get past the pain that racked my elbow. "I saw something odd, no big deal."

"Well, then. Up you go." He said, prodding me on.

People constantly telling me what to do made me want to scream. I sent him an icy look and turned to go up the stairs. My movements were slow, bearing pain as I climbed.

"Don't act so put off, Tessa. You brought this all on yourself."

"Stop talking, Kai."

I was livid when he laughed.

CHAPTER 21

*T*here's no event in life that will deliver a paradigm shift faster than someone trying to kill you. I felt I'd aged a lot in the last couple of weeks. Fun teenage years playing volleyball by the lake and deciding what I wanted to be when I grow up, gone. Kaput. Replaced by days of thinking about keeping myself and my best friend safe and free, and having my heart broken for the first time, while juggling a new life between being a human and a gargoyle.

Who'd ever think a gargoyle could cry? Or breathe for the matter. At least it was without physical pain. My body healed when I transformed at dusk the night before and then I'd slept the entire next day, waking up a couple times for water and then going back to bed. When I woke again I'd changed and slept crooked on one wing, which was far worse than waking with a stiff neck. I lay in the huge, over-stuffed bed in my latest prison wishing I was back in Austin with Brea, chatting over Skype about boys and new clothes. I'd had enough of the UK. The email I received from Professor Douglas that day had turned from the biggest blessing in my life into the biggest curse.

And my best friend was involved, lost somewhere in the vast, confining unknown of an insane man's domain.

I remembered the day last summer when I felt my life was going to change. *Substantially.*

I laughed through my tears, causing bit of clear mucus to spray into the air from my snout. *Guess it's safe to say it was a change for the worse.* Crying was going to help nothing, but it made me feel better. I wiped my snout on a scaly forearm and rolled upright.

It was time for Plan B, which would hopefully go much smoother than Plan A. I was ready to escape my room to search for Brea, find her and fly her back to the bookstore. My tail twitched at my feet. I wasn't emotionally recovered from the outcome of Plan A yet. Someone had tried to kill me. That, or they wanted to hurt me really bad. Scenarios twisted through my mind. I could have broken my neck on those murderous stairs.

I rose from my bed, stretching my wings so far the span made the boney tips scrape along one wall, gouging into the plaster. A small, childish grin formed as I watched paint chips and dust fall to the plush carpet.

In the library, the tile floor was cold even through the thick skin of my clawed feet. Moonlight glittered outside. Dew-laden fog gave way to a crisp, clear night. I opened the window and inhaled fresh air, closing my eyes, just breathing, trying to steel myself for my first, solo flight. Moonglow reflected through the trees, iridescent and silver. I leaned out, feeling the sill against my chest plate. The second my snout crossed the plane into the night air, electricity blasted my face like a hammer.

I coughed blood into the air. The cold tile pressed up on my side, as if the floor had risen up to meet me. The room went red around me and faded.

* * *

"You just don't learn do you?" Petra stood over me, pleased as punch. She hunched forward, claws resting on her thighs, wings twitching behind her. She smiled, bearing sharp teeth within a perfect set of gargoyle dimples. "Seriously, you are thick."

"Go away," I managed to whisper. Trying to speak made my eyes hurt.

"You don't mean that." Petra's large head cocked to the side, like a dog listening to someone speak.

"Trust me, I wouldn't steer you wrong here. I really want you to leave me alone." I sat up bracing on my knees and the bottom of my wings, then got to my feet. My head throbbed with my pulse. "Were you outside the window?" I turned on Petra, looking to deliver a payback. She wore a simple, cream colored dressing gown and looked ridiculous, not that I was ready to walk a runway in my cami and skirt. I pulled at the top, self-consciously.

"No, genius. The windows up here are warded against a pass-through from either direction."

"Warded?"

"He put a spell on them." She said it like I should know what she meant. "You got hit in the window."

"A spell." I was supposed to believe I'd been smacked in the face by a spell that guarded the library windows.

Petra nodded.

"Like a witch's spell?"

"Yes, Thickness. Takes you a moment to digest certain things, doesn't it?" She crossed her arms over her scaly chest, staring at me.

There was a special, added insult to being poked at by someone who spoke with a British accent. "Was that slime over the hallway door also a *ward?*" I used two clawed fingers on each hand to make air quotes. Doing such a human gesture with gargoyle talons had extra sarcastic zip. I'd made it through the slime and only threw up a couple times. Yay, me. But I'd only tried getting out the window once. Maybe it only worked on a second attempt.

"Yes. And that one was meant to be a warning. You keep surprising Kai."

"You don't like that, do you? Kai thinking about me?" I taunted.

"Look, you and I agree on one thing, and that's the fact that we both want you gone," she shot back. She hissed, nostrils flared. "And don't get ahead of yourself, Tessa. You've far from figured out what's bad and what's good out here. Things are soon to be really messy, and you need to get your fragile, little human friend out of here."

"So, what? Are you going to clue me in?" There was no way I was going to let her get me all riled up at that point. I touched the end of my snout to see if I was still bleeding. Pain shot from my nose into my throat. I hissed against the sting.

"So, I was on my way to your room when I heard you get hit. I can show you how to get out of here."

"I'm not leaving here without Brea," I retorted.

"I know where she is."

"There has to be a catch to this." I didn't trust Petra any farther than I could toss her. Overhand, like a football.

"The catch would be that you leave here tonight, with your friend, and you never come back." She put her claws on her hips. "You go back to London and stay put."

That sounded pretty good. I had to get to Brea and get her back home to her family before something terrible happened to her. I hesitated, but only for a second. There was a chance I'd never see Peter again. The thought of how he'd betrayed me stung. He'd known Kai had Brea. He'd driven us to Scotland. I'd heard him laughing with Kai in the courtyard.

"Deal." She could have her twisted little "happily-ever-after. Maybe her scheme would really work out. And I was fresh out of plans of my own.

"Let's go then."

* * *

PETRA WOULD TELL me to wait in one spot, normally tucked against a wall or in a corner, walk a little bit ahead and then motion for me to join her. It was impressive, considering she found places to conceal my large, gargoyle form. We made our way so slowly I twitched with impatience, but managed to contain my anxiety by thinking about finally getting to see Brea.

To my surprise, we headed back down to Kai's mineral springs cavern. My foot hit the first step going down like a magnet pushing through the field of a repelling, opposite pole. My senses screamed that I shouldn't go any farther. It was unexplainable and seemed unwarranted, except that I'd been injured down there. I ignored the foreboding although it was so bad I realized I'd been holding my breath. Continuing would be a risk. Petra could turn on me any time, but my imperative was to get Brea out of the mess I'd put her in and get out of Scotland.

The air smelled rich with sulfur and like the dark dirt under the nun's rosebushes in Austin. As we descended, Petra become human. The simple, frock style dress hung long around her skinny frame. I looked at my human hands, and back up the stairs to the starry, moonlit sky. Petra watched me.

"What's going on?" I wasn't complaining, but it was the first night in months I looked like myself.

"It's the water. Something in the minerals coming up from the aquifer mute the transformation," she said, gesturing back outside. "Don't get excited. Just as soon as you go back up those stairs, you'll change back to your true form."

I gaped. "Hello," I said, waving my hands in front of her face. "This *is* my true form."

"No." She said. "It's really not."

I didn't have what it took to argue that. I was a believer in the changes controlling me. But it was interesting to know there was a mineral able to mute the effects of my transformation.

"Do you know exactly what does the trick down here?"

"It's a mixture of elements. I'm not certain which." She continued into the cavern. "Stay here," she whispered.

I waited against the wall, peering in at the activities inside.

Humans swam in the pools. *Lots* of them. They gathered in corners and on furniture, totally at ease basking in warm humidity.

I considered the word "humans" and it sounded like some alien being, some foreign species. I was nothing if not completely, utterly conflicted.

Making out a familiar face in the foggy, broken light of the cavern was tricky. I didn't know where Petra had gone. Steam gushed in places. Water bubbled and flowed.

In one place, it rose a little higher out of the current, seeming to grow, or pile up. In seconds it was about six feet above the surface, churning in the air, forming human limbs. I blinked, remembering the woman who'd urged me to take a breath. I hoped it was her.

The form stepped forth, the outline of a human body glistening in the low light. Muscular and tall, and obviously, *not* female, it began walking in my direction, leaving wet footprints behind.

I searched faces but all others were oblivious.

It looked at me with liquid pupils, fixed and studious.

Without warning the watery man broke into a run, melting into a flow at another pool in the stream, right before it got to me. My legs trembled, but I stood my ground. Besides, I had no evidence it was bent on harm. More otherworldly entities lived in the cavern. I hoped whatever it was would be as kind as the woman who'd compelled me to fight for breath that day. There were no signs of him in the stream. He'd dissolved like sugar in a boiling pot.

About fifty people were visible and none let on that they'd seen what I had. They could all be gargoyles and I'd never know the difference. Music thrummed and my nervous trembling rocked me in place to the dark rhythm. Everyone seemed so happy, and I yearned to be a part of their fun. They swam and laughed, disappearing in groups and did things I was too shy to keep watching.

A small geyser spewed in the stream closest to me. I jumped. The water-man rose from the current again, looking at me with determination shining in his ethereal eyes. It was hard to tell, but I think he smiled at me before settling back into the water.

I tucked myself back inside the corner. I couldn't ask about what I'd seen without sounding like I'd lost the last remaining marbles knocking together in my head. I could just see myself asking Petra and enduring more of her condescending commentary and lilting laugh that accompanied. There was no way I'd put myself through that again, but I sort of wished she would show up because it was hard to stand still with everything happening around me. I made myself small in the darkness, but curiosity ruled me sometimes and I wasn't willing to miss much.

The lighting was spectacular, blending color with strobe. Grey fog clouded low on the dance floor, where college-aged humans gyrated slowly. The place held just enough people to make it interesting. They hung out casually, wearing swimsuits and drinking at the bar, partying together like they were at a beach club somewhere.

Possibly, some were human, not gargoyles. I was jealous. They were beautiful and small. Never changing like I did when I forfeited my true form at night. Seeing them touching each other as they danced was wonderful, knowing how smooth skin felt in their hands, devoid of hardened scales and sinewy, bulging muscle. They moved slowly, with determined motions, eyes fixated on each other. I didn't hear one of them make a sound over the heavy beat of the music.

Peter didn't appear to be down there but I kept looking, craning my neck to search the part of the room I hadn't scanned. Some humans didn't need the dance floor, holding and caressing each other wherever they deemed a good place. I loved dancing, for the brief time I'd been able to at the bookstore. Peter's skin had been smooth, the muscle bunching under my touch. I didn't want to admit to myself I missed him so much it hurt, so I didn't.

Darkness prevented making out details and I didn't realize I'd stepped out of my corner to watch until one of the guys broke away from a group near me, wandering close. His eyes were narrowed to slits. I panicked a little. One hand reached for me and I dodged his sluggish motions, sliding back to the corner. He followed like a drunk rabbit after a dandling carrot.

He was a beautiful human, shirtless and wearing a pair of board shorts. He closed the distance between us and reached for my waist with both hands. I began to wonder if I should shove him back into the room and act like nothing big had happened. He leaned in, hands moving slowly over the bare skin of my arms. I peeled his grip away.

"Please, just go back over there," I whispered.

He ignored me, close enough that I could smell a harsh, chemical aroma on his skin and breath. I pushed at him.

"Go away!" I whisper-shouted.

Petra appeared behind him. She yanked him backward. The guy staggered a little, then wandered onto the dance floor like nothing happened.

"What is wrong with these people?" I asked.

"Not a thing if you ask one of them. They all think they've found utopia. Kai has a supply of a tincture at the bar to keep them . . . fun."

A group shucked clothing beside one of the baths and eased into the water, oblivious of being watched, or just plain not caring.

"Do they know what we are?"

"They did at one time. Now, they don't give a damn." She continued to watch the antics on the dance floor.

"Have you ever seen anything like . . . odd swimming around

in the water?" I'd tried to make it sound casual but my words sounded crazy, like I imagined.

She shook her head slowly, watching me.

"Well?" I asked.

"No," she said. Petra looked toward the stream.

I was unconvinced. "Did you see him?" I asked, just above a whisper. Maybe I wasn't losing it.

"Did you?" Petra looked straight into my face.

"I don't know if we're talking about the same thing. I saw a man . . . like a water-being or something."

Petra shook her head, frowning. "It really amazes me how *you* see things most others can't. And you get past wards that most are repelled by so easily." She squinted at me with distaste. "He's a Tyren," she said, turning to face the water. "They live down here in the mineral springs." She traced the stream with her eyes, watching it meander around the cavern through rock, cascading into pool after pool. "The Tyrens keep a close watch on Kai. Never once have I seen him get in these baths. And you might think to be careful of them, as well."

"Why do they watch Kai?"

"They've been here for centuries." She sighed, looking the mouth of the stream.

It was possible I'd been a little wrong about Petra, after all. I'd never seen her react with genuine emotion before then, aside from being all pissy.

"Are you okay, Petra?" We'd got off on the wrong foot, but I didn't hate her. Maybe I was a sap, but she looked like she could use someone to talk to.

She flipped an emotional toggle. "Just get your friend and never come back here."

Welcome back, sweetness. That was precisely why I was a loner. I misjudged situations and people like a pro. We were quiet for a time, letting the new development gel. Some people didn't want anyone close to them. Petra and I had that in common.

"Your friend is over that way." She pointed toward a far wall, at an illuminated, steaming pool.

"Brea is one of these . . . freaking zombies?" More than one body was in that pool. I stepped out of the corner.

"Of course, she is." Petra grabbed my arm but I shook her off. "Be calm, or this will never work," she whispered from behind me.

That was good advice, and I took it. I walked slowly along the streams and over stone bridges, dodging approaching "zombies" and entered the large pool Petra indicated held my best friend. I wore my "go-to" skirt and camisole, which would have to do. I didn't have a swimsuit and there was no way I was getting in naked, like some of the others.

The water was warm and slick with soft minerals. I could see why everyone enjoyed the baths so much.

I squinted into the steam. There was more than one female human in the water. I waded my way along the edge of the chest deep mineral pool, ignoring the ones I knew couldn't be Brea. The possibility I nudged Tyrens out of the way as I walked was just plain creepy. I looked down to see if I could spot any.

My forehead bopped into the shoulder of a large man right in front of me.

He turned, and I froze.

Peter.

I looked away, feeling a large sting of pain punch my heart. I'd been so naïve about him.

He stared at me while I backpedaled mentally, trying to think of what to say. He opened his mouth to speak, but changed his mind, looking awkward and a little pained.

I did my best to ignore the pitiful way he searched for words. I'd busted him carousing in Kai's, naked-chick-a-plenty hot springs. No surprise after what I'd learned about him, but it still stung. I considered telling him how I felt, but all that came to mind was nicely-chosen parade of mean names, which wouldn't have been a quick process. I wouldn't waste my time.

A meandering, electric pink bikini top floated close on the surface of the pool, churning with the flow as water pushed against rather large, triangular cups. Peter and I watched as it hung up against his abdomen. I snorted, shaking my head. He looked down at the misplaced garment, brushing it away as if it was a used Kleenex. The strings twisted through the current as the top drifted away.

My shoulder smacked against his elbow as I pushed by. He never said a word, and that was fine by me.

Brea leaned on a smooth boulder just ahead. I was thrilled she wore a swimsuit. She stared at the grated window in the ceiling.

I continued toward her. When I was almost there and about to speak, she dipped into the water and came back up, clearing her long hair from her face.

"Get away from me." To my astonishment she moved to the other side of the huge rock and continued to stare up at the pre-dawn sky. She didn't even look at me.

She was waiting for the sun to come up. My heart leapt a little when I realized she wasn't under the same trance as the rest of the people in the baths.

"Brea! It's me," I whispered, following her to the other side of her hideout. She didn't hear me, but I had to be quiet so I didn't raise suspicion.

She turned toward the side of the long bath. Before I could get closer, she moved across the pool and stepped out.

I followed her from a distance.

Brea was a smart cookie. She wandered from pod to pod of zombified people, making her way toward the stairwell.

I dropped back and let her make headway, ready to shoot for the steps the moment she made it that far. A perfect, although temporary, plan formed. We'd make it out of the cavern, I'd follow and not approach her until the sun came up.

She cleared the last group of people and turned toward the

exit. The plan was working. I watched, drifting in the direction of the stairs.

One of the men saw her take the first step and began climbing the steps behind her. They were soon out of sight. Our plan had gone to hell quickly.

The hardest thing I'd done up to that point was be cool and act like my best friend wasn't being stalked in a stairwell. I needed the sun. I abandoned the attempt at being inconspicuous and bolted for the exit. The stairwell was empty.

Garging Out in that stairwell and knowing I was about to reveal my new form to my best friend made it the longest climb of my life. I clamored up the passage as quickly as possible with my large gargoyle feet missing some of the tiny little stairs and my wings scraping the walls. Right when I emerged sunshine flashed across the horizon. My eyes slammed shut. I shielded my face with a clawed hand as my form shrunk, scales mutating to faint, transparent skin over stringy tendons and muscle. I ran the path and found Brea, doing her best against her attacker. He was a gargoyle, skinless in the sun, holding her by a forearm.

She shrieked and beat against his chest with her free fist. I hated the way she looked exhausted, with terror keeping her awake and fighting. Water dripped and sprayed off them in the struggle. The black swim top she wore was coming loose. I was furious and couldn't get there quickly enough although my legs were a blur below me.

The man was a monstrosity of bared muscle and bone. Grey, tight lips peeled from his teeth as he grinned down at her trying to get free. He made a grab for her flailing hand, unsuspecting when I hit him.

I don't remember tearing his throat. Grey blood coated my hands. My fingers curled in replica of the taloned claws I wore each night. I took him to the ground quickly. He thrashed beneath my knee and I buried it deeper in his sternum. Gasping sounds gurgled from his mouth and nose as blood pulsed from a gaping hole in his neck, running black onto the grass in a thick pool. He stared up at me, fear prevailing briefly before pre-death glaze covered his eyes. I snarled, feeling my lips quivering against my bared teeth.

Then he stopped. Everything. Fighting. Spasming. Breathing.

An animalistic growl grated from my chest as I planted a heel to his ribs, feeling bone give like a bag of watered-down sand.

I stood panting with boiling blood coursing through my chest, feeling my face pulled into a tight, squinting stare. Something inside me raged, primal and deadly. Alive. Ragged breath was the only sound in my mind. I fought for clarity, control. The fabric of my skirt hung slick with blood that ran onto my skinless, grey legs. I peeled my cami loose from my torso where it stuck in splatter. I was a ghoul covered in gore.

My body trembled in the morning sunshine.

What have I done?

"Tessa?"

Brea trembled so badly I didn't know how she stayed on her feet. Her eyes were huge with shock, stomach withdrawn from lack of food.

"Brea! Yes! It's me," I said, around a sob, hoping the familiarity of my voice would count for something with her. I was careful not to approach her.

She shook her head, her hair clumpy and wet, steaming in the chill. She stepped back, faltering a little.

I tried to catch her as she fainted, going limp on the dewy, blood-soaked grass. I wiped my eyes and cheeks with fingers that showed thin bones. Of course she'd been scared. Just because the sun was shining didn't mean a thing.

I was still a monster.

CHAPTER 22

*B*rea was a little taller than me and, although she was slender, as I struggled to get her upstairs to my room I could tell she outweighed me. Carrying an unconscious person was hard, like carrying a huge sack of water and marbles. I moved fast, but by the time I topped the stairs, my arms and legs shook so badly I thought I might drop her. I thanked all that was good we encountered no other souls. When we got to the upper library by my room, I set her on the tile and drug her across the floor and onto the carpet in my room. If she had rug burns on her butt, she could be pissy with me later.

I pulled back the sheets and draped my bed with towels. Exhaustion sapped my strength and I almost dropped her onto the mattress. Arranging her limp form so she looked comfortable was completely awkward. I loved her, but I'd never handled another person that way. I watched her sleep, praying to whatever powers might be listening that she wouldn't remember anything she'd witnessed. Streaks of crimson dappled her skin in places since the guy's drying blood wasn't in the sun anymore, where it was grey before. I wet a washcloth in the bathroom and wiped it off her skin, but she would have to wash it out of her hair and swim suit when she woke up.

I covered her up and went for a shower.

Blood mixed with water at my feet, swirling into the shower drain while I scrubbed my shaking hands and arms. The bathroom smelled like rusted metal. I had a *lot* of the guy's blood on me. It poured from my hair and arms like I'd wallowed in it. Jagged bits of my humanity twisted down the drain, following the last of the man I'd murdered. I wiped my hands together hard, rinsed away pink puffs of lathered shampoo from my hair, over and over.

Out damn'd spot!

I'd have spent a lot longer in the shower trying to make myself feel clean if I wasn't so worried Brea would wake up and try to leave my room. I didn't cry. After I figured out how to get us to safety I would allow myself to come apart. I shampooed my hair one more time for good measure and emerged from the bathroom wrapped in a towel.

Brea hadn't moved, still wrapped up in bed like I'd left her. I'd half expected her to be gone, swiped again by Kai. He probably had one of his stoolies watching and already knew I had her. I'd been granted the blessing of keeping her with me and I wasn't about to look a gift horse in the mouth.

Unless I'd just disposed of that particular stoolie outside on the grass.

I grabbed my hairbrush and pulled through my hair on the way to my backpack to retrieve clean clothes, majorly looking forward to a fresh, clean pair of underwear.

"Aw, Tessa," Peter said from across the room.

I dropped my brush, losing my towel. Squatting to the floor quickly, I caught the two ends and wrapped them tight around my breasts, but I'd given him a good eyeful of flesh. I bunched the towel in one hand so I could get my brush.

"What are *you* doing here? Try knocking much?" I hissed.

Peter watched me, gaze caught on a place my towel covered again. He'd dressed in jeans and a shirt and his hair was still damp. His lips parted a little.

I tightened the grip on my towel.

His eyes narrowed, focusing on my fist bunched in the terrycloth at my chest, like a starved hunter measuring out prey. Meat and potatoes. That was me.

I threw my brush at his chest. "Stop staring!" I whisper-shouted, through gritted teeth.

He caught my brush before it struck, regaining his cool and stepping close. "I did knock, you never answered. Put something . . . ," he paused, eyeing my towel and soaked, ratted hair, "*bigger* on so we can talk."

"It's funny you chose to wear anything at all since you've already shown every girl in the place *all* your junk."

He ignored my observation. "I'll be just out in the library," he said, in a low voice.

I wondered if it was hard for him to walk away from me taunting him.

Peter silently closed the door behind him, the tension between us trailing on his heels.

Finally, I was able to breath.

Peter had come inside my room for a good reason, since he hadn't waited for me to answer the door, and that wasn't necessarily a good thing. I was relieved to see him even after all he'd done. The vice smashing my chest didn't feel so tight. I didn't feel as alone in the deadly situation I'd created for myself. At the same time, his betrayal still hurt.

Peter might have been another of Kai's lackeys. He didn't need to ask for directions when he drove us to Kelty. That really bothered me. He didn't make a wrong turn, driving as if he knew exactly how to get to Kai's ruined-castle-turned-mansion. I didn't trust him. But I needed him worse at that moment than I had at any other time before. I was heartsick. Besides that, I'd done something horrible, so was I any better of a person?

I dressed quickly, but wasn't looking forward to talking about the events of my morning. He was technically one of the bad guys. Disclosing information could be like ratting myself out to Kai. I had to keep myself in check with Peter no matter how much I wanted him on my side, which seemed to make me the underdog. My side consisted only of me, really, and Brea, but she was new to the game, human, and still in shock. I couldn't blame her there. She'd witnessed her best friend Garg Out into some lunatic monster and kill someone, on top of the fact that she'd been kidnapped and then thrown into a changed, mad world where she'd been attacked. She'd been hurt, badly, in ways that went far beyond physical pain because of my carelessness. That had to change.

Peter stood at the window outside the bedroom, bright sunlight making his skin and hair glow silver and grey-streaked ebony. Shadows played where the light bounced along the fabric of his untucked shirt, in time with his breathing.

Saying nothing, I walked across the room and got a bottle of water from the mini fridge. "I got rid of it," he told the room behind him.

"Of what?" He was getting zero information.

"The body."

Exuding no discomfort with the topic, I plopped into an over-stuffed chair in the shaded part of the room. I opened my water and sipped. "How long have you known your friend, Kai?"

"He's not my friend."

"Could've fooled me."

"Really, Tessa, you've murdered someone in the yard outside and you want to hash out a make-believe friendship between Kai and me?"

"Horse shit." If he'd seen what I'd done, he knew I had to do it. "I am *not* a murderer."

185

"Could've fooled me," he retorted.

"Why are you here, Peter?" I refused to let him bait me.

"I'm asking the questions."

I shrugged. "I'm sure I'll figure it out." Something deep inside me hoped there was a reasonable explanation for what he was doing at Kai's manor. The way he laughed with Kai convinced me they were old friends. And seeing him down in Kai's underground playhouse, swimming around with other girls—I didn't want to think about that again. Ever.

"Fine. I'm not discussing this with you, if you're not talking, either." I drank my water, swinging one bare foot from the chair.

"You don't want to talk about what I saw?" His tone said I was being ridiculous.

My look said I couldn't trust him.

He didn't have to say "Touché," it was clear enough on his face.

I remained silent, intent on hearing what he had to say rather than reveal something and betray myself. There was no guarantee he'd seen any-darned-thing at all.

"Tessa, you moved faster than I've ever seen anyone run in my life. You beat me to your friend and ripped that bastard's throat out while you jerked him away from wrestling with her." He shook his head, eyes narrowing on me. "You put a knee through his heart, and then you kicked him for fair measure!"

"Is that what this is about? I beat you to the punch and stole your glory?" That may have been generous. I didn't feel all that glorified.

"Stop dodging." A muscle worked in his jaw.

He had my attention. Completely. Hearing him recant the events brought the vision clear in my mind. What I couldn't remember before replayed in Blue-Ray while I watched myself snuff another soul. And he'd seen me do it. I sat forward on the chair, planting my elbows on my knees, covering my face with both hands, tough façade dissolving.

"Something is wrong with me, Peter. I'm different now." My

voice carried the qualities of a lost child. "I'm not just a gargoyle. I'm . . . evil in here somewhere."

"You're not evil, Tessa," he said.

His voice caressed me just enough to break me apart. I shook my head, keeping my hands firmly over my face.

"I'm a monster and you know it. You saw. I felt. . . ."

"What?"

I took in a shaky breath. "Relief. Like I'd been let out of a box." I cried softly into my hands. "It was amazing." I was shattering, out of control. "I'm so scared of this."

Peter pulled me from the chair. I buried my face in his shirt, wrapping my fingers in his long hair. His arms circled me tight.

"You did what was necessary," he whispered. "I was harsh before." It was as close to an apology as I'd get.

I clung to him, taking the comfort he offered before he took it away again.

"Well, this is cozy," Petra said, from the entryway.

Peter went rigid, stepping away. Cold air replaced him.

I dropped back into the chair, sliding back and glaring at Petra. "Please, come in." I wiped my eyes and tried to erase all evidence of emotion.

"Bungled things a bit, didn't you?" She glared back.

Great. Maybe Petra witnessed what I did to that guy, too. Might as well screw up the best I can and get it over with.

"You're still here, I mean," she continued.

Maybe not.

"Still here?" Peter asked, looking at Petra.

I laughed a little. "Peter, Petra," I said, introducing them with a wave of my water bottle.

"We know each other," Petra said.

I shot an accusing look at Peter. "You get around."

He rolled his eyes. "She's my sister."

"He's my brother," Petra said, at the same time.

I scowled at Peter. He had far too many secrets.

In the same room and not Garged Out, I could see a slight resemblance. It made sense the way they'd stared at each other the night Petra had trashed *Librorum Taberna*. I'd mistaken her confusion at seeing her brother as a different kind of fascination with him.

"If you're his sister, why'd you throw a fit at the bookstore?"

"I didn't know Peter would be there. I followed Kai one day after one of your chatty, little dates." Her gaze carried ice.

"Dates?" Peter asked. "With Kai?" He snorted. "You get around."

Okay, so I had that coming. I changed the subject, looking back to Petra.

"You didn't know Peter would be at the store, and now here you both are," I pointed out.

"You've really started something." Petra stepped closer. I was certain she did it so she could look down her nose at me. "I suppose I should be grateful. Kai told me Peter was dead, years ago."

"Where is Kai, anyway?" I asked.

"In his study," answered Petra. "I told him I saw you take Brea from the baths last night. Told him I followed you and that you had her up here so I came to check up on you."

I'd found the stoolie. "That way you stay out of trouble. Good thing I'm not going to tell on you for trying to get me to disappear," I said, smiling at her. "You trashed the bookstore because you were paranoid about what Kai was up to, not because you believed I was the one that changed you into a gargoyle."

She sent me a scathing look. I was right. She'd also acted out the whole scene at the bookstore the night I found her with Ezra, just to see what Kai was up to.

"Petra and I hadn't seen each other for over a century until that night," Peter added.

"Well, now that we're all caught up," Petra said. She looked at me with mock pity. "Poor dear, so slow at times." She tsked. "It was cute, the way you were protective of Peter. You're dreaming if you think you're anywhere near the caliber of girl my brother deserves."

That stung. Inwardly, I wasn't much in comparison to him. She was right about me. I was a mere throwaway in American society, saved only by governmental laws, not by the love of a single soul. Orphaned and owning nothing but a beat-up collection of literature. I had nothing to offer Peter. I peered down at the cracked old polish on my toenails. I used to rely on the fact that I was, at least, pretty. That seemed to be fading away to match the way I was nothing on the inside.

"Thought you'd see it my way. You're way out of your element. You're clueless here." She smiled viciously down at me.

That was the second time since I met Petra that she tried to make me feel like dirt. I'd had enough of her picking me apart. Heat grew in my chest, my new indicator of becoming volatile.

"You ringing the bell for round two?" I put my water on a side table and stood.

"Hold on, you two. That's going to help nothing." Peter stepped close to intercept my advance.

"And you, don't think for a second this excuses the things I've seen you do lately." I pushed him away. They could both screw off. I turned toward my room.

"Tess? What's going on?"

All three of us looked at Brea, standing in the bedroom doorway wrapped up in a blanket.

Petra snorted. "Now, it's a party."

I've never been more thankful for the shadows around me, allowing me to appear human. Brea and I ran at each other. We hugged for a long time. We cried, saying over and over how much we loved one another, not caring who watched us.

She was traumatized and exhausted, but she was unscathed, no bruises or bumps, aside from a handprint on her arm from being attacked hours ago.

Peter caught my attention, pulling Petra with him toward the door. "We'll go make an appearance with Kai."

That made sense. I didn't want Kai to get curious and needed a distraction so we could disappear.

We went back to my room, for lack of a better place to pull it together. It seemed easy for Brea to talk to me and hug me like the sister she claimed, but it was sort of dark in the room. Sunshine didn't betray me the way it could. My monster was hidden.

I had one, nearly full day to tell a darned convincing story about why I was going to get big, winged, and scaly when the sun went down. I fidgeted.

"You're one of them, aren't you?" Brea looked at me from her perch on the bed. I leaned against the wall on the floor, far from the window.

"Yes." I dropped my gaze to the floor. Not because I was ashamed, but because I didn't want her to be frightened of me.

Oh, Tess." She held her breath, a habit she had when she tried not to cry. I'd seen her do it half a dozen times at the sappy, chick flicks we watched, and one time when Jesse Perkins announced they should see other people.

"I'm still me . . . still the same girl inside." I hoped.

"No, you're not." She shook her head. Sky blue eyes brimmed with tears, breaking me down further.

"Sure I am. I'm still Tessa Conley. Book nerd and lover of all things purple, pink and food." I laughed unconvincingly, then sobbed a little.

"I know the situation, I mean, I know he was attacking me and God only knows what would've happened if you had not come at that moment." She trembled as she spoke. "You moved in a blur, like, I had trouble focusing on you. You looked like you were flying up out of the stairway . . .with wings, and long arms with claws. Then you shrunk some when you ran and the wings like, went away." She made her hands claw like. "It happened in a second, then he was dying." She wiped at her eyes. "I've never seen someone die before."

It wasn't the right time to tell her I had a tail, too. "Promise me something?" I rose to sit beside her on the bed. "No matter what, please remember and know it's me." I put a hand to my chest. "It always will be." My chin quivered and my voice shook. She was the most important person in my life. I needed her to continue to love me, whatever it took, because I loved her more than my heart could hold. Without her, I truly was nothing.

"I promise," she said.

"Thank you." I relaxed some. We lay back on the bed, staring up at the ceiling while tears trickled from the corners of our eyes to our ears. The silence, except for an occasional sniffle, was the best of comfortable silences. I'd kept my best friend.

"How long have you been in the UK?" I asked, after a few moments passed.

"My flight landed six days ago."

"You flew to London?" I rolled onto an elbow.

"I was worried about you." She started to cry again. "Looks like I had good reason to be. I was taken into London like I asked the cab driver. But then that guy, Kai?"

I nodded.

"He got in the car and we drove to that alley where I saw you in the window. Then he brought me here and put me in a room. I was there for one day then taken down to that hot springs place."

"That reminds me. How did you keep away from all the other people in there? The zombies, I mean? You're the only human that talked to me."

When I said "human" Brea looked at me, eyes wide.

"I mean, non-gargoyle type," I corrected.

"I don't know. I would start to feel kind of funny, like dizzy, shaky and tired all at the same time. But I was so scared. I would dip my head in the water to clear my senses, you know? And it kept working. I was starting to prune so bad my fingers hurt." She laughed, like music. "I was just trying to make it to another morning."

Memories of the last few days moved across her face like a projection screen. "Oh my God, Tessa what are we going to do?" She put her hands over her face. "This is terrible. How will we get back home with you like . . . *that?*"

I shook my head, ignoring her unintentional jab. "We'll figure it out. You're a genius, Brea. I watched your escape from the grotto. I was almost at the staircase when that Garged Out guy hopped up there with you."

"That thing hissed at me, and laughed. I managed to kick its claws off of me and that's how I made it out of the stairwell."

In my haste, I hadn't stopped to think he'd Garged Out on the stairs, right in front of her.

"If he would have got a good grip on me," she continued, "I can only imagine what would have happened." She started to cry harder. "And you're one of them."

"I'm okay, really . . . it will be okay. We're going to get out of here. We'll rest and I'll come up with a good way to escape at first light. We'll get back to London. I just need to think a little bit. Come up with a good plan, you know?" I did my best to sound upbeat and sure of myself.

That was a one-eighty from my turmoil. I was scared for my friend, and clueless about what to do. I didn't really know who to trust of the players involved. I started hashing out a mental list while I held onto Brea.

Kai—no, no trust for Kai. Enemy.

Peter—uncertain, limited trust but growing hope.

Petra—really uncertain, extremely limited trust with a strong dislike.

Bree—total trust. Good guy, like me. Fragile in this world.

Tessa—trusted, for the most part. Sort of a loose cannon at times.

The one that bothered me the most was Peter. Not long ago I trusted him. I wanted that back.

A knock sounded and Peter cracked the door. "Tessa?"

Speak of the devil. "Yeah, Peter."

He had a baby blue duffel bag, which he handed to Brea.

"Thank you." She took the bag gratefully. "I could use a shower. Lord only knows what was floating in that water down there."

"I'll bet if we asked Peter, he could tell us." Saccharine dripped from my words.

Brea looked from me to Peter, who sent me a crusty look. She shook her head. "You two should talk." Sliding back, she held the blanket clasped at her throat and scooted off the far side of the bed, heading toward the bathroom. "I think a long shower and some clean clothes are going to go a long way." The door clicked shut followed by the sound of water running in the shower.

"I was watching out for her," Peter said, defensively.

I laughed. "That's a likely story. You looked like the proverbial cat choking on the canary. You don't have to tell me about it because I could give a shit." I went to walk around him, looking forward to getting out of the corner I was in.

Peter snatched me by an arm, crushing me against his chest in an embrace that was hardly tender. Hot breath warmed my cheek. I'd pushed him, and regretted seeing the outcome.

"Let's get some clarity, yes?" A hand cradled my chin, amazingly gentle for the amount of pissed off energy he was throwing off.

"I. Touched. No one." He stared at me. Anger flashed. "But I think you know that." His hand left my face, tenderness gone. "And I am doing my best to keep in Kai's good graces to ensure I have at least limited liberty to walk the grounds. I had to drive your uppity little ass up here or he'd kill my sister." He shook his head, stepping away. "Let me apologize on behalf of the whole bloody universe for the fact that your happy little nail-polishing, pink-high-heel-wearing life has been tossed, Miss Conley."

"Is that really how you see me? Screw you," I said, without

allowing him to answer. Shame crept in, but I batted it back. At least he hadn't called me a "wannabe" again.

"You're not the only one with something at stake." His voice was cold, echoing back at me.

His frustration was tamped down by patience. The early-twenties, physical appearance was in stark contrast to the time-less, pained look evident in his eyes, barely kept in check by a flash of fury. They stood out, gaze haunted, bankrupt of any care-free aspects of life. It was so easy to forget his true age when he looked so close to mine. I don't know how I'd missed it before. So much had changed. Our time together wandering the under-ground tracks of London was no longer about me telling him good-bye that day. It was tortured for him, too. He'd known the whole time we were both being controlled by Kai, but said noth-ing, letting me think it was all about me. He was right. I was self-centered.

"Kai doesn't know we're together right now. It took some convincing, but Petra agreed to cover for me."

"That's big of her." I shook my head and looked away. "I don't want to know the things you've felt it necessary to do here."

"You're right about that."

I wasn't asking. I'd been through plenty and he could have been, too.

The events since I heard him laughing with Kai played through my mind in a series of sick vignettes. I'd waded through goo to try to get out and find Brea, I'd nearly been killed and then drowned, I'd been bashed in the face and knocked out by a ward. I had the pleasure of seeing Peter in a pool with saucer-eyed human girls, and that had been horrible, let alone getting my ass kicked by some guy with some poison on a towel, and I was again subject to more of Kai's charming demeanor. And then there was the fact that I'd murdered someone. How could I forget that part? I was a stone-cold blooded killer. I'd torn him apart and crushed his chest. I'd brutalized him. My chest locked up. Who—what the hell had I become?

"I killed . . . that man!" I bounced up and down a little, frantic, pushing away from Peter. Hyperventilation threatened. My chest exploded with heat.

I'm losing it.

"Take a breath." The familiar, calm quality I'd taken for granted was back in his voice. He crossed his arms over his chest, leaning a shoulder against the wall. "I was impressed."

"I wasn't." I sucked in a cold breath. "I didn't know what I was doing." Muscle memory pulled my fingers into claws. I stared at them, clenching fists to remove the feral quality, but knowing it was only a surface gesture. That animal nature was new part of me, embedded deep within, grappling with humanity and prevailing.

"You did the right thing. Calm down."

"I have to get Brea out of here, now. As soon as she's out of the shower, we run." I'd created worse odds for us both. Word would spread. They'd hunt me down. Hunt *us* down. Brea was frail. She was spunky and brilliant, but soft in a world of monsters. Human among beasts.

"Run where, Tessa?" Peter's stern words charged my panic with a call for reason. "They'll find you before you make it out of Scotland. This must be handled delicately, with some thought. And when was the last time you got some rest? You look like hell."

I sat on the bed, rocking in place, trying to calm down and ignore the part where he said I looked terrible. He had to be right about that one. I was exhausted and half starved. My surroundings were unfamiliar and in my current state I might get us both captured, or worse. Drastic things happened when I acted on impulse.

The water cut off in the bathroom. We looked at each other. Peter stepped toward the door. I stood up straight, taking a deep breath, feeling blessed composure settle over me.

Brea emerged from the bathroom wearing sweats and an over-sized Cookie Monster t-shirt. She looked at me as her concern grew, and then at Peter, as if for an answer. The composure didn't make it to my face, apparently.

"I'm okay. We're sorting some stuff out," I offered, trying to be convincing. "I'm just really tired."

Peter was back to the former, sweet guy I'd known. He smiled his agreement. "It's been a long couple of days," he added.

"So what's the plan." Brea searched our faces, fear wrestling with exhaustion behind her own tough façade. A few hours' sleep after being up for days wasn't much and every moment she lacked was obvious. That's one of the reasons I loved Brea. If for nothing else, her incredible tenacity when we both knew the world was kicking my butt and we were ever-so-screwed in our current situation.

"You have to be tired."

She blinked. "I'm good."

"We'll both be even better with some sleep." Even if we couldn't, we needed to hash out a plan. Sad as I was about it, Peter being absent from the meeting was likely best.

"I'll leave you two to get some rest then," Peter said, reaching for the door handle. "We can talk later."

"Where's your hoodie?" He hadn't worn one the last two times I saw him.

"I told Kai we saw each other and that you will have nothing to do with me. So there's no need to keep covered up out here at The Grotto now. You're the only reason he had me hiding."

"And he buys that story?" Kai wasn't stupid. Sooner or later we'd be hearing from him. I sensed it would be no picnic getting free from that place and back to London.

"For now, it appears he hasn't a problem with it." Peter smiled, but it wasn't the same smile he'd worn before. Our eyes locked for a moment, mutually acknowledging that change.

"Get some rest." He left without waiting for me to respond.

"Is everything okay with you two?" she asked.

"Yeah. You were right. We just needed to talk." I sighed. She probably knew it was only half the truth. "No." I gave a sarcastic laugh.

She dropped the topic and moved on. "We'll be okay here for a while, right? I mean, everyone knows where we are, and they don't seem to be worried as long as we're not trying to run away?"

I nodded. She sounded unsure of herself, a contrast from my friend who usually had the world by the tail. *Her* world, anyway. Her lids were already threatening to close. She yawned.

"We can get some sleep."

Brea dozed off in moments. I don't know how long I lay awake watching her. Being stuck in Scotland made me feel sort of powerless, not that I was the Queen of Resourceful before. I'd begun to have a good grasp of my bearings in London, was just settling in. I think I may have accepted things there eventually. Life at the bookstore suddenly didn't seem so bad, at all.

CHAPTER 23

*S*leep found me but only stayed for a while. I awoke later to the sensation of my skin tingling, signaling my change. Darkness tinted the room while we dozed. Brea's breath came in steady, slow beats. I slid out of bed snatching my old skirt and cami, and headed for the bathroom for some privacy.

I flipped on the light and my reflection caught me completely off-guard. My eyes were huge, the fleck of copper seeming to swirl or glint in a slow pulse. I picked up the ends of my hair, wondering why I'd ever had it trimmed or styled. The bright pink polish on my nails was suddenly disgusting. Coloring my fingers that way was childish. My physical appearance was perfection in its natural state, by the ages-old laws of divine creation. The t shirt I wore was an insult. I was confused, wondering where the new perspective and opinion of myself came from. Doing my best to shake it off, I turned on cold water and splashed my face.

I quickly patted dry on a hand towel. I felt better. I had no idea where the self-criticism came from, by my nails looked great and I was wearing a shirt with a big-eyed puppy on it. What could possibly have been wrong with a puppy?

My spine tingled, snapping me out of the confusion. I just

made it into the skirt and cami before I transformed. The parody of decency I kept up when I Garged Out struck me then. Clothes were useless as a gargoyle. The moments before and after becoming one kept me changing into the old outfit. The mirror showed how odd I looked, a stony, dark figure in ruined lace and pastels. My scales weren't the same color as before. Part of them shone deep grey, growing darker underneath. My face was dark, with cut features. The monster in me settled in, and my human side accommodated, blending. The resilience of human nature fought for survival, adapting. I craved being human again—appreciated daytime and sunlight more at that moment than ever before.

I left quietly, feeling cool air greet me on the other side of the door. Spines of books glinted in the low light. Sleet tapped at the glass, ice crystals gleaming and as they slid from the pane.

Headlights bobbed in the darkness toward the house, glinting through the storm. I walked to the window and crouched low to get a look at who'd driven up. I lowered the tops of my wings to keep out of sight.

A sleek, black Mercedes rolled to a stop. Kai got out of the backseat, dressed in a collared shirt and black pants, and tie that hung loose around his neck. His hair was tied back at the nape. He looked like he'd returned from some sort of business meeting as he reached into the car to retrieve a briefcase.

Kai walked beneath the courtyard lights toward the front door, on human feet. He was definitely no gargoyle. My tail twitched in agitation as I watched him until he was gone from view.

The front door pounded shut below me. He'd lied to me and it was time to get a better understanding of what he *was,* since I knew what he *wasn't.* He'd played me before. I would continue to be a monster, when Kai, rotten as he was, remained human. That got my goat.

* * *

I GLIDED over the bannister railing and landed quietly on the tile in the great room below. The more I thought about how he'd lied, connived and taken advantage of me the more incensed I became. Wishing I'd been able to explore the monstrosity of a house, I wandered the halls searching him out, intent on getting answers from him one way or another. Seeing him as a human changed things on the playing field. Being a gargoyle might give me the upper hand for once.

Kai's voice echoed in a wordless monotone through a hallway. I stopped, straining to listen. A female voice spoke low and calm, but I couldn't make out the conversation. I crept closer, trying to keep an eye on the hallway behind me. Soon, I stood outside the door to Kai's study, peeking inside through a crack in the doorway.

The female I'd heard talking was Petra. She stood before Kai, claws folded in front of her. Her tail twitched at her back, and her wings fluttered with small motions above her head. She was agitated. Or scared.

"I'm sorry, Kai—"

Slap!

The room fell silent. I leaned back against the wall. I breathed hard, thinking about running into the room. Between the two of us, surely we could beat the crap right out of him.

Before I stepped inside, Petra ran out of the room and down the opposite hall. She hadn't seen me. I flattened against the wall once more, trying to get a grip on my thoughts.

When I'd first met Kai, I would never have imagined him being such a monster. He'd been charming, and mysterious. Fun and polite. Hardly the type to kick a puppy. I snorted. Such a contrast. He was abusive, domineering and had apparently done something to keep Petra under his thumb.

Puppy kicker, extraordinaire.

I leaned off the wall and turned, taking one step into an

unmoving wall of hard scales. I looked up into the face of a snarling gargoyle.

I snorted, completely on accident and this big guy totally thought I was being sarcastic or something.

The giant looked shocked for about a millisecond. He snatched me by an elbow and flung me inside the study. My wings flew out of control behind me as I was jerked to a stop in front of Kai's desk. I rubbed my arm and glared up at the brute beside me.

Kai looked at me and shook his head with a sigh.

"Leave us," he said.

I turned on a heel and stepped toward the door. No one needed to tell me twice.

"Tessa!" Kai snarled.

I dropped my head and resigned to stand in front of his desk again.

The big gargoyle smirked. He left the room, leaving Kai and I alone. I stood precisely where Petra was moments before. Kai was livid.

I practiced stoicism as he paced to a sidebar and poured a drink from a decanter. Ben Thomlinson's face flashed through my mind as he'd poured himself multiple rocks glasses full of alcohol the day we'd met. That had not been a great day, either.

"What can I do for you this evening, Tessa?" He watched me with a rehearsed, calm smile.

"You lied to me."

"On which account?" He seated himself at his desk.

"It's nice to know I have choices."

He smirked, sipping from his glass.

"You're not a gargoyle." The tips of my wings twitched above my head, clicking softly.

"Ah, you caught me. I am not, indeed."

"But you were all see-through that day in London."

"You're the one that proclaimed I was a gargoyle, not I. I threw on a shroud." He shrugged as if it was no big deal.

"You threw on a shroud," I deadpanned. "I have no freaking idea what that means."

"I altered the appearance of my physical state to suit the situation. So in a sense, that was the lie. I was trying to make friends with you."

"Why? Someone like me should hardly matter to someone like you. I don't like you at all. You disgust me."

"There's that quirk you have, Tessa," he sipped from his glass and reclined in his expensive-looking desk chair. "I want for us to reunite. We've shared much."

I was about to give another snarky retort, but something in his voice stopped me. Behind the cocky attitude, there was a hint sorrow in his demeanor. I'd had the sense about him before. Whatever he felt, he was convinced it was real. We hadn't shared much time together, but Kai's eyes held a thousand years of affection. I looked at my feet. *Oh, shit.*

"Retrieving your friend emboldened you." He regarded me, staring from my eyes to my wings and claws. "You really think you've figured it all out."

"Don't even bother wasting your breath. You're a liar and I won't listen anyway." I was really lost. He'd made it seem like getting me there was his goal. It really figured I'd been misled, once again.

"I want my book back."

"What book?"

"The one that old fool has at Librorum Taberna." He removed two golden cufflinks from his shirt, rolling the sleeves against his forearms. "The fact he used *that* book to transform *you* into a gargoyle is the most absurd alignment of events possible."

Cryptic blather from Kai, the way he placed intonation on certain words when he spoke, wasn't something I'd entertain anymore. "So it's okay for you to play with people, but no one else? And I don't even know where your stupid book is," I shot back. "As if Ezra tells me every-dang-thing around the place."

My mistake was obvious a moment too late. I should have known not to get sarcastic with Kai. In the next second I found myself floating above the floor, unable to move as my body leveled out, going horizontal. I couldn't make myself stop shaking from sheer terror. My stomach heaved. I glided atop the air, growing closer to Kai's desk. He stood, taking my right hand, which had changed to human form along with the rest of me. My stained skirt and camisole hung against my chest and hips.

"This spell that makes you change at night?" He didn't wait for an answer. It belongs to me. It's part of you. Do the math."

"I'm sorry," I whispered through tears. "I really am."

"Sweet girl, you are," he touched my cheek gently. "You will learn to watch your tongue around me." He traced my bottom lip with a fingertip and placed his hand over my mouth.

I cried against his skin, begging him to stop.

"You're blind to your own potential and have absolutely no idea what you're dealing with."

He gripped my little finger and snapped it.

Jagged, wet bone grated together. I screamed. Tears streamed toward my ears, dampening my hair. I continued to hover, trembling and helpless. Kai released my fractured finger and wrapped his hand around the ring finger on the same hand. I cried out again, muffled in the stillness of his study. He leaned over my face.

"Shhh . . . ," he nodded, waiting for me to nod my understanding.

The delicate bone in my finger snapped quickly, like a soggy Popsicle stick. He tightened his grip on my mouth when I screamed at the new pain. I drew ragged breaths sobbing quietly, not knowing which was worse; the terror of being helplessly tortured or the pain in my hand. My body trembled so hard I felt my hair and skirt swinging in the open air beneath me.

"Here's how this will work." He squeezed my middle finger hard, selecting the next bone to splinter. "Are you listening to me?" He moved his palm from my mouth.

"Yes," I said, after inhaling a quivering breath. "Please don't."

"You will go to London and get my book. You will bring it here to me in two days' time. Brea will stay here with me, Petra and the boys." He snorted and shook his head slightly. "That reminds me of something we need to discuss." He leaned in again. "You have the gift of surprising me. That's a quality I've missed seeing in anyone for centuries. It's one of the things I admire about you, Tessa." His eyes scanned my face while one hand stroked my hair. "Don't make it a habit to kill my boys." The pressure was back on my finger.

"Okay," I agreed, hastily. It hadn't been a highpoint in my life, anyway.

"So let's recap, shall we? You will bring me my book. Brea will remain here with me, in one of my suites. She will have the best of care, food, everything. You will refrain from habitually killing anyone else around here. Do we agree?

"Yes."

"Good girl. I'll even throw in a driver, as a token of good faith. But I feel it needs said that if you get any ideas to deviate from our agreement, I will kill your friend and hunt you down."

I locked onto his eyes and met sincerity. He meant every syllable of what he said, without a doubt. He'd placed my best friend's life in my hands. I felt horribly inadequate. Brea being threatened was entirely on me.

"Kai, will you do something for me when I give you your book?" I knew I was in no position to ask for perks but I had to try. I tried my best to engage him with sincerity through my tears and pain.

"Again, a surprise. Please, humor me," he said, smiling down at me.

"Will you send Brea back home? That's all I'll ever ask for. She doesn't deserve any of this. Just put her on a plane back to Austin and never contact her again."

"Of course," he said gently, stroking my brow. "You've such a big heart." He kissed me softly.

I was horrified by that. I would never understand how Kai could be so tender while he tortured me.

"I'm not a monster, Tessa."

That was the thing with Kai—he looked and spoke like a normal, sane human. No helter-skelter eyes. No face of evil, or little voices playing with his expressions as they dictated his motives. All bad guys should look the part. Twist a mustache while they laughed in maniacal tones or something equally tell-tale. I apparently needed more to go on, because Kai's warning signs didn't scare me off until it was far too late. The last few moments had done the trick. He was purely vile.

I was a believer.

And Kai, was also. He was convinced he was a good guy; that he'd been stolen from. Victimized. His state of mind sealed a cap over a really big bottle of "Psycho".

I was lowered slowly to the floor. My bare toes touched down lightly. Kai held my wrist, moving the hand with my fractured fingers into the center of both our lines of sight. The tips pointed at sick angles toward the floor. I could barely stand looking at them.

He touched the base of one broken bone and I panicked.

"Nonono Kai, please don't!"

"Shhhh," he hissed as the pain left my hand. "You shouldn't force me to do such things to you." Broken bone fused together and my pinky reset against my other fingers, with the ring finger following suit. I shook, sweat growing heavy on my brow and upper lip. I was suddenly freezing, but numb.

He caressed my hand. "Good as new," he whispered.

"Hamish!" his shout burst toward the door behind me. I was startled by the thunder in his voice. Kai held my hand, keeping me in place.

A moment later the door swung open and the hulking

gargoyle approached us. I took a careful look at him as he came to stand next to me. He towered over Kai, with a wide, plated torso. Waist-length blond hair was tied at his nape, subtle hints of copper as if he'd spent time in a swimming pool that contained too much chlorine. Two long, spiraling horns pointed from his forehead, curving back like a goat's. His face held no emotion at all, like a soldier who'd been trained to uphold duty above anything else. A spiked tail twitched against the floor, darting between the heels of his elongated, clawed feet. He looked straight ahead, as if I wasn't in the room at all. Hamish had a lethal quality about him that was barely contained. His ability to make me feel nonexistent terrified me, like he could do away with me and carry on without missing a beat in his neatly, Garged Out world.

"Tomorrow you will take Tessa into London so she can get some of her things from Ezra's book store—"

Hamish broke character, huffing.

"Kai," I cut in. "Please." There was no way I would be able to endure that long ride trapped in the same space as Hamish. I would have to find another way to get Brea out of there if Kai disagreed.

"Ugh," Hamish grunted, peering down at me with blatant disgust curling his lip.

I bristled. "Screw you." The night had gone completely south and I was in no mood to be "Ughed" at. I turned to face Kai, who squinted, watching me.

Hamish continued to stare at me like he'd stepped up beside a steaming cow pie. I couldn't concentrate with hate flowing so freely and from such a close distance. He tried to intimidate me, to make me feel unsubstantial in the shadow of his huge body.

"What's your problem?" I returned the nasty look.

Hamish snorted his distaste. "I'll not waste good breath on a woman who needs to be put in her place, for good," he snarled.

The slap was rocket-fast, landing so hard against his rough cheek that my hand stung past the wrist, feeling like flames burst from the many pores of my palm. A blackened handprint marred Hamish's face where I'd landed the blow with a searing sound like water dancing on a griddle.

Oddly, I was the only one surprised by the speed and result of my action. Kai erupted with laughter, telling Hamish, "You earned that one."

Hamish jerked, standing rigid, facing Kai, The handprint on his burnt cheek pointing right at me. I needed to look for a good hiding place. The psycho gargoyle would seek revenge. It was high time to plead my case.

"I've seen Peter around. Could he take me? I don't know how Ezra will react to a stranger showing up at the bookstore, and Peter knows the place well. I'll need help locating your book." I shot a look at Hamish. "And I don't trust him with my safety." I played on the hopes that Kai didn't trust Hamish, either, especially since I'd dug my own, fresh grave by hitting him. And Peter coming to the bookstore with me would make more sense to Ezra, seem more natural, especially since Peter did Kai's bidding to keep Petra alive.

"You have my word I will come right back." I swallowed hard. "On my friend's life."

I must've said something right. He searched my face for sincerity then nodded like I was the Queen of the Obvious.

"I would offer to accompany you for the ride," he looked at me, just long enough to make me break out in a new dousing of sweat. "Although, I feel you owe me this, so I'll attend business here and await your prompt return. Don't forget what I said about the fate of your friend, should you decide to deviate from our agreement." He stared at me, so cold I could have got brain freeze. At that moment I understood him with sheer clarity. I wouldn't mess him around and he knew it.

"Off with you now, and get some rest. Big day tomorrow." Kai looked meaningfully at Hamish.

I frowned. Big day, indeed. I turned to go, stepping toward the door. Hamish followed me out.

"I know the way to my room. You can go away now," I told him. He followed too closely for my comfort.

"Kai wants to be sure you stay put in your room until morning." His voice was monotone, all business, each word a grunted snarl.

"Well you don't need to follow me to be sure of that. We have an agreement, and I won't do anything to mess it up."

"Just the same, I'll walk you back."

"Here's the deal," I stopped and glared up, *way* up, at him. "Go away. I don't need any more cheap shots." My voice shook, making it hard to sound demanding, rather than pleading.

He smiled, knowingly. "No' a chance." The gargoyle stepped forward, peering nearly straight down on me. "You need to be taught your place, lass. And I be the perfect one to show ye, so don't push me." His green eyes gleamed with venom, forked tongue sliding across his teeth as he spoke.

I stood my ground. Where did he get off telling me "my place"? He didn't know me like that, and I was certain "my place" was nowhere near the big bastard. He could end me, true enough. But that didn't mean I had to agree and turn mousy in the meantime. Kai wanted me alive, with *working* body parts, and Hamish needed to remember that.

"I'm apparently not like other girls you know. I won't take orders from you, or anyone unless it suits me for a very good reason. *You* can go die in a hole. Leave me *alone*." I blustered, giving my best shot at showing him I wasn't afraid when inside I was cringing. *Goawaygoawaypleeeeeeasejustgoaway* . . . .

Hamish was silent for a second, then threw his head back and laughed like a rabid hyena. "Turn and walk or I'll be sure you get to your room the hard way. Seeing how the only thing that's kept you alive this long is Kai's amusement with you, I'd take each breath as a gift from the gods." He rapped my sternum hard with a talon, pushing me off balance. "Now. March, before I change my mind and have to come up with a good excuse for killing you where you stand. Believe me, every drop of your spilled blood would be worth it."

That was convincing enough to get me moving toward my room upstairs. I may try to talk tough, but there was a time when I needed to play it safe for the sake of self-preservation. Mousy me.

Sometime before I reached for the bedroom door, I changed back to a gargoyle. I was in such shock that I hadn't even felt the transformation. Becoming Garged Out was really beginning to feel second nature, in the truest sense of the statement.

Hamish drifted toward the couch as I walked through the library. I was intent on slamming my bedroom door right in his face if he tried to follow me in.

When I stepped inside, I scanned the room. My heart sank to my feet.

Kai had already taken Brea.

CHAPTER 24

*N*ot being able to tell my friend what was about to happen pushed me too far. I was determined to take control. Little ol' me was going to do something drastic. My body heated up the second Brea's absence greeted me. I wanted answers, and was going to make allies.

Fear tactics and duress were the ways of operation at The Grotto. Physical torture, abuse, and coercion were Kai's tools for keeping order. I got the point. That didn't mean it wasn't working. Hamish completely freaked me out.

I tried not to think about it hours later when I tested the situation to see if he was still out on the couch in the library. The door opened painfully slowly, but that was the only way I could get the handle and hinges to be silent. The back of the couch was to my room and I didn't see Hamish on it, but wasn't about to rule out his presence. He could have been lying down, even though he seemed much bigger than the furniture. Besides, he wouldn't maul me too badly, because then I wouldn't be in any shape to retrieve Kai's book. I crept out of the library on my claws and knees, moving so slowly, I wanted to pee the whole time. An hour passed easily in the time it took to get into the hallway, and by then, I was done hiding. I leapt over the bannister, stretching my wings wide to soar in a tight circle. My crouched landing was perfectly placed on a sofa, then I slipping outside into the cool, moonlit air.

A Tyren had spoken to me once. Maybe I would be lucky twice, not that they were all-knowing or something, but it wouldn't hurt to pick one's brain. I didn't slink toward my destination, I sprinted two running steps, caught the wind and shot across the grounds like a missile, moving so fast my eyes narrowed to slits and watered as I blew through the air. Adrenaline was truly addicting. I could have soared into the night and stayed there until I fell to the earth when the sun rose.

Music greeted me halfway down the stairs. Moonlight dimmed as I descended, and by the time I took the bottom step into the cavern I was in human form. I straightened my skirt and walked toward the small area behind the staircase. I didn't want anyone to notice me, but it was really hard not to look around.

Some of the people beside the bar, and a few more on the dance floor, seriously needed to get a room. The air was damp with warm humidity and my sense of smell struggled but finally adjusted to the sulfuric minerals that weighed down the air. I sped along, padding on bare feet across the tile and smooth stone walkway, ducking behind the stairwell.

Memories flooded my mind from waking up half dead in the shallow eddy there. The pain I suffered that day was the worst I'd endured in my young life. The gushing sounds of the hot springs were much quieter there. I circled the pool to the side where I woke up that day, when I'd looked into the face of the Tyren.

"Hello?" I called, low. My voice echoed a little off the stone around me. No one was in view, so I called again.

After a couple more times, it was confirmed, I was an idiot, calling out to no one. Risking my life didn't seem like such a bright idea when there wasn't a payoff. Not noble at all. Who did I think I was? I needed to get past the identity crisis quickly, before I got someone killed. I sat at the water's edge, and let my toes wander the pebbles, contemplating sneaking back into my room.

The more I thought about it the angrier I got at myself for even trying to find a Tyren. I picked up a smooth river rock, flinging it hard to skip across the pool.

The projectile skidded once, then stopped, suspended by a watery hand. Relief coated my frazzled nerves. I hoped I hadn't ticked someone off by breaking an unknown rule about not throwing rocks. I figured no one was around in Tyren-ville.

Shimmering water rose into the form of a man who paced my way. He paused inches from me, gazing down before dropping the smooth stone in my lap and sitting on the pebble beach.

I ran my thumbs over the flat of the tumbled limestone, wondering what to do next. *How does one start up a conversation with a supernatural being?* 'How 'bout those Longhorns?' didn't seem appropriate.

He stuck his feet in the water next to mine and they disappeared to the ankle. I wondered if they were gone, or just camouflaged by the water. He seemed comfortable enough, so I broke the ice.

"Sorry if I bothered you." I said, looking over at him. "I just need to know what would happen if I gave Kai his magic book back." He watched me, but didn't reply. "Do you know what I'm talking about?" I fidgeted, waiting. "Is he going to turn the whole world into monsters? I mean, what else can he do if he gets it?"

He remained quiet. I was pretty sure Tyrens could talk. I straightened my knees, putting my legs in the warm water. The tattered hem of my skirt was like a sponge, soaking the back of my thighs.

"Maybe I'm losing it." I laughed. "What's left of 'it', I mean. I'm going to get my best friend killed." I folded my legs against my chest and put my chin on my knees.

The Tyren still didn't answer. He just sat, gazing at the pool and the walls. I sighed loudly, without realizing it at first. He turned his head and smiled.

I was beginning to think we had a language barrier or something. At least he showed up. He stood, walking a ways into the water. When he was nearly waist deep, he looked over his shoulder at me. He gestured with a hand, urging me to follow him.

I wasn't so sure that was a good idea. From what I knew about Tyrens, they were basically good guys. Last time I was at that spot, the female Tyren could have let me drown, rather than try to get me to breathe. I wondered if they were like people, some good and some not-so-good. Like she could have been a good Tyren and the new guy could be like The Joker of the Tyren world, waiting for me to trust him and then turn on me and cackle while he drowned me.

He cocked his head with look like *"Awe, come on, really?"*

I sighed and got up, following a supernatural being to the depths, hoping I hadn't made a decision that cost me my life and Brea hers.

I was waist deep when he turned and smiled at me. I smiled back. He pointed down.

I looked into the water, but didn't see anything. "What?" I looked at him and then back down, still seeing nothing but the pebbly bottom and my bare feet.

He pinched his nose—as if he really needed to—and went under, beckoning with a hand for me to follow. I held my breath and submerged. Only his silvery silhouette was visible under the surface. The sound of water flowing filled my ears. My hair billowed around my head and I had to clear it from my face to keep the Tyren in my sight.

"The book is not his to claim." he said.

"You need water to speak!" My words gurgled together in a mass of bubbling syllables.

I'd been half submerged with the female Tyren when she spoke to me. I smiled and stood up straight for a quick breath. The air in the cavern was chilly compared to the temperature of the water. His head popped up a few feet from me. He grinned, and was gone.

"So whose is it?" I received no answer when I looked for him in the water. "Please don't leave me yet," I called. There was no sight of him. He'd left me to ponder things by myself.

Of course the book wasn't really Kai's. Water splashed onto the dry pebbles when I trudged from the pool. Risking my life to hear something I could've guessed wasn't the information I'd hoped for. I'd hardly hit pay dirt. Whether the book he wanted was truly Kai's or not was beside the point. Kai's demand to bring it to him to trade for Brea still held firm. Soaked and angry, I realized I'd have to sneak past Hamish and wait for dawn.

Golden light flickered ahead from a tunnel in the rocks behind the path leading to the secluded pond. There was an additional part of the grotto I'd failed to see when I was there before. I followed like a moth, tracing the light to an immense, chiseled doorway. Dim torchlight peppered a row of squatting forms with yellowed illumination. Water dripped inside, echoing in a soft patter. Stone gleamed underneath from a pedestal knapped in limestone. Six stone gargoyles hulked, statuesque, all crouching on haunches with unfurled, massive wings creating a regal halo at their backs. Large claws clutched heavy swords that shone platinum. Spiked horns sprouted from the foreheads of each one. I paced forward, examining the "place-holder" of Hamish and five others that matched his huge form in size, some going beyond in mass, others more lethal, demonic, but all equally tormented in facial expression. I placed a hand to the cheek where I'd struck Hamish earlier in the night. Cool, scaly stone warmed to my touch in an instant.

I exhaled into the dank air. A twinge of recognition pulled at the back of my mind. Not only was Hamish familiar to me, I'd also seen the others somewhere. I paced between them, an odd reunion taking place as I studied them individually, working my way across the long, crypt-like hall.

Soft, cracking sounds carried from farther inside the new cavern, just loud enough to drown the patter of dripping water. The doorway out beckoned with safety behind me, a reminder that I would make a choice to leave it behind if I continued down the darkened hall to satisfy my curiosity. I'd snuck out for answers and struck out with the Tyrens. In a few short hours I would trek back to London to return bearing a tool of possible destruction into the hands of a lunatic. I could skulk back to my room and act like I'd never found the mysterious tomb holding the gargoyles, never heard curious sounds. Never tried and failed.

The smell of decay should have warned me off but I walked on, carefully picking my way across the gravel strewn floor, listening as noise was defined into recognizable categories—tearing fabric, and chopping on wood. Splatter. The hall widened into a room.

Torchlight sconces illuminated the place, bringing into view a tall plank table, streaked with black and crimson blood in various states of dryness and rot. A cleaving blade smacked down into the thick wood. Splatter erupted, coating the table, the floor and the skin of men accustomed to the spray. I could tell, because not one of them flinched when it hit them. Long, matted hair hung down the backs of two that faced away. A sticky flip flop worked loose from still, suntanned toes on the table and clopped to the gooey floor. Pink and red flesh was lifted to a Viking-like mouth on the flat of a short blade. Lips smacked. Lifeless, human eyes stared in my direction, jerking with the chopping and pulling. They were blue. The hair sandy, light brown.

Not one barbaric, feasting man witnessed my entry. I felt behind me, stepping back with one timid foot after another. Gravel crackled under my weight and a set of cannibal eyes lifted to meet mine.

"There's your girl," one of the men said. He gave a stained grin and a nod in my direction.

Hamish twisted from the table, bloodied to the elbow. Our gazes met briefly enough to convey a short message between us—he was incensed and I was ever-so-sorry for being out of my room. He slapped a blade flat against the sticky table and stepped toward me.

My feet didn't feel the jagged stones beneath me when I ran. Adrenaline beat in my chest and I pumped my arms, reaching, lengthening my stride. Heavy footfalls gained ground, but detail began to blur as I flew past the stone gargoyles. The sound of running water was a garble in the wind and the rhythm of dark music by the bar sounded offbeat against the pounding of my stride. I took the steps two at a time, diving toward moonlight at the end of the winding staircase, stealing a look behind me as my wings burst from my shoulder blades and I shot high into the air.

Hamish and two other gargoyles emerged seconds later, exploding into winged beasts behind me, but I moved lightning fast. I pulled the manor door open, stepped inside and flew over the banister, watching over the wooden handrail for Hamish to follow.

Seconds ticked, turtle style, but no one came through the door below. I stood. They'd done what they intended. I'd been scared back to my room.

CHAPTER 25

The same time the previous year I'd never have imagined I'd live in a world where words like *warded*, *shroud* (not the "executioner" type), *Garged Out* (okay so that one was mine, a Tessa-ism) and *grotto*, would become part of my vocabulary; part of everyday conversation that I said casually, as if I was saying "How's it going?" or "Dang, it's hot." I found it crazy how life could switch up all on its own and drag me along like a bucking horse with my foot caught in a stirrup. Life could force me to pick myself up out of the dirt, dust myself off, and see what still worked.

I'd become Tessa Marie Conley; darkened even further at the heart, and able to take another person's life, given a reason and opportunity. I had a love-hate relationship with New Tessa. She was extreme, but at least she wasn't a pushover.

Peter and I left at first light since Kai wouldn't give us the keys until daybreak. He seemed to derive a large amount of glee reciting the rules of our deal, and the possible outcome if I didn't hold up my end. We would travel in human form. I wouldn't want gargoyles tearing up the leather inside my Aston Martin, either.

Peter and I rode in silence. Occasionally he looked over at me as I stared ahead at the open road. The car purred along, oblivious to the turmoil inside the cockpit. I amazed myself by not crying. I'd felt something snap inside me, or maybe something inside me had begun to click, rather, which would be a good thing. I didn't want to play a further part in any of the madness that went on at The Grotto, but there I was, on the way to do Kai's bidding to save my friend.

Without thinking about it, I snorted at the irony, jarring both of us.

Peter looked at me, surprised. "What's funny?"

"Sorry, I was just thinking. Not in a funny ha ha kind of way. More in a like, weird way. Why doesn't Kai go get this dumb book himself? I mean Ezra seems pretty harmless after the last few days."

"As harmless as Ezra seems, it's going to be hard as hell to find that book. He's apparently placed very strong wards around it. Kai can't get into the store. He didn't send Petra in after it because he knew I was there."

"Why didn't you go looking for her?"

Peter didn't answer right away. I shouldn't have asked such a sensitive question.

"Kai and Ezra battled once, just after she disappeared. Mayhap a week after. We'd only been . . . possibly eight years old. Ezra had brought us both in off the streets of London after catching me stealing dried fish," he smiled a little. "After the transformation, Petra and Ezra fought horribly. She ran away, and was found by Kai. It was said that Kai killed her to get back at Ezra." He quieted, looked out the windshield at more than just the road ahead. "And now she's back from the dead."

"That's a horrible story," I said. "I'm sorry, Peter." We'd endured similarities as children. One difference was, he got his sister back.

"So, you're twins?" That was sort of cool. They looked a little bit alike, but far from identical.

"We are." He watched the road and we proceeded in silence, both lost in our tormented worlds.

"Explain the ward thing again? I'm trying to understand this stuff."

"It's Apotropaic magic. Wards are magical spells that are placed around an object, or even an entire place as protection from certain people or things. A ward can be a very powerful tool, and is not a toy. You've been extremely lucky so far." He glanced over at me. "Or something." He shook his head.

"Don't ask me," I said, holding up my hands. "I don't get it either." At least I made it through the wards, without being hurt too badly. Peter acted as if it could've ended much worse.

"So, if the book is warded, and the wards don't work as well on me, it's possibly I've seen the book Kai wants and not even know it."

"Exactly. I can't see it through the wards and Ezra will not be willing to assist."

"Am I the only one freaking out because we're going to search for this frickin' thing in a bookstore?" It would be like looking for a needle in a stack of needles.

Peter didn't bother with an answer, so apparently I wasn't alone there.

"What is Ezra? I mean is he human?"

Peter sent me an ironic look.

"Don't act like you don't know what I mean. He acts all . . . bijiggity. The guy doesn't even have pupils."

"Ezra just *is*."

I waited. He had nothing to add, apparently.

"Well okay, then," The whole situation was amazing. I laughed a little. "I have no freaking idea what the heck I'm doing."

"You, Tessa, are a mystery to us all." He searched my face, tracing a finger along my jaw. After a moment, I turned to the window, reminded of Kai touching me like that.

Whoa, Nellie. I needed a good therapist.

We arrived at the junction in Kelty. The day was young, so the sidewalks were still deserted, save for shop owners preparing for the day, setting out displays and signs. I noticed one of those squatty, red post boxes on the roadside.

"Stop here, okay?" I pulled a postcard out of my bag. Kai had given specific instructions that it must be posted that day. The card was hand-written from Brea to her parents back home in Austin.

I hopped out of the car and dropped the card in the slot on the post box, determined to live up to my end of the deal for Brea. I had to have faith that Kai would keep up his side of our bargain, as well. Her safety was my biggest concern, not so much that Kai might break my fingers again, or some bigger part of my anatomy. I'd made it a point to omit the part about broken fingers when I told Peter about my deal with Kai. Apparently, the two of them had already talked by then because Peter knew he was to drive me to the bookstore to get the book. I seriously doubted Kai would tell Peter that he tortured me. Or that he kissed me while he did it. I'd developed a deep, fear-based respect for Kai. He could do things that frightened me on a new level. Out of so many super-natural elements and beings from my new life in the UK, Kai was the hardest of them all to understand. The way he was able control people was just plain eerie, but the fact that he liked doing *things* to me, could caress me after he hurt me, made him a whole new kind of monster.

The way he'd looked at me in his study stirred something deep in my memory, like I'd seen him look at me that way many times before. It wasn't the first time he'd hinted that way. I scoffed, mentally. There was no way. I'd known Kai for a short time during the early summer. Being told we'd known each other for a long time was obviously beginning to wear on my mind. If a person was told the sky was green long enough, they'd eventually step outside and check.

The way I used to spend so much time with Kai sickened me

inside. To my credit, he'd been hiding his true nature and acting like a normal, incredibly hot, fun-loving guy. He'd exuded a charm so profound I'd been drawn in, a magnet to steel.

"What are you going to do about the fact that Petra's with Kai?"

"Petra and I hardly know each other. She says she's done with him," he snapped.

"She's still your sister. Doesn't it worry you?" My tone was soft, words carefully chosen.

"Pick a new topic."

"Well, excuse me for being concerned."

Peter said nothing, again only warming up when it suited him. He'd changed so much from the time when we worked together at the bookstore. It must have been hard to act friendly and affectionate when he was really all business.

I took his advice and moved on. "I'm worried about what it might be like after Kai gets the book back." If Kai was being held back because it was missing, that meant the guy I'd been dealing with was Tame Kai compared to what he would be when he had it back again.

"Ezra has had that book for the better part of two centuries. Kai hasn't created another gargoyle for at least that long. That grotto, castle and all belonged to a clan that was like family to Ezra for centuries. The place has an ancient, charmed history." Peter looked for my reaction, waiting for my curiosity to be piqued. He'd nailed it. I was glued to his every word. I blinked expectantly, waiting for him to continue.

"The standing stones go back to their ancestry, an ancient place of ritual and worship."

"Could you imagine having that kind of timeless faith? I mean the kind that made you believe with your soul, to the point of ritual." I shook my head. "Religion today just doesn't have that devotion, if you ask me. I mean they've got ritual in going to church and studying the bible, but so many only go through the motions. Like it's only a way of life when someone's looking." And as for growing up with a group of nuns watching over me, I didn't buy in to blind faith.

"The ancients lived their lives according to lore and the power of the natural world. And to answer your question, Kai would traipse around taking whatever he wanted, whenever he wanted it. The world as we know it exists merely because Ezra's held the bastard at bay by stashing away that book. Kai has done away with some of Ezra's clansmen for it."

"So we're talking what, a few hundred years ago there was a war between some Scots?"

"Hardly the case. More the nature of about eleven hundred years. And Kai isn't a Scot."

"He talks like one."

"Kai isn't human, like us."

I couldn't help it, I started to laugh. "Human?" That was a stretch.

Peter wasn't impressed with my humor. He remained silent, looking out over the wheel with a slight frown.

"Human, that's us," I said when I'd calmed enough for coherent speech.

"What you need to know is Kai is an Ancient. Been wandering the planet for eons."

"And then he lost the big book of mojo." I added.

"Exactly. It deflated his abilities monumentally. Even the wickedest of powerful men fall victim to misplaced trust. One of his own stole away with his book." He looked over with a tight, satisfied smile. "He's able to work small charms, manipulate things a bit and maintain things he'd created before the book was taken, but he is weak in comparison to before. If he gets that book back, we may as well bid farewell to the rest of the world as it stands. Kiss our asses goodbye."

"He's older than you?" I regretted the words the second they hung in the air between us. I'd risked Peter announcing another demand I change the subject, but it was increasing hard to wrap my head around the way no one around me seemed to age. Ever. And it chafed thinking about Kai getting what he wanted, especially since I knew he'd been using me because I was close to Ezra.

"Easy," he teased, "you're not going to age now either. And yes, he's much older."

Kai skulking around the earth for ages spooked me. I didn't believe in ghosts, vampires, werewolves, witches, anything like that growing up. There was no monster in my closet ready to eat me when I turned out the light, nothing lurking under my bed, ready to swipe at my ankles. Kai had likely seen countless souls come and go in his life, making them common, just another consciousness taking in a full life's experience and then fizzing out. Whether he valued life, or didn't for that matter, made him a complete loose cannon.

"There was a time when Kai was feared as a god," Peter continued.

"Demon, more likely." I was getting pretty uneasy about the task I'd been set to do. If I gave Kai the book, he would change the world, and not for the better. He wasn't the kind of guy who would use his powers to find a cure for cancer or discover the secret for world peace.

"It's so weird Ezra has that book." I had no idea how the old weirdo had managed to keep it away from Kai for so long, wards aside.

"Don't underestimate Ezra. He may seem feeble, and even unstable, but he is a quick study. He got the recipe for his wards from that very book, and that really digs a hole in Kai. Ezra changed Petra right before he changed me."

"Wow."

"She didn't know I was next. Had no idea I was there, too. Next time I saw her she was tossing hunks of elephant sculpture through the windows at *Librorum Taberna*. I've always thought Kai hung out close to Ezra in hopes Ezra would let his wards down.

So that's how Kai found Petra. Ezra kept me hidden and safe until I was much older."

That explained why Ezra was completely stunned when he saw Petra collapsed in the bookstore. And Kai thought I was the key to recovering what he'd lost. "And then I came along, just in time for Kai to think up a good way to get his book back."

"His plan wouldn't work with just anyone."

"What do you mean?"

"Remember the night I took you out to teach you how to fly?"

"Yeah, of course. What about it?"

"Ezra warded the entire bookstore to keep you inside."

"So. . . ." I'd been able to fly off the roof that night the same as Peter. From my recent experience, when I had trouble with a ward of some kind, it either slimed me to the point of making me vomit or blasted me in the face so hard it knocked me out.

"I didn't know at the time." Peter looked over at me expectantly.

"And?" I snapped. I wasn't putting it all together.

"And you can make it through Kai's wards, too, which in essence are the same ward spells that Ezra uses from that book, just juiced up. Neither of them understands it. The difference between the two of them is remarkable though, in the way they've decided to deal with you."

"So the wards work on you?"

"Absolutely. I'm unable to locate Kai's book at the shop because the wards do their job and deter me whenever I get close to it."

"Holy hell," I breathed. "Kai told me he knew why I am the way I am when we first met. I wonder if it has anything to do with the wards not working."

"What do you mean, 'the way you are'?" he asked, perturbed.

"I've struggled with fevers since I was little. No one could ever figure out why, but my body heats up to crazy temperatures. I just learned this, but one time when I was like, two, I got so hot that the fever put me in a coma for almost a year. Kai says I heat up because I have an old soul that's trying to get even. Like, it's angry."

"You confuse him. Pretty big blow to his ego having you tromp right through his ward in the hallway." Peter smiled, like he remembered hearing a funny story.

"Tromped? I hardly tromped. I had to run as fast as I could, from clear across the room straight at that doorway to make it through that slime, then I threw up. That's hardly tromping."

"You're unique, Tessa. And as for the rest," he looked at me, shaking his head in wonder. "There's something *inside* your soul that needs to get out. Your soul's in your heart, right where it belongs. Kai hasn't had the honor of knowing you the way I do." He watched the road.

Peter seemed to find the perfect words when it was so important to me to hear how he felt. I didn't know why, especially after the way he'd become so moody, but his opinion of me was important.

"Kai should feel fortunate he can still work small bits of magic at all," he said, moments later.

"He can do enough to scare me." I sat on my hands, remembering the feel of bone splintering inside my fingers.

"Do you know what Ezra said when we talked about you breaking through the wards?" Peter glanced at me quickly before putting his eyes back in front of us.

"What's that?" Ezra was an odd, old dude so it was hard to tell.

"'You see, Peter, I told you keeping her was best. She's charmed and has no bloody idea,'" Peter said, in his best imitation of Ezra.

I laughed. "That was pretty good."

"Ezra was happy you were with us. He considers you a blessing. Like a daughter."

I inhaled sharply and looked out the window. *Like a daughter.* I disagreed.

"Quite the similarities between them though. They both have a use for me. And they've both taken things from me, too." I continued to watch outside as rolling green met forest and returned to more hills, grass, and wild flowers.

"Ezra, the 'nut-job' may have saved you, bringing you into a new life at the bookstore."

We rode in comfortable silence for miles. I'd overlooked Ezra's deed in the face of his absurd, sometimes grumpy, quirkiness. But the biggest epiphany was, I would break the bargain with Kai.

"There's no way I'm giving Kai that book."

"I never thought for a moment you would."

CHAPTER 26

*P*eter guided us to a purring stop behind the bookstore six hours later. I'd left finger prints over virtually every part of the interior during the remainder of the trip. The cockpit of the car fascinated me, all bells, whistles and soft leather. It passed time much better than dwelling on the elephant in there with us. The Plan Fairy needed to make an appearance because I had nothing at that point.

Peter's key still worked on the back door.

"I guess this means he's not too mad about us being gone." I actually hoped Ezra wasn't at the bookstore. Maybe he was out for one of his "business abroad" trips that took him away for nearly a full week at a time.

No such luck.

Ezra manned the post behind the register, wearing dark glasses and fawning over a music mag with a teen-aged couple. When he saw Peter and I approach from the back of the store, he escalated the speed of the purchase.

"Off you go," he said as he handed the bagged magazine over the counter.

"Thanks Mr. Finfrock," the female of the pair said.

Ezra followed the two to the front door, flipped the sign, and turned on us.

"Charmed you could join." He pushed the dark glasses to the top of his head and glared at Peter, and me too this time, all white eyes and attitude.

"You got the windows all fixed up," I hoped changing to a positive note might help diffuse the situation.

"How was The Grotto?" He said the name of Kai's domain as if he spoke about someone's armpit. Ezra wasn't smiling but he wasn't all tight-lipped like he got when he was mad at me.

"Interesting," my small, guilty voice answered.

Ezra amazed me once more by knowing what we'd been doing and where we'd been. He searched us with darting, colorless eyes, then sighed. "I'll get some tea warming and you can tell me about it." He guided us to the drink station behind the store's front-end with an unmasked air of importance.

"I'm going to run upstairs to my room. I'll be back down in a sec." I didn't wait for a response.

Kai had given me an extremely detailed description of the book. I had about a day and a half to get the thing found in the vast bookstore and get my behind back to Scotland. There were parts of *Librorum Taberna* I hadn't explored yet.

The tome I searched for was close to three inches thick and about two feet square, and covered in bruised, brown leather. Its pages were made of vellum. Kai hadn't specified, but I'd wager it weighed close to twenty pounds, give or take. I, of course, was not permitted to open it.

There were latches around the book that were cast from electrum, a natural occurring alloy of gold and silver, commonly used to create royal jewelry by Iron Age Celts. Kai said it was silver in color. I imagine that's what that torc he wore around his throat was made of.

Dealing with Kai's *"Pinky and the Brain"* syndrome was going to be tricky. I had a huge problem and I didn't know how things were going to play out with him trying taking over the world, but the long car ride had done me well. I'd had hours to think.

First thing I did when I entered my room was change into clean jeans and a fresh shirt. I dumped my backpack out on my bed and rolled fresh clothes to pack, this time taking every clean pair of underwear I had in my drawer. I smashed my bag flat, put my worn Garged Out cami and skirt back in along with some more socks. Changing to a gargoyle and being naked at the same time really shouldn't have been a big deal, but it still felt better wearing *something*.

I ran down the stairs to meet up with Peter. We needed to get started looking.

The two men sat at the tea bar, both their faces marked with concern.

I ignored their worried vibe, dropped my bag and filled a mug of Earl Grey. Keeping upbeat was the only way I would stay motivated.

"So, looks like we all know what's going on." I looked pointedly at Peter. We should have talked about whether we were going to tell Ezra or not. I wasn't sure it was the best move, but the cat was out of the bag, growling and hissing, from the looks of Ezra.

"There is no way I could help you look with the wards in place around that book, Tessa, and this building is far too large for you to search in one day, yes?"

He had a point, but I thought keeping Ezra, who was digging through a box of pastries, oblivious was best. "Nice job," I mouthed at him.

"You can't simply hand that book over to Kai. There's a reason I've kept it hidden so well, dear girl." Ezra spoke with an even tone, around a mouthful of some kind of bread. He sipped his tea calmly, which worried me. He should throw a fit, make crappy comments, scream and yell.

I bit the inside of my cheek and glanced at Peter. "You can't see it? At all?"

"It repels me." He looked pointedly at Ezra. "I have a stake here, as well."

That opened the door for me to get my two cents in. I needed help, and convincing Ezra was the only way to get it. "There's no way in heck I'm going to give that psycho any ammunition." I sounded tough. Determined. Matter-of-fact. Old Tessa cringed inside me, unsure. Concentrating on holding my cup steady, I took a deep breath and sipped my tea. I grabbed a scone from the box of day old breakfast and took a healthy bite.

Ezra cleared his throat.

I looked up at him. I never knew what to expect from Ezra Finrock.

He shook his head slowly, smiling. "I've never met a young person with such resolve," he said. "I'd suggest changing into your running shoes, young lady. You're in deep. You may need them."

"Good idea." I set my mug on the bar and headed back to the stairs, taking them two at a time. I ran into my room, hopping on one foot while I untied the laces of one high-top Chuck Taylor, looking frantically around the room for my Asics. I saw the toe of one peeking out from under the edge of my bed. Hitting my knees on the carpet, I reached under to retrieve my shoes.

A huge book lay on the carpet under there, pushed up close to the wall underneath the head of the bed. Silver hinges and locks gleamed in the low light.

Ezra was a smart old codger, but I didn't get why he'd place the book under my bed when he knew Kai wanted it so badly. *I* didn't even trust myself that much. How did he know everything?

When I pulled the book to me the aroma of old leather blended muskily with ancient intrigue. Something inside me started purring like a kitten. I bent, putting my nose flat to the mottled leather cover. The scent was intoxicating, alluring, like stepping into a room that smelled like heaven. I'd smelled it some-where before but I couldn't think of where. Maybe it matched the smell I remembered when I first found *Librorum Taberna*. The tome's cover warmed to my touch. Silver-gold latches and corner enforcements flashed. Patina blotched the leather, adding a well-used appeal to the overall appearance. An ornate keyhole gaped in the center of the largest latch. Touching something so powerful, an object that could enable one person to accomplish the incredible realities I learned existed in the UK, was so very humbling.

"A clansman of mine brought me that book just before his death," Ezra said from behind me. "He'd been changed to a gargoyle, but I knew him as my nephew." He leaned in the doorway. "To head off a question before you draw air to inquire, I've grown tired, dear girl. These past centuries were my greatest trial." He stepped past the book and I to perch on the edge of my bed. White eyes watched me closely from above. "It's time for a change."

I returned my attention to the soft leather beneath my fingers, realizing I'd been petting the cover a little as he spoke. "It's beautiful," I admitted. "So the gargoyle died when he gave it to you?"

"He died as a *result* of giving it to me. He was convinced Kai was preparing to do something horrific. Being one of Kia's most trusted creations, he gained access to the book and ran to safety. He paid with his life and saved many." He dropped his gaze to his boots.

For a second I wanted to hug him because his heart remembered the hurt from so long ago.

"I performed many warding spells around the tome and have done my best to maintain them, to hold Kai at an arm's distance. Tis fortunate the book lets me open it. It doesn't take to everyone," Ezra watched me caress the warm leather. He sighed softly. "It was only a matter of short time before you found it. Or it found you, rather. Kai knows this. He sees the same potential in you as I. I made it available to you in hopes of explaining it to you before you learned about it otherwise."

"It locks," I baited.

"The keyhole is only a representation. The tome can either

remain sealed or be cracked open. When the book is held, it senses the things it craves."

"It's so warm." I reached for the corner of the cover.

Ezra stilled my motion with one of his boney, gnarled hands. "Ask yourself, Tessa Marie Conley, are you so comfortable with what life's become lately that you wish to endure more of the unknown?"

He seemed one hundred percent sure the book would open up for me. I hadn't been. I relaxed my hand. "So the book craves something inside me?"

"Think of it more as . . . it craves the potential with which you could use it. It craves a soul's ability to wield its powers."

I'd changed a lot lately. Done a couple things that didn't make me feel right about myself. If the book didn't distinguish between good and bad, just craved the user's ability, I might not be the best candidate to hold it. "Does that make me one of the good guys, Ezra?"

He threw his head back and laughed, heartily. Tears formed in his eyes. "Dear girl, you are, doubtlessly, the best of *guys*," he managed through his fit of hysterics.

Ezra was odd, but I was beginning to admire his quirks.

"Power corrupts the weak-hearted, Tessa. I have something for you." He out a leather scabbard. A jeweled knife handle protruded from the sheath. I took it with care, feeling the heavy weight of the weapon.

"Is it a dagger?" I grasped the handle and pulled the blade free. Fine metal chimed as the blade slid from the hardened, leather casing. Two strips of pliant rawhide hung from the top and bottom of the scabbard, to tie in place and conceal the weapon.

"Of sorts. It's a dirk. And a very sharp one."

I grinned. Ezra had handed over a book that could ruin the world with his total trust, but then warned me against cutting myself like I was a kid.

I held the gem encrusted handle up to the light. Green and

blue stones encircled a smooth ruby at the end of the handle. An inscription glinted on the blade but it was written in a language I'd never seen before. "What does this say?" I got up on my knees, holding the blade so Ezra could see the lettering.

"It's an old adage of the Gaels. It says 'When the sky falls, we'll make larks'."

That didn't sound nearly as cool as it could have. "I was expecting something like, about, well . . . something tough, you know?"

"It is one of the best to live by. It means, 'Always look for an opportunity to change things around, even when life crashes down around you.'" He smiled knowingly at me.

"When life hands you lemons, make lemonade."

"Precisely." He winked. "I couldn't think of a better suited owner for a weapon with such character."

"Thank you, Ezra." I continued to examine the blade, awed that he would give me something so precious.

"Don't be afraid to use it, Tessa. It's meant as protection. Wield it like it will save your life."

"I will." I pulled up the leg of my jeans and began tying the straps around my calf. The end of the scabbard rested perfectly against the inside of my shoe.

"That," he pointed a boney finger at the tome beside me on the carpet, "cares not about good or bad. It craves the ability of usage, not the directive. It senses an entity's ability to work its magic and it seeks a bond."

I looked back down at the huge volume. "It sees ability in me?"

"If it was my decision, if it was me in your shoes, I'd put that thing in a box, bury it, and never turn one page." Hindsight glittered in his eyes. The laughter was gone from his demeanor. There was no twist to his words that time. He was serious as death. "It will take a token payment for the ability to use it."

"A token?"

"Kai paid with his humanity. He was kind-hearted, a compassionate soul before he crossed paths with the book and its maker."

"What about you? You seem okay. I mean not all . . . evil." I acknowledged the new way I viewed Ezra with subtlety.

Ezra blinked at me with his pearl eyes, gesturing with one hand toward his face.

"Holy—," I whispered. "It took your eyes?"

"The book marked me, when it could have done much more."

Good enough for me. I pulled my hands away and stood.

"There's a special element to you, dear girl. Be warned. It can sense something in you just as surely as I."

We both stared as is if it was a sleeping crocodile.

"I'll load it in the car," he said, carrying the momentum to stash the book away again.

"We could get Peter do carry it down." Ezra's frail appearance worried me at times and besides that, I needed Peter to be able to see the thing.

"Peter won't see it. He wouldn't be able to hold onto it."

"The wards."

"Yes, and I've no intention of removing them."

"Please, Ezra? It would make me feel better if he could help out with it."

"No damned way."

I sighed. He was dead-set.

"Are you human, Ezra? I mean. . . ." He couldn't explain *me*, but the decision to ask about *him* suddenly seemed like a really bad idea. My words trailed off, reminding me of a fish out of water, flopping and fading in the sand.

"I am good, dear girl. I assure you, my humanity is intact, be it torn, weighed by centuries of existence and memories. Alas, I am just a man."

Ezra delivered the best thing he could've said. My chin quivered as I looked away. "I'm scared, Ezra. I feel like such a child."

"You're so much more, Tessa. Never doubt that. At times faith is all that is within reach. It may seem fleeting, but other elements merely stand in the way." He gave a smile. "Things fall apart." He laughed, ironically. "Faith remains."

How could he sound so sure, when I felt unsubstantial against the monstrous challenge that awaited my arriving with that book in Scotland? I did my best to convey some confidence despite the sick feeling in my gut. "I'll just have to see how persuasive I can be holding our book."

"Our?" One of his bushy eyebrows quirked.

"Well, it's certainly not Kai's."

CHAPTER 27

urned out, Ezra never had the intention of letting us take the book back to Scotland without him. He went downstairs, locked his skinny grip onto the handle of an oversized suitcase-on-wheels and loaded it in the trunk, right next to the book. He'd probably packed at the same time I was upstairs getting more clothes, after his conversation with Peter.

For the first time in several nights, Peter and I changed into gargoyles at *Librorum Taberna*. The trip back to The Grotto would have to wait until morning, but it was a small relief to know we wouldn't go crazy searching the store. We walked upstairs to the familiarity of our old bedrooms. My room was foreign in its familiarity, like it was so safe, such a sanctuary that it couldn't possibly belong in the dangerous mess my life had become. Not wanting to be alone and craving Peter's company, I asked him to stay with me until I wound down. We leaned back on the pile of pillows against the headboard of my bed. I curled close to him, laying my head on his plated chest, causing our human forms to become visible.

"Thank you, Peter."

"For?" He caressed my back and shoulders.

"So many things. The comfort. Sticking with me, I guess." I turned my head so I could look at him. "You make me feel like it's all going to be okay."

He watched me with lowered lids, making his eyes look black, devoid of the brilliant grey I loved. "It will be. Have faith in yourself."

I shook my head, watching my fingers trace the stitching on the comforter. "How can you say that? I feel like a complete jellyfish."

He laughed at that. "You have no idea how strong you are." He tipped my chin up. "You're amazing." His gaze travelled my face as he lowered his lips to brush with mine. "I would protect you with my life."

He deepened the kiss, pulling me closer. I wrapped my arms around his neck, pushing my fingers into his thick hair. I needed to be as close to him as I could get. One large, beautiful hand cradled the back of my head, letting my hair slip through his fingers, the other caressing the tender skin of my jawbone with a thumb. Sliding his hand forward on my chin, he parted my lips, tasting my tongue with his. My heartbeat began to race as I tilted my head, accepting him. Our bodies entwined tightly against one another. Warmth built in my chest along with a warning that it was time to stop. Peter's hand smoothed down the back of my arm. My skin flushed as heat broke free, surging through my veins. I stilled. If I heated up because of what he did to me inside, I didn't know what the outcome might be.

Peter broke the kiss gently, sliding back up on the bed. I rested my head against his chest, listening and feeling his heart pounding. "You all right?" he asked, peering down at me. He ran a hand through my hair, clearing it from my forehead, testing the skin there.

"I'm okay." I wrapped my hand in his shirt. "Just got a little heated up, is all."

"Does this happen?"

"I've never done this before." I turned my face away, a little embarrassed.

"Tessa," he said, tipping my chin up. He was smiling. I couldn't help but smile back. "It bothers you more than it does me."

I pulled his hand close, placing a kiss in his palm.

"We should get some rest," he said.

"Okay, I replied, secretly grateful. My thoughts whipped around like they blustered inside a wind tunnel. I still had to get Brea to safety. Ensuring Kai didn't get his hands on the book would not be easy. I wanted to work on a plan, but found myself too exhausted to think clearly. My eyes threatened to stay closed each time I blinked.

I WOKE up as dawn broke, feeling like I'd run a marathon rather than slept. Peter was gone. I was up and dressed fast, nervous energy speeding me through a quick rendition of my morning routine. I twisted my hair into a messy bun, brushed my teeth and went straight out to the car to wait for Peter and Ezra, but they were already getting settled for the ride. We locked up and left quickly.

Ezra sat shotgun, pushing buttons and singing along to songs he knew, dialing a new station the second something started playing that he didn't like. The interior of the car became entirely too hot as a result of the passing hours with Ezra over-adjusting the heater, and Peter looked like he may snap the next time he was told to keep both hands on the wheel.

The whole way to Kelty I would have preferred to sprout wings out of my hiney and fly, rather than spend one more second in the back seat. I tried sleeping but the antics in the front wouldn't let that happen. I turned my attention out the window to help bide time.

Rays of sunshine rebelled against thin clouds to streak the day with shafts of enthusiastic gold light. Even through the tint of the car windows Peter's dark hair shone with metallic grey and silver-streaked black. His hands bunched with network muscle of charcoal and dark sinew as he used one hand to drive and the other to pull a hood over his head.

We hadn't worried about sunlight at the bookstore. Other than the front, the place had few windows, so we were kept out of natural light and looked human during the day. Out in the open, even in a car we showed our changes. I was confined in my own skin, finding one more way I was imprisoned in my world. I hunched in my seat, twisting a thick strand of hair in and out of a sunray, watching it turn from honey blond to grey and silver. I slid lower to hide from the sun completely. The act was polar to my nature as a sun worshiping Austinite.

Uncomfortable and too anxious to hold still, I scooted far left on the backseat and jerked up my hood. I reached for the window controls and let fresh, cool air buffet my face since we rode on the outside of the traffic. Rolling green raced by outside, broken up by occasional farm houses or barns.

Peter adjusted the rear view mirror so I was in his line of sight. I maintained eye contact, my gaze pleading, telling him things from my soul, about how my greatest fear was failing. How I needed him by my side, and how sorry I was for doubting him. He winked from deep beneath the fabric of his hood, watching me a moment longer before his gaze moved back to the road ahead. He urged the car forward, releasing the horses beneath the hood, sending them racing through the miles. The sooner we made it to Kelty, the more daylight we'd have to work with.

And the fewer "other" gargoyles we'd have to work against.

Worry about Brea and my decision to try to trick Kai twisted my nerves into a screaming network of stressed-out anxiety. I fidgeted with the seatbelt and watched the miles tick by on the gauge in the cockpit. "What-if" scenarios paraded through my imagination like Heffalumps in one of Winnie the Pooh's nightmares. I was a wreck. Taking a long, exhausting run sounded better then, than any other time before. I hated it, but my mind kept returning to my pact with Kai, and all the ways it could be made better. He could get hit by a bus, for instance. Game over. Deal's off.

Kai had given our bargain some serious planning, as far as time was concerned. We were given two days to get back to his place with the book. A good portion of that time was spent on the road.

We were over half way there and I was doing my best to come up with a plan. I wasn't equipped to bargain for the life of another person, let alone my best friend, with a tool that could end the world as we knew it.

As if sensing my mental wheels spinning in the seat behind him, Peter spoke up, frustration heavy in his tone. "This whole thing would be a lot less complicated if I could help with that damned book. I say the wards are taken off. Kai will know we've brought it back with us anyway." He turned toward Ezra on the seat beside him. "I can't even *see* the bloody thing."

"Taking down the wards would be devastating to us, once we arrive," Ezra said.

"Isn't there some way you could make wards that only worked on Kai and his groupies?" I sounded naïve, but it needed asking.

"Wards do not work that way," he responded.

I kind of felt like that might be a half truth, but didn't want to start off arguing. "So basically, when we get there, we can put the thing wherever we want and Kai will have no idea where it is?"

"Precisely. We must take advantage of any opportunity to stay a step ahead of him." Ezra twisted on the seat, looking at me.

"We put it inside the grotto." I didn't have a clue how to get it there, but it seemed like a logical answer. "Ezra could take it down there, which works because Kai won't expect him to be with us and we won't have to worry about gargoyles." I slid forward on the seat. I didn't mention how Petra told me Kai avoided Tyrens like the plague. We needed every advantage we could muster, and placing the book in the grotto might throw him off a little.

Ezra continued. "I will be hidden from sight while I carry the book, although the second I no longer have it in my hands, the wards will let me be seen. I lack the skill to cast shroud over myself. I'll use the wards to conceal my body."

I leaned close to Peter. "Well, that's something at least. So, when we get there, I go get Kai and tell him the book is in the cavern. Ezra will be hidden down there and between the two of us, we can use the element of surprise and ambush him. While we're doing that, you go find Brea. We meet back at the car after we each complete our part of the plan and we drive home. I mean to the bookstore."

My words came rapid-fire, reminding me of either Alvin, or another of the Chipmunks. I chewed my bottom lip. It would be really, really great if Kai would just go down to the cavern to get his book. That easy. Nobody else in the car said anything. Peter had quite the job to do locating Brea, but he was most familiar with the manor. Ezra would have a big challenge making it back to hide in the car until we were together and ready to escape.

"I'm taking Petra out of there with us." Peter said from the front seat.

"Of course," Ezra confirmed.

"Sounds like a plan." I tried to sound sure of myself despite the sense that something was going to go horribly wrong.

"Faith," Ezra reminded.

I took a deep, steeling breath. "We got this." *Buckle up . . . It's going to be a train-wreck.*

CHAPTER 28

*I*n another life I would've considered the town of Kelty, Scotland completely charming.

The sun was shining as we passed through so we had the tinted windows up. I fought the urge to lean against the glass to read the names of the shops along Main Street. I could see myself traumatizing small children by pressing my transparent-skinned face to the window as we drove through town like a freakish float in a Dias de los Mortos parade.

Ensconced against the leather, I hid myself from view beneath my hoodie. Peter steered the car by gripping the bottom of the wheel so his hands weren't in view. Ezra peered out his window with the gusto of a six-year-old whose parents had just pulled the family car into a parking spot at Disney Land.

The right turn onto Black Road took us toward Loch Ore, which we skirted with the solemnity of a funeral procession. I'd begun reading every road sign I could see miles ago to try to keep my senses. Pent up, anxious energy made it hard to sit still. I sat forward on the seat, close to Peter's back.

"Do you know where to look for Brea?" I broke the silence, but didn't really want to. I was still a little doubtful of the success of our plan. People ate other people out there.

"I've a fairly good idea she'll be close to Petra's room in the house. Kai will have Petra watching her."

"Well that would make things easier," I told him, softly.

"I imagine you'll have an easy time getting Kai to follow you into the cavern." His words were clipped, tidying up a loaded statement into an efficient little jab.

"That was a little terse, don't ya think?" He'd sounded down-right pissy.

"Just stating the obvious." He didn't look at me.

"Do you have a better idea?"

"No, and that's why this whole thing is so bloody pitchy." He sighed. "I don't want the bastard touching you."

"I know, Peter."

"I don't think you've a good grasp of how bad this could get."

"Let's just stick to the plan. Ezra takes the book into the cavern, you find Brea and Petra, I get Kai down in the hole, we ambush him, we wait for each other at the car," I huffed and shook my head. "We sneak in and we sneak out. It's mechanical, like a play-by-play."

Peter knew the countless ways it could go wrong as surely as I did. I wondered if he had scenarios playing through his head like vignettes inside a haunted house, too. I glanced at Ezra, who remained quiet. Who could guess what was going through *his* mind. Sweat ran inside my hoodie. My knees bounced with my emotions, jittering my frame on the seat.

"Don't make it a habit to kill my boys." Kai's voice played in my mind through a decrepit phonograph. There were touchy elements to each of our parts.

"What about Osgar and his friends? Won't they want to help defeat Kai?"

"Osgar would be more than willing to help get rid of Kai. They're held in check by threats against the lives of remaining kin. I've watched over the centuries as the clan has dwindled in numbers. Now they stay and do Kai's bidding to preserve what's left, lest Kai kills off more."

"Why has Kai kept them alive this long?" Crappy question, but I needed to know what was going on. The whole story.

Ezra turned to face me. "He would have done away with the whole clan, but for the brave soul who stole that book and brought it to me that day, centuries ago. Kai couldn't make any more gargoyles after that, so his plans were cut short."

"It's the book that makes gargoyles. Not Kai. And not you, either." My statement was met with silence. The will of the user made the book a weapon in the same sense as any other weapon verses the whim of the one wielding it. I let my point rest, moving on. "So the only thing keeping Osgar and the others alive for the past thousand years is you keeping the book hidden."

"Kai can't see it when it's warded. Neither can Hamish or any of the others. Kai is a master at manipulating people. Just look at how fast he was to find a way to get you to retrieve the book for him." Ezra looked out his window, frowning. "When he found that you are somehow immune to most magic, he kidnapped your friend."

"Don't you feel better knowing we're not alone in this? Because I do."

"No one else knows we're headed back with the book," Peter reasoned.

"Why don't you guys carry cell phones?" A gusty sigh accompanied my words.

Peter and Ezra exchanged puzzled glances.

"There's likely no cellular service out that far," Peter said, at last. "I'll get Brea to the car first, then go back for Petra if I don't find her along the way." The car continued forward at a slow pace. Peter was giving us time to sort out the last bits of the plan before we got out. "And how will you ensure Kai buys in?"

"Well he won't know where his book is without me showing

him, right? I mean, because of the wards?"

"Yes." Ezra agreed.

"Then he'll have to go down there to get it." I felt the outline of the dirk along my calf. "The first he can see of me will be when I come out of the stairs, because he'll think I carried the book into the cavern, not Ezra. I'll need to be quick."

I glanced at the feeble looking man in the front seat. Hopefully Kai would never even know Ezra was there.

I didn't see Ezra as the cruel sorcerer I had before. The psychotic edge had faded from my impression of him. He was still quirky and downright odd, but those things endeared him to me. Living for so long had taken a toll on the man. He struggled for sanity, often reverting to childish behavior, almost like an odd form of senility.

"Ezra, why are you risking Kai getting his book just to help me save Brea?" The question had been bothering me. Brea and I were only two people. If Kai got control of his book, the two of us would be two small casualties in a world of chaos.

"Tessa." Peter gave me a stern look in the rear view.

"Well seriously, Peter. Think about it. It's like the good of the many should be way more important than just us two."

He looked away.

"This has gone on long enough," Ezra stated. "This life has exhausted me and taken too big a price from my kin." He looked down at his clunky boots. "You've given me hope that we will come out victorious."

I wasn't much to get one's hopes up over. Tessa Conley was just a girl in a world of beasts.

We pulled onto the winding drive toward The Grotto. I dropped my hood since we were out of sight of anyone who might need therapy after seeing my thin-skinned, sinewy face in the sunshine. Peter pulled the car off the road and popped the trunk so Ezra could retrieve the book. We all got out. I needed to stretch my legs desperately.

"Ezra?" Peter said.

"Tessa, tell him I'm beside the door here."

"He's back up here," I told Peter. *Wow.* It hadn't occurred to me that Ezra wouldn't be seen *or heard* by anyone but me when he was wrapped in the wards surrounding the book. "This is going to be interesting."

"I'm going to take the book into the cavern. You can lead Kai to it, although he won't see it until he can find a way around the wards. That should be the end."

The end. At that point Ezra would be a target to Kai and his "boys" as he called them, until he made his way back to the car. I forced thoughts of a bad ending from my mind. We would all meet back at the car. No one would be hurt. I had to keep my glass half full or I'd go crazy.

Peter looked across the car at me, worry etching his dark features. A low breeze caught his long ebony hair, scattering it in a rich cascade over his jaw and neck. The effect against his silver-grey eyes and transparent skin was amazing. He looked more *savage* than *horror*, more otherworldly god than beast. I really wanted to feel the security of being tucked away in his arms one more time before we parted, but it would be incredibly awkward with Ezra standing there with us. I stared back, trying my best to hold my ground against the urge. We didn't have a lot of time as things stood.

I turned to Ezra, trying to emit confidence I wish I owned. "Here goes."

"Not to worry, I'll be right back with you, dear girl." He looked over at Peter and was quiet for a long moment. "Tell Peter I'll see him soon, please. And that I controlled what he read in an attempt to make him forget, even after he requested I stop. He'd been through so much when I found him and his sister. Then she was taken away. I thought it best. I apologize if I was wrong." He opened his mouth as if to say something else, but changed his mind. Instead, he shut the car door.

Ezra walked into the trees, large boots clomping through brush and leaves. His white hair waved with his steps, stark in the dark cover of forest.

I leaned my elbows on the car and looked at Peter. "He said he'll see you soon, and that he was trying to protect you by choosing what you read, so you wouldn't be sad. He wanted you to be happy, so he let you read things he thought wouldn't remind you of the past."

He stared quietly ahead into the lush forest and ivy.

"He'll be okay Peter, don't worry." I added. I reminded myself of a cheerleader, rooting for a team constantly on defense. *Go team, go.*

I swallowed hard as warmth hatched in my chest. Eerily, a small part of me was looking forward to an altercation ahead. I'd warmed to the rush of bloodshed, before guilt set in. That made me wonder just who—or what I'd become. At least before then I could identify with myself, knew the hand I'd been dealt. Everything was switched. I sighed loudly in a shaky rush. Peter glanced at me.

"I don't know what's wrong with me," I said, feeling a flood of tears behind my eyes. "I mean shouldn't I be scared to face a monster that could potentially ruin parts of the world? I'm worried about losing Brea and your sister, but I'm not scared of being hurt or killed. And I should be." I jammed my fingers into my hair, rubbing my temples. "I don't know how to explain it, but it's almost like I'm looking forward to the confrontation with Kai." I wiped my face on the sleeves of my hoodie. I'd never been one to thrive on conflict. "I think something went wrong with me, or got turned loose when I killed that guy."

"Something is different in you," he said, nodding. "But that's not necessarily the worst thing. It's good you don't want to run from a fight, yes? You've got a bit of steel to you, Miss Conley." Peter nodded with a tight-lipped smile. "Not that I'm in love with the idea of you being in the same room with that . . . Kai." He eyed the roof of the car as he spoke. "Be careful, Tessa," he looked into my eyes. "Just do what you have to and get to the car. If I'm not there, Brea will be and I'll be right along with Petra."

"I don't love the thought of you being hurt, either."

Our gazes locked, loaded silence carrying thoughts that neither of us was ready to say.

"I'd better head out before I lose Ezra."

"Keep at a run." His words were selective. My battered emotions basked in the knowledge that he was in my corner, that I was not alone. That he cared about me and whether I continued in life.

I turned in the direction Ezra had taken into the trees and broke into a fast run through the underbrush, dodging low branches and skirting outgrowths of ivy and brush. I stretched out my legs and pounded the soft forest floor as I sprinted. I caught up with him easily, just as he came to a crouch behind an outcropping of the ruined castle proper. The grounds were in plain view.

I fidgeted in place, rocking on my feet. "I'm going to wait till I hear Peter pull up before I come out of the stairwell. The car should get Kai's attention."

"We've got this." Ezra winked.

I couldn't help laughing a little. He'd said it, trying his best to mimic my casually drawled phrase by dropping his accent.

We walked to the edge of the jagged rock wall, joining hands so we were both hidden by the book's wards. I peeked around the edge. Not a soul was in the yard. The stairs to the cavern were close ahead, so Ezra would be down at his post in plenty of time.

I closed my eyes. *Please, please let this work.*

I breathed in my resolve as we stepped around the rock wall and walked toward the stairway. We were both far too nervous to talk.

The plan was in motion.

CHAPTER 29

*E*zra left me to descend the stairs into the cavern. I waited a few moments a couple steps down, listening hard for the sound of the Aston Martin to pull up next to the garage and hoping I encountered no one on the stairs. When tires sounded on gravel, I started out of the stairwell toward the house. I opened the front door and made it inside when I saw Kai stalk into the foyer. Just like I'd thought, he eagerly waited at the front stoop after seeing Peter show up with the car.

"I assume since I can see you, you've relieved yourself of my book, Tessa. Where is it?" His eyes narrowed on me.

"Carrying it around made me feel jittery, so I stashed it."

"Where?" he asked, tight lipped.

"I figured down by the baths would be a good place. I mean, that's where you left me for safe-keeping when I tried to escape." I couldn't help getting a little smart-assery in. I was still angry he'd left me down there so long.

"That's ridiculous. You could have brought it straight to me."

"As if I knew where you'd be or something. I sort of expected you to be waiting by the garage or at the front door. I didn't see you, and I thought it would be a good idea to hide it. I don't know all the rules with those ward things. Someone, or something out here could have seen that book the second I took it out of the car." I'd never hoped to sound stupid before, but that time, I prayed I appeared dumb as a brick.

"If you're attempting to deceive me, your friend will pay the price," he warned.

A twinge of intimidation bit at me. Neither of us doubted how he would murder another person. That was a kind of understanding I never thought I'd have with someone. "Come, Tessa. There's something I want you to see," he said, gesturing to the door outside.

Worry carved into my face and I tried to relax the muscles of my brow. It was like knowing I'd wiped paint on my cheek but couldn't do a measly thing about it until I could get to a mirror. Donning a poker face in the same room as Kai was a trick.

"I'm fine here, thanks," I answered, calmly.

"I insist." Kai grasped my arm above the elbow and drug me down the long set of steps to the front yard. "There, you see?" He pointed to a wrought iron balcony, backed by a set of glass French doors. Brea stood in plain sight through the windows. Kai waved and one door swung wide. She was shoved onto the landing. A man who was at least six inches shorter than she was stepped out behind her, tossing and catching a small dagger. Sun glinted off the blade each time it caught air before he'd catch it with a quick hand and sent it flipping up again. The man smiled down at me with the kind of grin I associated with a psychopath. And a murderer. His features were blackened beneath transparent skin, muscle and sinew pulling tight with each movement of his face, arms and hands. One hand rested on Brea's elbow and when he saw I was watching he began to caress the skin of her arm.

Brea jerked away, keeping her eyes locked on me. Her captor snarled, white teeth gleaming inside blackened gums and lips. He grabbed her again, shaking her elbow hard. She stumbled backward.

"There's something more assuring in older forms of insurance, don't you agree?" Kai looked down his shoulder at me.

I met his gaze. "I just want you to know that if that sawed-off little bastard hurts my friend, I'll burn this place to the ground." I didn't blink, and neither did he. "And I'll make sure you're in there with him." We continued to stare for a few moments longer.

I'd never spoken in such a way to anyone, but Kai. The first time had been when he insisted that one day I'd love him and I told him I would never. I really hoped he didn't doubt my conviction. Because I didn't.

"The beauty of this, Tessa," he said, "is that soon, you'll give me what's mine, and I will change your mind about the whole situation." He pulled me toward the stairs leading down to the grotto. I looked over my shoulder one last time at Brea and the psycho. She stood still beside him, a picture of stagnant emotion. Kai jerked me hard by an elbow, crushing my arm and making me stumble against him, reminding me how tall and strong he was. We crossed the yard and started down the winding stairs, descending into the room that held the key to the end of things in the world, or else the end of my best friend.

* * *

NOCTURNAL HUMANS DOZED on chaises and chairs, sleeping the day away in preparation for nightfall when the party would start again. I scanned the place, looking for Ezra and found him waving me forward, book in hand. Kai continued after me, unable to see Ezra, staying close because he trusted me about as much as I trusted him.

Ezra sat the book on a table beside a large chair, making sure I was watching his motions. One hand remained on the cover, keeping him out of sight.

"Where is it?" Kai was losing patience. He grabbed my shoulders, spinning me to face him. "Give me what's mine, right this moment or I might do something you won't enjoy," he warned. He shook me hard for emphasis.

"It's over there," I gritted. "On that table." I pointed in Ezra's direction best I could with him gripping me so hard.

He released my shoulders in exchange for a wrist, dragging me as he stalked toward the table. Ezra was nowhere that I could see, having left the safety of the tome's wards to stash himself away somewhere. Not seeing Ezra made me panic. I struggled against Kai's grip, forcing him to pull me along as we came nearer.

"Put your hand on it so I can see it," he commanded.

"W-what?" That would be a show-stopper. Our plan didn't contain steps that read "What to do if psycho gets his book back".

"Bring me inside the wards so I can take the bloody things off or I won't be able to see it," he snarled. "Put a hand on it *now*." He squeezed the delicate bones in my wrist, forcing me to cry out. I nearly went to my knees in pain.

"Okay!" I cried. He released the pressure. I sent my free hand slowly questing toward the leather cover.

Beyond where the book rested on the table, a face formed in the water. The features of the female Tyren who'd saved me came into view. She rose from the surface with fluid silence. A watery finger pressed to her lips in a universal gesture to remain silent. I didn't see what she could possibly do to help the situation, being made of water. And besides that, she was about twenty-five feet away from us. I was losing hope. She continued to materialize, a transparent, glistening form above the surface. Water surged, trapped beneath her skin, like a see-through pot full of boiling water. My heart raced as I watched my shaking hand touch the book.

Kai saw the leather tome on the table that instant. His face lit up, a kid at Christmas. It was over. We'd lost. I'd sealed our fates by giving him sight of his tool of devastation.

For a split second he smiled.

His grin faded when Peter hit him with the spirit of a professional linebacker, running hard and sending them both to the ground with a series of *smacks* as solid bone met the hard tile. My wrist popped loose of Kai's grip as they went down. The two tumbled, throwing punches and grappling. Peter landed a mean sounding hook to Kai's chin. Both men regained footing, slugging it out. Peter hit Kai's torso hard, his upper body tight with bulging muscle that sent his fists pounding like steel. Kai swung back at the perfect moment, catching Peter straight on, splitting open his bottom lip, sending him spinning to the floor. Peter was on his feet quick as Kai advanced and the two went at it again, striking each other with vicious, horrible sounding blows, with rage finally released after more than a century of hatred churned and grew for the other.

The sound of boiling water erupted as the Tyren drug herself forward with her arms, the rest of her body trailing in a malformed pool of transmuting limbs and faces. She wrapped her arms around the men, taking them down.

"No! Peter!" I screamed. They continued to thrash, coated with water that clung to their bodies rather than falling away with gravity. I lunged forward, intent on grasping onto him somehow to free him from the Tyren's grip. I grabbed him around the waist, ducking blows from Kai and pulling Peter back as hard as I could.

"Let go Tessa, before you get yourself hurt," Peter growled.

I held fast, feeling water hesitate for a second, as if it was repelled by my touch. Peter and I fell backward, free of the Tyrens as they covered Kai's thrashing body.

"Are you okay?" Peter was on his feet in an instant, pulling me in front of him, checking my wrist and scanning my face. His nose bled a little from one side, adding to the stream from his lip. A long, angry scratch ran the length of one side of his neck. He panted, turning my face in his hands, searching for any sign of injury.

"What are you doing here?" I felt like crying. If he was in the cavern, no one was getting Brea away from the psycho with the knife.

"You shouldn't have believed for one second I'd leave you on your own down here. I found Osgar and he knows where Petra is," he said, nodding down at me.

"What about Brea? This nut with a knife has her!"

"They're going to get her," he said, turning to look at Kai and the Tyren.

Kai wasn't going down without a fight. He growled and flung his arms to get free, managing to make it to his feet, dragging the liquid form up with him. The water-being's multiple faces melted away into a sack of bubbling, churning liquid.

"Holy hell," There was more than one Tyren in the pool that escaped the stream. They'd clung together somehow. As Kai stood, more Tyrens materialized, breaking off from the main body. They wrapped themselves firmly around each part of him as if translucent anacondas decided to work together to take down a gorilla.

Kai glared at Peter. "You," he spat. He eyed me, huddled, tiny beside Peter. Kai's eyes softened, rage deserting him and leaving nothing but sorrow.

I knew it for what it was; a mixture of heartbreak and resignation. He'd missed me and he'd never stop. Mistakes were made, recognized. His face held an apology. "Remember," he whispered.

Each syllable of the word resonated inside me. My ears buzzed as it sounded again and again. I stumbled forward, gripping my head. Kai's face floated in my mind's eye. I stood in front of him, reaching up to caress his cheek with my hands. He caught one and placed a kiss in my palm. I grew warm, enjoying the contact with him, knowing we'd done it before, just like that, hundreds of times. From a haze, I was aware that Kai struggled for breath. He called for me. I had to save him. . . .

I spun on Kai and the Tyren, reaching, with intentions of

prying the bitch off him. I couldn't let him be killed. We were to be together. Just as my hand touched a watery arm, something hit me from the side, cradling me tight and drove me straight toward the stream. I thrashed as I sank deep, touched down on the riverbed and shot forth, up and out of the water. I floated to the floor.

A Tyren lay on the bank, feeble from attempting to take me down. His essence leaked around him as he tried to hold form. I bent, sending a fist through his chest. Water exploded around my arm and he was gone.

"Tessa!" Peter called for me as I stalked back toward Kai. "Tessa, stop.

I turned to him, shaking, water steaming away from me. I looked at my hands. I'd killed again.

"Tessa? Can you hear me?"

I nodded as tears cascaded onto my cheeks.

"Come away from the water," Peter said.

That sounded like a good idea. I ran to him. "I killed him," I said, hating myself a little bit more.

"It's going to be alright."

Kai thrashed in the Tyren's grip. Watery arms gripped his shoulders, stilling him. His eyes shot wide and he grew quite, jaw snapping shut.

Everything just *stopped*. No sounds of struggle. No gushing mineral stream. The baths rested unmoving, mirroring the celling of the cavern like glassy lakes at sunrise. Kai no longer flailed to be free of the Tyrens and they ceased moving around him. Foreboding hung in the sulfur-laced air like a black veil.

The Tyrens seemed to shrink. I thought maybe there was only a certain amount of time they could stay out of the stream without evaporating.

Kai's face began to bulge in places as if tumors grew in seconds under his skin. On his neck and hands, flesh seemed to develop sagging cysts where soft tissue gave way. His body began to tremble as all parts of him swelled and skin gained impossible elasticity. His eyes rolled to the ceiling as blood and clear fluids began to ooze from the orifices on his face and ears, then leak from his fingernails.

The Tyrens were nearly invisible against his skin, deflated to a shimmering coat of moisture that clung like spray lacquer.

"Ugh," I said in disbelief. The Tyrens pushed through the pores in Kai's skin. His entire body was completely filled with water. A *lot* of it. I couldn't imagine what that felt like. I shuddered.

Silence gave way to sounds of cloth tearing and membrane separating from muscle and tissue.

I took the first tentative step backward.

Kai's head rocked back and his jaw fell open as a geyser of water spewed forth. Blood pooled in each pore of his skin, soon coating him in crimson. I wondered how much more his body could stand just as water split through the softer parts of his form, starting with the thin flesh beneath his arms, under his eyes, and neck.

A *pop* sounded. All the water found its way out. Simultaneously.

I averted my face a beat before I was pelted with things ranging from blood and liquefied bone, to bile and off-colored water. I cried and jumped back, but it was too late. My body was covered with fluids. Had I not turned my head at the right moment, my face would have been plastered, too. Luckily, there was so much water mixed in, that other things sloughed off me, but they still left disgusting trails of goo that smelled worse than anything I'd ever encountered. I took off running and threw up with gusto.

The sound of the stream moving overtook the grotto in seconds. My heart pounded in my ears. I glanced at Peter through watering eyes.

"Aw," he said. "Damn." He flung his hands hard toward the

floor, dispelling clinging streams of flesh. Multihued blobs of gook clung to his shirt and dripped from his soaking hair.

I gagged.

He looked over at me, instant worry crossing his features, even though he was just as covered in crap as I was. He began wiping at my clothes to help get it all off, but when he touched it, the fluid pressed through the cloth, coming into contact with my skin. I continued to retch, turning away and waving him off.

After a few moments, I was able to approach him again, although my eyes watered and nausea rested at the back of my throat.

Peter reached slowly to brush at my shoulder, picking my hair out of solidified chunk of matter there. "You have a little bit of . . ." he trailed off, still wiping at me.

"Ewwww! I have Kai on my shoulder?" I shuttered. I felt like I was going to cry, wanting to sprint in circles to try to control the panic in my chest.

"Go straight to the car," he said.

All I could do was nod, which I did, enthusiastically.

The gold torc Kai had worn boiled to the surface of the water. Peter bent to retrieve it, turning the precious cuff in his hand. The finality of what happened began to settle.

"Best go," he said, gesturing toward the stairs.

I did as he said, so numb from the shock of what I'd seen that I didn't really feel the gooey way my clothes clung to my legs as I stepped.

"What about you?" I called to him.

"I'll get the humans out of here and meet at the car. Leave. Now Tessa," he urged.

I sprinted up the stairs into the afternoon sun.

The sound of gushing water roared from the grate-covered hole over the cavern. Electricity popped as if lightning struck. I was certain I'd just heard the stream break free, overflowing the rocky bed holding it in place below ground. A crystalline geyser exploded upward in the courtyard, topping the bars of the grate and began flooding the grass, gushing onto the grounds.

I was disoriented, standing in plain daylight, covered with things I didn't want to think about, watching a small typhoon erupt from a hole in the grass like a water-filled volcano. Faces formed in the swirling geyser but they were Tyren's I'd never seen before.

I searched the balcony, but saw no trace of Brea. A crumpled form lay beneath the wrought iron railing, blackened skin visible in the waning sunlight. Someone had rescued her. I rejoiced with a couple excited hops before I found my senses.

Stick to the plan. Ezra words shot through my mind. I turned toward the garage and ran to where we'd agreed to meet. I dove behind the car, out of view of the house. I hoped Osgar was able to find Brea and Petra and that I saw Ezra appear soon. I fought the urge to run to the house and look for the others, but I knew that could cause problems if I was seen by Hamish or another of Kai's lackeys. I stayed put with the worst of scenarios playing through my imagination, stretching the minutes into what seemed like hours as I waited for anyone else to show up. Daylight would be scarce soon. I couldn't stand the smell of my skin and clothes. I fought the urge to retch.

The sound of many pairs of feet pounding gravel grew louder by the second. The humans that slept in the cavern sprinted past me, down the drive in various stages of undress. Peter had apparently sobered them up and put the fear of a higher power into them because not a single one looked back as they ran out of sight, toward Kelty.

Time dragged on painfully as I waited for someone else to meet me. I had a clear view of the outer courtyard wall where the flow of water crashed against stone, churning back onto itself in a frothy tube. The fledgling current roared with new life, carving a new bed, disappearing into the forest beyond the driveway. I worried the cavern had been flooded far too long to support life. There was still no sign of Ezra.

I fidgeted anxiously, watching as the afternoon sun waned.

Something was wrong. No longer able to wait, I stepped out from between the car and the wall, ready to sprint toward the house to help Peter find Brea and Petra. It was going to be dark soon, and I didn't want to think about what would happen when the grounds crawled with gargoyles.

A man I'd never seen before watched me rise from beside the Aston. He'd been heading from the direction of the house toward the stairs leading to the underground baths, likely to investigate the eruption of mineral water. I'd stepped from the safety of the car with impeccably bad timing.

We stared at each other, both a little shocked.

Please be a good guy. . . .

"Ah the girl prodigy. I suppose you're behind this," he gestured to the flooding yard and rushing, detoured stream, stepping toward me.

I instinctively stepped back. Something about him was hard to read. He wasn't acting all that friendly, but he hadn't threatened my life, which gave him at least one point on the "good guy" board. He spoke distinctively British, what the Scots would consider a "lowlander". The skin of his face was dirty against a frame of greasy, dishwater hair. He wore a motley blend of modern clothing that could use a good laundering.

"What the hell happened to you?" he asked, curling his lip in disgust.

I found that terribly ironic coming from a guy who looked like he made a home in a Dumpster. I could just shower and change clothes. That guy needed to be boiled, bleached and spend a couple days with a dentist who had a hammer and chisel.

He made a grab for my elbow, but I dodged it.

"Come on then, Kai will be looking for you."

Not so much, I thought. I backed up against the wall of the garage, not sure where to go. His possible "good guy" point was revoked.

A quick check of my options to bail myself out came back entirely lacking. I pushed away from the wall to sprint toward the house and find Peter, hoping to be able to outrun the nasty guy. He didn't look too healthy so I thought maybe I'd be faster. My foot caught on something and I hit the gravel so hard my neck popped with the force of impact. Air left my body, locking my lungs. A deafening siren shrilled in my head while lights flashed, outlining objects in my view.

The grungy guy yanked me off the ground by the back of my soiled hoodie.

"Where you off too so fast?" He pulled me to standing with a huge, yellowed smile. "Can't have you running away. Let's go have a look at what you've done," he gritted.

I did my best to shake him off but he hung onto the fabric of my jacket tight with one hand. He laughed. I swung my elbows furiously to free myself. I couldn't let one guy and my inability to sit tight ruin the chances of us getting out of there. One elbow connected with his chest.

He grunted and stepped back, releasing my sweatshirt. Awkward silence grew between us while the fact that I'd struck him registered. He swung fast, slapping me across the face so hard I spun and doubled over to keep my feet. My jaw exploded with stinging pain. Blood dripped from the tip of my nose to the gravel and the stained net toes of my Asics. He hit me in the back of the neck, taking me to my knees. I fell onto my side, hoping he wouldn't do anything else so I had a second to recover. Running away wasn't going to work.

He paced a tight arc around me against the wall of the garage.

I lay curled in a ball, ragged breath dragging blood into my mouth. My face throbbed. The shock of being tripped and landing so hard wore off quickly because of pain and fear. I felt along the inside of my shin for the dirk Ezra gave me. My hand worked quickly at the slimy leg of my jeans to slide the dagger from the sheath as if I rubbed a bruised shin. The knife slid free against my leg while I worked it lower, the blade poking at the top of my shoe. I curled up tighter and pulled it loose, gripping the jeweled handle tight.

He was going to have to come down to get me. I waited.

My nose still bled a little, but adrenaline was working for me. I could have been much worse off. That thought bolstered my determination.

"Get up." He kicked gravel, spraying me with small rocks.

I didn't.

"Get the bloody hell up right now," he growled. He grabbed the back of my hoodie again, yanking me upward.

I spun at him and stuck the blade into his arm twice with two quick jabs.

He stared wildly, as if he didn't believe I'd fight back.

I stuck the blade out again not really having a target in mind, retracting my hand and thrusting it out again and again, so fast it was a blur. I don't remember coming to my feet. A smile widened across my face, causing dried blood and goo to crack on my skin. I grabbed his shirt with my free hand to hold him up. His blood was all over both of us. He tried to run but I held him, catching a flailing arm so hard I felt the bone snap and pop up toward my palm.

"Please! Let me live," he said.

"Uh uh." I shook my head, incensed.

He wept but swung one last fist at me, popping my lip open.

Gotta take those shots while they're hot, buddy.

I stabbed my dirk deep into one kidney, realizing I laughed in a voice that sounded like it belonged to someone else, someone deranged. But there was no stopping. I had the same feeling when I fought off Brea's attacker that day fueling each strike of the dirk. I stood over him as he bled out. Gashes littered his torso, arms and face. At least his eyes were closed. My last victim's weren't.

I pulled my ruined hoodie over my head and left it inside-out, using it to wipe blood and goop from my face and hands. I wiped my dirk clean and sheathed it. My Smurfette t-shirt would have to do. Crouched once again behind the car, I waited, having learned my lesson about making myself seen.

The unmoving body beside me ran dry of blood.

What a cruel beast I'd become.

CHAPTER 30

*A*t least twenty minutes had passed since I'd seen Peter and Ezra. I remained behind the car, waiting. Surely Peter could have made it back with one, if not both Brea and Petra by then. The thought that Ezra could have drowned was something I wouldn't allow myself to entertain. The dead man beside me became morbid fascination, and the fact that I'd made him that way was seriously messing with my mind. Self-defense was a hard call when it felt good killing him.

I crawled forward and peeked around the car.

Ezra was there, making his way across the yard. I had no idea how he'd ended up in the courtyard and I didn't care, really. I was just happy to see him alive. The flow of water across the yard had stopped, so the soaked grounds glittered as if they'd been soaked with dew in the day's late sun.

Standing up so he could see me, I waved, grinning wide. I never thought I'd be so elated to see the old guy. Clouds flitted over the sun, pouting then bowing in the light, sending fleeting rays onto the yard. Sunshine glinted off Ezra's white shirt and yellowed hair. When he saw me, he began flipping a dagger in the air, and catching it over and over, smiling knowingly. He'd saved Brea. I beamed at him.

My smile faded. Hamish must have been waiting for one of us to show because the moment Ezra took the first step in my direction, he appeared from beside the house. Lethal sword in hand, he stalked Ezra with the stealth of an ancient warrior.

That's when it all slowed down. My heart sunk deep. I was helpless to save Ezra.

Time crept and silence took over as I pushed my arms into the air, waving furiously. Ezra carried the large book beneath one arm. A split second seemed to take a full minute. I yelled to him to run while I waited for one of my feet to hit the gravel in front of me and begin my sprint in his direction.

"Behind you, Ezra! Run!" I screamed so loud the words seemed inaudible.

Hamish approached Ezra too quickly. My feet finally pounded the ground. I grew closer to them. Crimson flooded Ezra's chest, giving way to blackened burgundy against the stark white of his linen shirt. Blood-streaked silver glinted in the sun, protruding brutally from his sternum. His smile faded, melting to an expression of shock. The blade jerked free. Ezra looked up at me with a resigned stare. His face took on relief, all too easily.

I screamed and time caught up.

My gaze followed the blade as Hamish pulled it free. Ezra's lips drew into a slow smile. I continued to sprint toward him, but the lines dividing him from his surrounding grew fuzzy and blended. He leapt straight up—*way* up, dropping the book, human form bending and shrinking, arms stretching at his sides. A shriek sounded across the courtyard as what was left of Ezra became a huge, white and grey owl, flapping its wings hard. The raptor was gone behind the standing stones in a moment. My hands fell limply to my sides as I watched him vanish.

Hamish yelled after Ezra, apparently feeling robbed.

Rage built inside me, surging lava replacing my blood. I slowed briefly, bent at the knee and removed my dirk from its leather holster and began to sprint straight at Hamish, racing as my inner fire ignited into a burst of hell-bent speed. He was going to pay.

Hamish stared at me, eyes growing wide at the speed of my approach. He dropped back on one foot, the other rested, cocked at the hip into a defensive pose. He leveled the sword in my direction.

A millisecond later I let the dirk fly in a white ray of light that erupted from my hand on release. The blade embedded to the hilt in Hamish's right arm. I continued to sprint, a short second later ripping the dirk free as I passed. I spun on him, standing face-to-face with an armed giant, David braving it with a dirk against a towering Goliath and claymore. A bad joke about bringing a knife to a gun fight came to mind, but I was small and *really* quick. And I'd surprised him. I grinned.

Blood pulsed from the wound gashing his biceps, but Hamish smiled. "What's that you've got there, lass? Looking for some taties to be peelin'?" One booted foot was placed in a cross-step in front of the other as he began to circle me.

Keeping my face to him, I wasn't willing to be hunted while standing still. Ezra's expression as he'd been run through was branded on my mind, tainting every action. I locked my eyes on Hamish's intent gaze and lunged forward, blind with anger, intending to put my blade through his ribs. The butt of his sword cracked across my cheek, spinning me away. I rolled from my knees to a crouch, blade held in one hand. Tears ran freely from my right eye. I blinked, trying to hold together against the ringing in my head and the numb sensation creeping across my face and jaw. I regrouped quickly but dizziness threatened to pull me down onto my butt. The blow had rocked me hard. I was far from all-powerful. Hamish was dangerous and I needed to remember I was just a little chick from Texas, no matter how pissed off I was. Speed was my only advantage and I needed to keep my eyes wide open.

Advancing with the opportunity, he swung the massive sword at my shoulders. I barely dodged it, spinning with my dirk, slicing upward and deep into his sword arm below the other wound. Dark blood spilled down his arm onto his leg like I'd torn open a sack of pus. The sword fell forward in his limp grasp. I'd cut deep enough to sever a tendon. Perseverance paid off a little but I was growing woozy from the strike to the head.

The world darkened as my right eye lost focus. I was badly injured and adrenaline gave way to the damage my body endured. The whole side of my face throbbed with heat. I backed away, trying to clear my senses. The anger that befriended me and made me stronger was abandoning me in the face of fear.

Clouds shrouded the sun once more, showing the scene for what it truly was; a bloodied giant of a man with a sword almost as tall as I was, towering over my small frame and preparing to kill me. There was irony in seeing how our blood matched crimson tones in the lack of sunlight.

Hamish reached with his other hand to grab the sword, the injured arm hanging lifelessly at his side, heart still pumping fluid from the gash. His long, matted hair was stuck to his arm and shoulder in places. He snarled.

"You die this day," he gritted.

"You're talking pretty tough for a guy with one freakin' arm." I might not be a big, bad, swordfighter, but I was a few other things. *Know your strengths.* I was tenacious, really pissy, in bloodlust, and a complete smartass. The bigger issue was I was punch drunk and injured badly. My head grew cloudier by the second. My right eye was in bad shape and continued to water. I wiped at the tears on my face, only to pull back a bloodied sleeve. I'd misjudged my injury. Seeing that much of my own blood staggered me.

Sensing another opportunity, Hamish came at me, a little slower with his off hand. I stepped out of the way while the clumsy swipe of his sword whooshed by, but lost my footing, going down hard. Trying to roll to my feet didn't work. As soon as

I got a foot under me I became so dizzy I went back to the ground. I tried again, doing my best to ignore fast spinning vertigo and ringing in my ears. The metallic taste of copper pennies crept into my mouth again. My hair clung in sticky strands to my neck and face. On my hands and knees, I kept one eye moving with Hamish.

He laughed, low and manically.

One more attempt to get up was stopped as he drove a knee into my side. Two quick pops spasmed through my chest before sharp pain seared my ribs and back. I took a blow to the face, either with a fist or the sword's handle again, I couldn't tell which. My body spun. A splintering sensation erupted inside my shoulder as I slammed down hard on my back. The world tilted and suddenly I weighed a ton.

Hamish ran his blade into the grass where he stood and walked toward me. He doubled over, lowering his face to mine. Sharp pain sliced through my shoulder, forcing a cry from deep in my chest. He held my dirk over my face, having removed it from my shoulder. I'd fallen on it.

"A warrior passes between worlds with no honor, being killed with his own blade," he told me.

I swallowed a mouthful of clotting blood, watching pleasure grace his face. He was going to end my life, and he was elated at the thought.

Of all the ways I thought I'd die, being stabbed by a psychotic gargoyle in Scotland would never be on the list, back at the beginning of summer. Everyone imagined how they might someday pass away, or possibly go out in a blaze of glory while enjoying their favorite extreme sport. I hadn't even begun to live yet. Fate played cruel tricks and I wanted to know why.

An ironic laugh escaped my throat, throwing me into a racking coughing fit. My breath was crushed inside my chest. I rolled to my side and spit blood. A pool had built up around my right eye and when I rolled to my left the blood ran into the only eye that wasn't swollen up. I flattened against the grass and used the one hand I could still move to wipe my left eye in an attempt to see.

The smile Hamish had been wearing was gone. All that was left on his face was monster and rage. He put the dirk to my throat, having waited until I could see so I could watch him kill me.

He didn't get that, too. I slammed my left eye shut, not wanting to give him the satisfaction of seeing my fear.

I waited to feel the blade slice through my neck, wondering if it was going to hurt to die.

Will my parents be waiting for me somewhere on the other side? And how will they know it's me? And Robbie, will he be there, too? Dressed in his Dress Blues, beautiful, like in his picture on the Thomlinson's wall? We'll be a family over there, on the other side. A conjured image of what my mom might have looked like smiled at me with the love I was sure could only come from a mother. She looked like me. My father grinned and put an arm across Robbie's shoulders. I smiled.

. . .

A feral scream drove the image from my mind. The blade never reached me. I pried my blood-crusted eyes open the best I could and saw bright sunshine where Hamish blocked it out before. A loud hissing, gurgling sound came from somewhere to my right.

Petra stood beyond where I lay, fists doubled on the hilt of Hamish's sword. I couldn't see Hamish anymore. I guessed Petra had killed him. *So sad for a "warrior" to pass, being killed with his own blade. . . .*

Pain coated every inch of my body but I was too weak to cry out as I rolled to my side to see what I'd missed when I'd drifted off. Many feet approached, beating the turf. Beside Hamish's severed head, just out of my reach, lay the large, gilded leather book.

I reached for it.

"Tessa, No!" Peter's voice sounded from somewhere behind me.

When did he get here?

My fingers grazed the comfort of soft leather. I scooted closer, using my good arm and one foot to propel myself.

Footsteps grew closer.

"Tessa!" Peter called again. He was close, but so were many others. A frantic feeling hung heavy in the courtyard. The sun was beginning to set. Soon gloaming would urge gargoyles from human forms. Terrible things would come about, with bloodshed, pain and centuries-old lust for power through battle.

"Something wicked this way comes."

The thought that I wouldn't be around to see the battle skipped through my mind like a smooth stone on a choppy lake. I couldn't get enough air in my lungs and I grew weaker, but I couldn't risk the book falling back into the wrong hands. The last few centuries of Ezra's life would have been in vain.

I pulled the book closer and felt its warmth push through my hand, coursing up my arm. Fear gave way to relief. My chest tingled and became lighter suddenly, and it was easier to breathe. I sat up as heat cascaded across my body into my wounded shoulder. My right eye gained focus as the heavy swelling lifted from my once shrouded eyesight. I jerked the book into my lap. Energy thrummed through my being in a rush of elation. I hugged it to my chest, realizing the familiarity I knew was innate. Things were as they should be. The book *belonged* in my hands, and although I didn't understand, it was the most incredible feeling of power. My senses roared to life, enhanced in the absence of physical pain. I was renewed.

Dried blood cracked on my face as I threw my head back and laughed.

Peter's face came into view as he reached for me. "Don't you do it," he yelled.

I opened the book.

CHAPTER 31

*T*he din quieted. I knew warmth and safety. They were my creation. All pain left me; my body was whole again and my soul light as the day I first knew sentience. No grass lie beneath me, I floated effortlessly and weightless. The air smelled sweet, like the hyacinths that grew in the yard behind the Home. I was calm, and not alone, seeing through the eyes of another who knew what it was to live out of reach of worldly anguish. She enjoyed a deity's perspective and shared with a generous heart.

We watched together, omniscience fused into one.

A child toddled on clumsy, soiled feet below, chasing a springing insect from clusters of blossoming gorse to thick banks of heather. Beads caught sunlight, gleaming from bound tips of her plaited hair. Giggles burst free and tiny hands clapped each time the cricket sprung to life, spreading delight far into the air, touching my heart. I craved more innocence, drifting close, keeping a distance so the precious scene would continue.

Thick Lycanthrope mingled through air sweetened by wildflowers near the squealing child, growing heavy, encroaching. I drifted lower, catching quadruped footfalls crackling downed leaves, bending brush against matted fur. The hunter's gut growled in anticipation. Earthen, biological nature ran a course of survival that I did not interrupt.

Disturbed once more, the cricket hopped away from a probing, curious finger. More spritely laughter danced to my senses. The wolf lunged.

So did I, admitting my growing weakness, my love for innocent mortals. What was done, was done. Soft grasses broke underfoot when I stepped forth, taking mortal form as my essence made contact with carbon-borne earth.

The wolf's wet nose sizzled against my hand. The beautiful creature backed away from contact with my palm, white heat disrupting the planned meal. A quick shot of flame at a nearby bramble provided a deterrent, ousting two fat hares, eyes narrowed on the pouncing wolf. Smoke billowed in slight waves as I tamped out any hope of fire spreading.

The child watched the animals chase away, green eyes coming to rest on me. She smiled, approaching. I held out my arms as she fell into my embrace, tiny hands grasping fistfuls of my hair. I breathed in the scent of true contentment, innocence, and love, rocking her.

"Wolf!" A man neared quickly, followed by his mate. I stole a last, sweet breath, prying tiny, reluctant finger loose of my robe and hair, grasping a small hand in mine. I bowed my head, waiting.

The woman screamed. I remained still, youthful innocence next to me seeing tranquility in my beautiful, human form, and tainted humanity seeing a winged, leathered beast grasping the hand of their offspring.

"Aine!" The woman wept. I shook loose of the baby's grasp, willing her to her mother. Tiny feet stepped away. The man drew an arrow and snapped it at an impressive speed at my plated chest. The projectile puffed into flame as I batted it down and defied earthen gravity, taking flight. Wind buffeted the tiny one's frock as my wings beat air. The family ran from me.

I wept for ages. My dark, winged form became the stuff of haunted, human minds, transcending their sense of time as my likeness was communicated through centuries— engraved, sculpted, sketched, mounted to advancing architecture. Titled.

Gargoyle.

But I was eternally more. I saved another child, rescued her as her consciousness threatened to abandon life. I wouldn't give away the love of another without a fight this time. I fused our existence.

An annoyance, her physical pain was dissolved. I rested deep within, next to her tiny, lively heart, keeping a watch as humanity claimed our small form. They took us to the safety of harmlessly confused religion that was a suitable safekeeping. I knew happiness in her growth. I love her. . . .

"Tessa!" Peter called, ripping me back toward the ground.

I focused on nothing but the book in my lap, opened to the first, blank page. We were reunited, a forsaken bond replaced. This was the family I searched for, my home. I belonged in the vast possibilities of what the many pages held. They were the stuff of my existence. There was a need of nothing, and I ached for no fulfillment, having found the source of all I desired. I flipped another leaf, to find more gleaming, untouched vellum. Pristine, unmarked pages replaced etchings I expected to remain. Three words formed in fine silvery print, as if an unseen quill marked the parchment.

"*Bandia na Teasa*," I read out loud. I read it again, a little faster. They were the words the man who'd burned in my dreams said before he caught fire. He'd bent the last word, "Teasa", pronouncing it as my name, Tessa. New words appeared. *"We long for your return."* The tome belonged with me. Pages would soon hold my will once more. I was so very misunderstood by everyone around me.

"Tessa!" A familiar voice pulled at me from outside. I yearned to follow, closing the cover, willing myself to return to him.

Chaos erupted around my small form back in the courtyard as I sat cradling the huge book to my chest.

"Tessa!" Peter called again.

"I'm here." He searched for me, frantic until his eyes met mine.

"Bloody hell, Tessa, hide that thing." His eyes shot to the horizon as the sun winked out, silver light glinting through trees. "Get to the car, now!"

I ran hard toward the Aston on winged, light feet, feeling amazing although dried blood and fluid cracked and clung to my skin and hair. I sprinted to the garage-side of the car, knelt, and slipped the book inside, clicking the door latch softly.

My skin tingled as scales erupted across my body. Gloaming closed the day and ushered in sweet nightfall. Wings unfurled at my back, yearning to chase wind. The twilit grounds became heavily contrast in my focus. I'd changed quickly being amped up, barely feeling the transformation.

I'd never watched Peter change before. He became a gargoyle in under a second, taking to the air in the process. There was a huge size difference in his human form and his gargoyle. He twisted to look above his head.

The air became thick with the sound of beating of wings. Three soaring forms circled the courtyard. Peter reacted quickly, pumping his wings, gaining altitude above the grounds.

Hamish's sword dropped to the turf from Petra's clawed grip with a muffled, metallic *thump*. Serpentine eyes watched the circling gargoyles. She snarled low, taking flight. Petra picked up speed at an amazing rate, gaining altitude and smashing into one of the scouting gargoyles like a hawk hitting a pigeon. They tangled in the air, tearing at scaled flesh with talons, shrieking. The two bodies plummeted to the ground in front of the house, brawling as if they didn't notice the fall. Petra suffered a punch to the throat as the other gargoyle took flight, jetting into the cover of trees beyond the manor. She rolled to her feet, launching herself in the direction the other had fled.

Peter neared another gargoyle, soaring fast, claws distended in front of his body. Just as he grew near, a larger gargoyle hit him with the force and sound of two cars colliding, knocking him away from his intended target. The two churned in the air, audibly landing blows against plated flesh. They spiraled in the air, losing control of flight. The two winged bodies smashed down onto the roof of the house, rolling to the ground with the clatter of armored bodies, nearly crushing the small form of a human huddled against the wall.

"Brea!" I drew a tight breath. Time stilled as I searched the scene around her. Gargoyles were really close. Fear for her life took me back to feeling like a helpless human in a beat. I prayed she stayed close to the house for cover.

No such luck. When Peter and the other gargoyle fell in front of her, she screamed, running from the tussle, putting her frail human body in plain sight of everything on the grounds and in the air.

"No! Brea!" I screamed toward her. She acted like she hadn't heard me, turning in a circle as she watched the darkening sky above her. The gargoyle Peter had missed in the sky twisted in the air, changing the trajectory of flight when he saw her. He laughed. Looking at the car, Brea took off toward me at a dead run. My clawed feet tore at the gravel as I leapt into the air. I beat my wings as hard as I could, doing my best to keep level and stay against the ground rather than get higher in the air. It worked. I sped toward Brea.

So did the other gargoyle. He'd seen me and was plummeting from the sky straight at us.

"Nooo . . . ," I moaned as I sped up. I had to make it to Brea before he did. If he hit her with the force and speed he had behind him it would end her. I quit watching him and locked my eyes on Brea. She'd seen me coming and was running hard toward me. Her eyes were frantic. I hated seeing her so scared. I extended my arms, ready to catch her hands.

Airborne bodies collided above us in the fading light when Brea and I grabbed onto each other. "Get her out of here, Tessa," Osgar yelled from above us. He hit the other gargoyle with such force that they shot away from us, onto the grass where they fought like animals, tearing at each other.

My claws scratched the flesh of Brea's forearms as I clutched her protectively to my chest and flew as hard as I could toward the garage. She clung to my shoulders, feeling tiny in my grip. I needed to get her to the car.

"You made it!" She cried between ragged breaths.

"Barely," I said.

I alit between the Aston and the garage wall, setting her gently on the ground. I squatted, furling my wings.

"Get in the car and stay down, okay?"

She nodded and hopped in. "Be careful Tessa! Get Peter and let's get out of here!" She sounded impossibly young with so much fear in her voice. I wondered if I'd ever been that young. The door clicked shut and I heard the lock sound. Brea was out of sight behind the dark tinted glass. I turned to find Peter.

I stilled. The blood in my veins iced.

A gargoyle I'd seen in the long hall the day I found Hamish and the others dining on human flesh stood in front of the car, tail lashing, a long, heavy sword held in a clawed grip. A black gaze looked from me to the backseat, where I'd stashed Brea and the book. Stalking forward, it peered darkly at me with undersized, gleaming eyes from beneath a lowered brow. A pair of glistening, black horns jutted from its forehead while it examined my small existence.

Seeing myself as a beast's prey was an eye opener. The monster gargoyle seemed to have lost what humanity it once had. If any.

I stepped closer to the car. The thing was going to have to go through me to get to Brea. Not that it appeared to be a difficulty. The beast towered above me, drawing nearer. Adrenaline surged, making me tremble. I did my best to look bigger, curling my claws into fists and unfurling my wings. "Get back," I growled.

The beast let its head roll back laughing, an ancient evil thing, a demon that matched its appearance. Lowering its face again, it continued to smile wickedly, bringing the blade into view between us. Stepping back, it leveled the sword at shoulder height, measuring me out.

"Kai isn't around to protect you now, is he?"

I hadn't thought of it that way at all. Maybe Kai had been holding the monsters up there at bay. I hiccupped, instantly hating my nervous tick. It laughed again.

This thing is going to end me.

I swung a fist hard on impulse, connecting fast with its jaw. I screamed, which came out more like a lethal sounding siren. I pounded it with another fist, rocking the monster's head to the side. I used my wings each time I swung to reach, taking flight and putting as much momentum as I could behind each strike. The thing didn't try to stop me from hitting it. Instead, it smiled.

Infuriated, I stepped back, breathing hard. Blood dripped from one of its nostrils, gleaming black in the low light, matching the color of the things scales. I glared.

The thick blade flashed in warning before it swung, I crouched, ready to dodge or to feel the cold bite somewhere in my flesh. Somehow it missed. The blade whipped through the air at an awkward angle, flying far off target.

The gargoyle spun away from me to face another of equal size. Light grey scales gleamed as the new gargoyle stalked forth. Sword held high, it wasted no time laying into the brute, striking two rapid blows into the dark flesh of the other.

I backed away as a lethal sword fight took place between the silver toned gargoyle and the ebony scaled beast who'd intended to chop me up with a sword. The new guy was much faster on his feet. The fight would be over quickly. Dark blood splattered the Aston and the gravel with each slicing, sword strike.

"Run, Tessa," a familiar voice urged, mid-swing.

"Crispin!" I was amazed. He didn't respond, continuing to dodge the strikes of the lumbering black gargoyle.

I leapt into the air, looking back once as he ended the fight, severing the blocky head from the dark gargoyle's body with a graceful, spinning slash of his sword. I'd just seen a warrior in action. He'd saved my life.

Fighting erupted across the grounds like hot spots in a grass fire. The sickening sounds of fists and claws striking bodies, screams of triumph and pain, and the clashing of airborne gargoyles created a din that brought my senses to a new level of awareness. Things were dying, and others were killing. Distant moonglow was the only light on the grounds and that, together with my amped up gargoyle sight, still didn't make it easy to see everything that went on. I suspected every noise in the darkness, and tried to look everywhere all at once.

Osgar still fought against the gargoyle that nearly caught up with Brea. The two grappled furiously, with Osgar holding his own. He placed a kick to the other gargoyle's midsection, causing him to double over for a millisecond before he turned to try to fly away.

Osgar fought to hold on to the other when it fled, losing his grip on first a bloodied arm, then a forked tail. The other gargoyle kicked and beat his wings hard, breaking Osgar's hold. He soared into the darkness, vanishing from sight. I flew toward the house to find Peter in the melee.

Something reflected silvery in the moonlight below me. I dipped close to the grass, seeing my dirk winking at me like a little beacon. I snatched it from the ground without landing.

Peter fought with a different gargoyle. The one that had hit him in the air lay unmoving on the grass. He saw me nearing him and called out, mid-swing. "Tessa! Get down!"

I turned in the air, too late to avoid getting hit. A missile knocked me to the ground. I tumbled on the grass with another gargoyle. We wrestled, flashing from human form back to gargoyle when we grew close enough. I struggled to get a clear view of my assailant, but I was crushed against the ground right then, my neck held firmly under the other gargoyle's elbow. I twisted hard, trying to smash to any body part in reach while I sliced at anything with my dagger. I managed to get an arm between us, and planted a knee in the grass, flipping us over. I bit down hard when part of a wing covered my face. We rolled over, clawing at each other. I was struck so hard in the abdomen that reflex pulled me into a tight ball. My back and ribs took two additional kicks. I screamed, trying to get up. Something cracked hard against my face and the world went fuzzy. I covered my head with my arms, becoming familiar once more with the possibility of my own death.

"Get off her," Peter growled low. I didn't move my claws from my face but I'd never been so happy to hear Peter's voice. The other gargoyle grunted and his weight lifted from my back. I chanced a look to see Peter fling him to the ground beside me. I rolled away and managed to get to my feet while I watched Peter pummel the other gargoyle. Soon, it quit moving.

Peter looked at me, drawing quick breaths. He walked toward me. "You all right?" he asked, reaching.

"Yeah," I said quietly. I was dizzy and exhausted. My back and wings hurt and I tasted blood again. He pulled me vertical and my head screamed.

The sound of wings huffed overhead. I fought off vertigo and a pounding cranium, searched the dark sky. The silhouette of a single gargoyle flew over the circle of stones beyond, followed by two more. When they'd flown out of sight, I followed Peter into the air toward the manor to find Petra. She stood beside Osgar, along with Crispin and another gargoyle I'd never met. Two more landed with them before we touched down. Our war was over, and it appeared we'd won.

CHAPTER 32

*M*orning sunshine glinted across dew covered grass as I blew warm air onto my numb fingers, wishing I had a sense of control over my burst of heat. Just as quickly as the sun lit the sky, clouds took the light into gloom. Ironically, I wasn't tired at all. I was a little sore in places, but the transformation had healed my wounds for the most part. My emotions drug through the morning, hanging up on any little thing. We'd spent the night constructing a funeral pyre.

The bodies of fallen gargoyles rested atop the tall arrangement of brush and poles. Ravenous flame consumed the wooden stand like manna. In moments, fire licked at the mourning sky. Shadows ricocheted between the standing monoliths of the sacred circle.

Solemn faces encircled the cremation from a distance. Some mourned, and we all paid respect. Peter stood between Petra and I. Brea leaned close and gripped my hand.

Crispin stood next to Osgar, who looked at me and bowed his head, closing his eyes for a brief moment. I didn't know what to say, honored by his actions. The last time I'd seen he and Osgar, they were in direct sunlight so I couldn't tell what they looked like as humans. Crispin was taller with green eyes and freckles that matched his auburn hair. Osgar's ice blue eyes could melt fog. He was the first man I'd seen wear a kilt. Standing a few inches shorter than Crispin did nothing to diminish his athletic build and the way I'd seen the warrior side of him, fighting to free his home and family.

Peter broke away from us. He took the torc from his neck and handed it to Osgar, who bowed his head again, sliding the twisting, thin metal cuff around his throat. No words passed between them. Peter dipped his head slowly, then returned to stand beside me. I gripped his hand tight, tears filling my eyes. They were all hurting, and I hadn't been able to meet any who'd died so the rest of us could live on. There was some guilt attached to that.

Peter pulled his hand away from mine, replacing it a second later with a cold, silver pocket watch. I recognized it as Ezra's, from the first time we'd spoken, what seemed like a year ago.

"He'd want you to have it," Peter said before I could refuse. "He gave me my timepiece when I was young. He thought of you as family."

The gesture did the trick, pushing me over the emotional edge. Tears ran freely. It wouldn't have done any good to try to stop them. An odd sense of relief prevailed, letting emotion show rather than keeping it bottled up. I slid my hand inside my pocket, keeping the watch wrapped in my grip.

The fire hissed, the heat of flame growing as it lusted over its newborn life.

* * *

LIFE'S BALL field had changed entirely, with a whole new roster of players, for me especially.

Magical, unexplainable things lived among us.

I hadn't slept well after the fight that day. Seeing that much death and almost being one of the dead, twice, rattled me. I was grateful for sunrise.

A breeze filtered through my hair, reviving my spirits some. I walked the grounds, enjoying the magnificent gardens without Kai's shadow dulling out natural beauty. When I'd first arrived, the place had seemed shrouded by an overlying air of darkness, but it became brighter, as if a breath of new life had been pumped into the environment. I saw potential, rather than waste. I broke into a run, skirting the ruined castle wall, rethinking the events of the last week.

A grove of trees crowded the stones so I cut through them. Lush forest created a canopy. The trees breathed with happily buzzing wildlife. Insects chirped and birds flitted from limbs. I stopped running, standing still and enjoying my time in the moment. Low branches created passages, tucked away beside thickets entwined with ivy. Trails were beat into the grass, weaving around the bases of trees and through tunnels in brush. I began to walk, stepping outside the cover to see the bluest expanse of still water sparkling with dappled sunlight.

The castle had been constructed on a hillside, and just below lapped the crystal clear waters of Loch Ore. Tears burned the back of my eyes as the artistry of my surroundings inspired awe at the powers of nature. I was humbled. Change had brought me there against the will of Fate. Somewhere, something vast and controlling graced my small existence with the ability to continue, and the presence of mind to acknowledge a blessing when I saw it. There was magic in such beauty.

I pulled myself away to go back inside, breaking into a run again to make good time getting back. I couldn't wait to show Peter what I'd found on the west side of the castle ruins.

I skirted the main hall, overhearing a bit of conversation between Petra, Osgar and Peter.

"There's no way he's dead," Peter said, pointedly.

"The hunt will heal Ezra. 'T'will take time." Osgar's voice was reassuring.

"How could you possibly know that?" Petra asked.

I slowed my pace a little, hoping to hear the answer. Petra's tone might have been condescending, but she had a good question.

A moment of silence ensued. Finally, Peter answered. "A druid. He continues with the old practices. Shape shifting included."

I kept walking, making a mental note to pursue that information later. Scents of nutmeg and cinnamon warmed the air as I continued the short distance to the kitchen. I pulled a bottle of water from the refrigerator and leaned against the cabinet. Not knowing so much about the world I'd been brought into was intimidating, in a way. I'd read about druids. I hadn't realized I'd meet one in an urban setting while shopping for a good book.

I sipped my water, cooling down from running, pondering the way I viewed the existence of the human race. Some of the vastness was gone. The species hardly rested at the top of the figurative food chain, or held the title for being the most powerful. As a human, I'd been subject to the whims of the universe.

The counter tops gleamed in the sunken lighting of the kitchen. The beautiful manor would be leveled and that was a shame, but I completely understood the motivation. Clan Logan, as I'd learned, was free. They would rebuild Castle Logan and rid the grounds of anything Kai had built in the midst of their home.

"What's wrong, Tessa?" Peter asked. He leaned against the refrigerator, looking at me intently.

I couldn't help but smile. Peter was magnetic. I searched the warm expression on his handsome face. The dark outline surrounding the light grey part of his eyes contrasted intensely. He'd let his hair hang loose over his shoulders. He really could make my mouth water.

He smiled wide. He knew it.

"Nothing's really wrong, I just have a lot to think about. Sort of an identity crisis, I guess." I laughed a little. "I've learned a lot about myself since I got here."

"Anything I might be able to help with?"

"I don't know, Peter. It's stuff like, why magic doesn't work on me, along with Kai telling me I am an old soul . . . why the book likes me enough to let me open it and the memories or flashbacks I've been having. They belong to someone else, a really, really old presence in my mind. It's all got me confused and worried, I guess."

"Were you able to read from the book?"

"That's the thing," I said, peering up at him. "I was able to open it, but it only said a couple of things."

"What were they?"

"'Bandia na Teasa', was the first thing, like that was my name. Then it said, 'We long for your return'."

"Where did you hear that?" Osgar had just come into the kitchen. "Sorry, I wasn't trying to overhear, you said that when I walked in," he explained.

I smiled at him. "It was written in the book when I opened it. Or, well, it formed on the page while I watched it being written, if that makes sense."

Osgar looked from me to Peter and back. "Do you know what that means?" He asked.

"Well, obviously the first part of it is a name," Peter added.

"I don't know," I added. It was hard to sound sure of myself. "I remember a man in a dream I had saying it to me once recently."

"It means to Goddess of Warmth. Some translations may cite it as Goddess of Fire."

No one spoke for a moment. I toed the tile, thinking, trying to digest what he was telling me. I didn't feel much like a Goddess of anything, if that's what the book, Osgar and the burning man from my dream were trying to tell me.

"This is just nuts." I looked up at Osgar.

He shook his head. "Crazy how you'll buy in to little things and others suffer the need to convince you the hard way."

"My life is just one big freaking learning curve, these days," I retorted. I was going to need some major convincing to believe I was a reincarnated goddess of anything besides bad luck.

"I have something that may help," he said. "I'll be right back."

Osgar walked from the room. I sighed really loudly without realizing it until Peter glanced at me.

"It can't be all bad. Try to stop with the gloom and doom."

"Why do you do that?"

"Why must you look at the worst in any situation?" he countered.

"That's over-the-top judgmental of you." It wasn't him with the problems.

"I think it would be best to listen to what Osgar can offer," he said, adding a little sympathy to his words. "And we can't ignore the fevers and the other anomalies. Ezra saw things in you from the start."

The word "anomalies" bothered me. A lot.

Crispin stuck his head into the kitchen. "Osgar's asking for you two in the library." I walked toward the stairs, apprehension building like I was in trouble for something when I was a kid. One time I'd got into trouble at the Home during lunch. I'd eaten my whole meal and I was still hungry. They'd given us bananas that day, whole, big ripe ones that were delicious and quite the treat. I figured one more banana would fill me up. I went to the kitchen and put my tray on a stack of dirties, turned to the lady who'd served us our food and told her a bold-faced lie about how I'd dropped my peeled banana on the floor and had to throw it away. She gave me another. I don't know why I didn't stop to think that one of the nuns in the room could have been watching while I ate the first one. At any rate, I got caught lying, and had to wait a half hour before they decided my punishment.

I had the same feeling walking up the stairs to hear who Osgar deemed I had been in a previous life. It was the same as when I turned to walk back to my seat holding the stolen banana. I was at the mercy of the forces that existed around me.

CHAPTER 33

Osgar sat on the big chair by the library kitchenette, having drug a massive table between two more chairs. Open volumes were strewn around and he eagerly waved us over to sit.

I began looking at some of the articles, cocking my head and picking out words here and there. We waited for Osgar to finish reading the page he was on.

"Teigan knows the lore front and back." The three of us glanced up at Crispin, who looked like he wished he'd kept his mouth shut.

"Who's Teigan?" I waited for an answer from Crispin but he didn't say anything else.

"He's my brother." Osgar finally said. He put his nose right back in the book.

I wanted to ask if he was around, but was afraid "Teigan" was one of the casualties during the fight. My face must have betrayed me because Crispin answered the question.

"It was his turn in the cell." Crispin sighed, dragging another chair close by. "Poetic really, since he always tried to get us all to allow him our turn inside."

"What's poetic?" And why hadn't they opened the "cell" if Kai was gone? A raw feeling started in my stomach, building into a knot. Something wasn't right.

"He volunteered to guard your door the first night after your arrival. That was the night the moon began a new cycle." Osgar looked at me, waiting as I digested what he'd said.

"For my protection." The guy guarding me that night had been one of the good guys after all. He'd tried so hard to make me realize I should stay inside, to keep safe, even roughed me up some to make me reconsider an escape.

"You must to be taught so many things, and need to remember so many more, lass." I hadn't understood then. Teigan did know things about me, and about this goddess we researched. He'd spent his last free night protecting me from the evils at The Grotto, and I'd given him nothing but grief for it. I dropped my face in my hands.

"Don't beat yourself up over it. There's no way you could have known if he didn't tell you, Tessa," Peter said.

It was easy for him to say. Guilt would round off the nice gamut of emotions I'd endured over the last few months. I sighed hard. "My God, that sucks." I sat back in the chair, trying to compose myself.

"We all know there's a chance we won't make it out each time we go in, Tessa," Osgar offered. "Teigan may have been gruff, but he meant well. And he was right about you." He tapped the page of the book he held. "I knew I remembered seeing this," he said "This is the only reference I can find about Teasa."

Crispin whistled low. "You're a strong resemblance," he said, looking over my shoulder.

Two drawings dissected the article, one of a gargoyle in flight and the other of a young woman clad in a long wrap of flowing cloth. The sketch was reflective, as if *I* stood there on the page. A crown of small blossoms encircled her head. Hair nearly grazed the ground at her feet. I leaned in closer when I saw the talisman hanging around her neck. An arrangement of feathers shaped the head of an owl around a stone set in the center, like the one worn by the burning man in my dream.

"Who wrote this?" Or at least who *illustrated* the book? The drawing was detailed, sketched with a skilled hand.

"Kai." Osgar looked at me for a second, then nodded. "At some point in time, Kai had seen this goddess. And it wasn't just a glimpse, he'd gotten a good, up-close look."

A red flag flapped at me when remembering the vignette from my encounter opening the book in the courtyard. No other than an innocent child saw the goddess's mortal form. Was Kai different? Could he ever have been an innocent? Or a child, for that matter?

"That talisman is interesting," Peter added.

"Look at that big crystal." Crispin pointed at the drawing.

"It's an amethyst." The words were out of my mouth and gone before I even thought to shut up. There was no bringing them back, like sending an email into cyberspace, realizing it's going to the wrong person. There was nothing to be done but explain. I leaned back in the chair a little. All three men looked at me, expectantly.

"When I nearly died in the cavern, I had a dream. I was in a meadow somewhere, lying in the grass in my human form, although the sun was shining through the trees. An old man knelt in the grass beside me." I swallowed hard, remembering the way he screamed. "He was wearing the same kind of robe and had a matching owl talisman. The stone in the middle there," I nodded toward the page, "is an amethyst."

They were silent, staring.

"What?" I snapped.

"Do you remember anything else?" asked Osgar.

"He said, '*Bandia na Teasa*'," I replied. I sighed. "And he caught on fire."

All three sets of eyes in the room grew wide when I said that last bit.

I frowned, looking at my feet. "It was so real. And that smell," I shook my head to oust the memory. "And then all the birds fell in the water with me and just floated. I couldn't move. I watched the smoke billow up into the trees, and the birds didn't even struggle, they landed in the water and died. Like they'd given up living. It wasn't natural."

"Whoa," said Crispin.

"I really don't want to talk about this anymore," I whispered.

"It's fine." Osgar smiled, warmly.

I moved on to more pressing questions. "Why haven't you released Teigan? Is the cell locked or something? Maybe we could break him out."

"It's not that kind of cell." Crispin gave a sad smile. "It's a veiled place, hidden from sight and sound. We've looked for centuries. You wake up there, then at the end of the cycle, you wake up here."

"So he'll just like, stay there?"

They nodded.

"How? I mean, we can't just leave him." I searched faces. No one spoke.

Osgar sighed, dropping his gaze back to the pages before him. "In a nutshell, this explains that Teasa was a goddess that was celebrated, and feared by the Picts, or the Caledonians. They worshipped Teasa as a daughter of Lugh, the sun god, to provide them with a fertile season for planting. Beltane is her time of power. She is a goddess of warmth with the power to oust winter in the spring, but has also been referenced here as a goddess of fire if she is incited. It might be related to the worry that she wasn't pleased with the offerings they left for her."

"The clans likely thought she was responsible for lightning striking and causing a fire in the spring, or something to do with a disaster that they felt accountable for, if they didn't leave her the best sacrifices at Beltane," Peter added.

"Actually the article references the goddess growing angry and becoming a burning light in the night sky at times," Osgar said, tracing the lines of text with a finger. "This all makes sense considering the wards around here didn't work on you."

"She also sees the Tyrens," Petra said from the doorway. She paced across the floor, sliding into the oversized chair beside Peter.

"Kai mentioned trying some sort of coercion a couple times. He was pissy because it didn't work," I added.

Peter sat up a little straighter. "What sort of coercions," he growled.

"I'm not sure, but I think he wanted me to trust him so I would go to Librorum Taberna and steal the book back for him."

Petra snorted. We all looked at her. "Sorry, that's hilarious. Kai was livid," she said, grinning.

I shook my head at her. "Well, if he knew I had some sort of a tie to *Bandia na Teasa*, that would explain his fixation. I mean I didn't know a thing about it, so I was an easy target."

"It is said Kai killed a clan elder and took the book, someplace close to Hadrian's Wall around 180 AD."

I struggled with that after holding the book, *bonding* with it. For some reason that part of the story didn't sound right. More information never hurt, so I fished. "Where did that book come from, anyway? I mean who wrote it?"

"The Lore states the book was written by a Roman warrior-turned-scribe. It was a journal, of sorts that the scribe added to when coming into contact with the Caledonians. He described the appearances of the inhabitants of Northern Scotland, as well as the rolls and powers of the druids in their society. War broke out between the encroaching Romans and the native Caledonians, and the warrior who'd been recording in the book was killed. His blood spilt across the pages. At the same moment, a Caledonian warrior was struck down, and the life blood of the two mingled, soaking into the pages of that book, creating a sentience of sorts within the pages recording the bloody war."

Osgar looked up from the article sending me a look of warning.

I shrugged a little. Along for the ride. That was me.

He clapped his book shut and continued, reciting from memory. "The book was recovered by none other than Lugh's daughter, *Bandia na Teasa*, who took it to her home in the trees among the Dryads. Kai, a Roman, followed, and when her back was turned, he stole the book and ran. He disappeared for a time, showing up nearly eight centuries later with Hamish as a henchman along with a couple other ancients, tome in hand, chanting his magic and turning Clan Logan into a clan of gargoyles."

Ancients. I got hung up there. "They have horns because they're ancient." I looked at Peter. "You're going to sprout horns," I teased.

"So are you." He smiled curtly.

My grin faded and I put my hands in my lap. "Funcrusher."

Osgar nodded. "They are *very* ancient. After they took the castle, one of the Clan grabbed the book, apparently being able to see through Kai's wards, like you," he gestured to me, "and brought it to London, where a distant descendant named Ezra Finfrock keeps a store of literature."

"And you know the rest of the story," Petra said.

"You must be careful with that book," Osgar warned. "It creates monsters."

"I can handle it," I said. The book had shown me very little in the beginning, and I had no reason it would affect the very depth of my character. I was a good person, and I knew that in my heart. So far, so good. I wasn't going to look at it with a negative light. A token would be paid to use it, but it would be worth it.

My skin began to tingle. The room had begun to darken.

"It's time to turn in. I'll catch you guys in the morning. I stood, heading for the bedroom I'd slept in with Brea, for lack of a better place. I hoped I would be more comfortable there since Kai was gone. All the men in the room stood when I did. "What was Brea doing when you came up, Petra?"

"She's fine. Iain dotes on her as we speak, entertaining her with stories from before the castle was brought down, and what it's like to change into a gargoyle. She's quite interested." Petra grinned.

"I might have something to add." Crispin headed toward the stairs.

"Sure you do." Petra rolled her eyes.

I shook my head, smiling. At least Brea was in good hands.

"I'll fetch her and bring her up soon," Petra added.

"Thank you, Petra." I still didn't get the best vibe from her all the time, and it bothered me a little. But I would want the perfect girl for my brother, too. And neither of us saw me as perfect. Not even close.

Peter intercepted me on the way to the stairs. "You alright?" he whispered against my ear.

"Yeah, I don't want to change in front of everyone. I need to think for a while and let all this gel," I whispered back.

"Okay then. I'll be here in the library if you can't sleep."

"Thank you, Peter." I kissed his cheek. "I'll see you in the morning."

Inside my bedroom at the castle, I shut the door and pulled the book from beneath the bed where I'd stashed it when we'd all come in after the battle. The time had come to have a little heart-to-heart with a Pict and a Roman.

* * *

HEARING MY THIN, streaming voice as a toddler was extremely jarring and surreal, but I had no trouble understanding that it was me I heard when I entered the book's trance, coming-to inside of the earliest childhood memory I'd experienced. The overwhelming smell of spilled gasoline, the lack of light, and confused adults shouting put me right into a horrific scene that I couldn't get my bearings in until an explosion ripped through the darkness, prairie grass and vehicles bursting into raging flames on the roadside.

And my brother was there.

I was confused, bleeding—dying rather, and viewed chaos through the eyes of a baby.

What was that loud boom? And now there is a big fire, too. Hot! Don't touch! And there is a stranger. Robbie's crying and where did Daddy go to get Momma? There are more strangers and now there are amlances and a real fire truck. . . . I got a big bleed now . . . I don't want to sleep now. . .

Robbie's yelling!

"Don't touch her! I'm watching Tessa! Our dad will be right back with our mom and we have to sit right here 'cause we promised."

We're being good and sitting here like Daddy said to. . . .

I HUNG my feet from the tall, ruined rock wall of the castle proper. My running shoes dangled about fifty feet from the grass and brush below. I'd needed a place to be alone and think so I'd climbed the crumbling walls from the inside the ruins, surprised at the height of the castle from the back by Loch Ore. Sun prickled my bare shoulders, reminding me that the tan I used to be so proud of when I was human was destined to fade into sun-damaged, pasty white skin in the immortal shadows.

My mind had opened up to me when I peeled back the heavy, patinaed cover of the ancient book. I had no idea which of the two warriors wrote to me at what time, but they were forthcoming with my answer to the question about where my parents had gone when I was little. They were dead.

I was able to put the pieces together. That's when the goddess had saved me from dying, too.

I was blessed, but wounded. Tears chilled my cheeks in the cool wind gusting up from the surface of the loch. Majestic beauty blended bittersweet with my emotions, making it easy to cry.

The pages of the book were blank after that. I knew it might change, but I was comfortable with it for the time being. The book blessed me by unblocking memories that were too painful for my mind to replay. The tome was a hypnotist. A few of my early memories were free and my question answered like replaying a scene from a movie.

The little blond boy beside me in the orphanage intake photograph sprung to life in my mind's eye, singing Christmas carols while we strung cranberries and popcorn. He popped the head off my favorite baby doll then cried because I cried when he did it. He held my little hands tightly in his determined grip and danced me around a tiny kitchen to Eric Clapton singing "Change the World".

Our dad worked hard. Our mom loved us better than anyone else could have. We lived at the whim of the open road, travelling the country from Daddy's new job, to new job.

I loved the memories despite the pain. Wiping my eyes, I untied my shoes, placed them beside me and stood on the edge of the limestone wall, looking out across the lake at sunset. The wind picked up, gusting through my hair and blowing my stained camisole against my aching chest. I'd never forget the rich, loamy smell of the wind coming off that the loch that day as I continued to replay those memories. I had the answer to where my family had gone. To why I was eventually left with no one.

The fiery wreck that killed our parents destroyed the only home we'd ever known when the truck and travel trailer exploded from the fuel spill. Being a loner and a runaway, our parents loved each other, us kids, and no one else. They were all they had, along with Robbie and me.

The sun set lower and lower in time with the pounding of my heart, winking out as my wings sprouted in lavender twilight. I sucked a chilled breath in through my fangs and smiled.

We'd been fifty-five miles north of Austin, Texas when Change first drew her bow along my strings of time. Fate gave a me a long, slow smile that day, holding my young life, rocking my cradle to the melody of Change. I'd been wrong about them both. Change and I were no strangers, we'd just lost touch. And Fate, well she'd better buckle up. It was time for me to fly.

EPILOGUE

The book sat under my bed, where Ezra had kept it. No one but Peter and I knew. I'd replaced the wards on my own, by simply asking how to do it. I found the ease of power to do that really unsettling. Power created monsters, I'd learned.

I'd asked the pages questions for hours, getting no answers. After a full day of trying I figured it out. The answers weren't the problem, it was the fact that I still asked questions I knew better than asking. My family was gone. That was that. But I wouldn't stop asking about Teigan. I'd shake the book like a Magic 8 Ball until I learned his fate and how to find him.

The tome would not make me all-powerful or all-knowing. I was grateful. That would be a large burden to bear for someone who merely wanted happiness around her. But then, happiness is not a stagnant thing. Most states of mind are fleeting, dependent on other elements. I breathed in deep, steel and resolve behind my desire to be good in the world, and not blight like Kai was.

I will be a blessing, not a bane.

There was one question I managed to get an answer to. The human body would not survive a reversal of base molecular change. My mortality was replaced by a stone statue. I didn't know if anyone else had thought to ask, or if I was ahead of the curve because I had access to the book. I wanted to know if I had the option of being human again. I'd found my answer. We would be gargoyles forever.

Peter approached the window where I stood gazing at beautiful London while she slept. We'd been back for nearly four days, and I'd let the memory from my family's car accident, the one that had claimed the lives of Robbie's and my parents, replay in my mind whenever it started, beginning to end. I didn't cry anymore. A gift shouldn't make me cry.

"How's today?"

"It's good." I couldn't help but smile, remembering the first time I'd seen him. He'd been Garged Out, and had bowed like a Victorian gentleman when he introduced himself to me. This Peter was so different. The playful demeanor was gone, replaced by steel and protective determination. He'd shown me he was brilliant. Timeless.

We'd both changed so much. Old Tessa retained a child's heart, innocent, the center of her own universe, be it a simple one. New Tessa saw what the universe could offer if the right elements and entities aligned. And it scared the hell out of me that I liked it. Peter and I embraced Change, together in our solitude. Destroying the boundaries of youth and fear together.

He must have sensed my thoughts because he pulled one of my hands up to place a soft kiss in my palm. I closed my hand around it.

"Peter," I said quietly. "What am I? Really?" I searched his eyes for tell-tale signs that he knew something he wasn't willing to tell me.

He ran a thumb over my cheek. "We'll figure the rest out as we go." He smiled down at me. "We should get going soon. Quite the drive, yes?"

We'd decided to go back to Logan Castle to bring Petra back to London for a while. I was anxious to see how the rebuild was coming along. I hoped I could help for a while before we headed back to London. I zipped up a lavender hoodie, shouldered my bag, and we headed downstairs.

Brea was at the register, sipping on a mug of hot chocolate. She'd proclaimed Earl Grey "was not very tasty." Her face lit with a smile when she saw me. "Hey!"

Crispin stood behind the counter with her, ready to learn to run the register. I grinned. He was my favorite of the Clan so far. We were becoming good friends. And then there was the fact that he'd saved my life. Big Brownie points for Crispin.

"Did you get ahold of your parents last night?" I asked Brea. She'd been leaving messages since the day we left Scotland. Their housekeeper was in charge because the couple had taken an early season ski trip to Colorado.

"Yes, *finally*. They got the postcard you guys sent out just before they left. Things were a little tense because I only called once after my flight landed, but they're better now. And they like the idea of you and I working at a bookstore in SoHo."

"Nice. We'll get Internet in here so we can Skype with them."

The bard's bells jingled at the shop entrance. Brea stepped around the sales counter to greet the morning patrons. A man stood there, tall and wearing a chopper style hat. He had a silver beard and close cut hair. He wore blue jeans and a white shirt with plain, brown shoes.

Dazed familiarity drew me toward him as Brea pointed my direction, and the man stepped farther inside the bookstore. Bright blue eyes sparkled. A wide smile broke out across his face.

I began to cry and run, dropping my backpack. My beloved Professor Douglas was in London, holding his arms open wide for me to fall right into. He smelled like his office, stale coffee and Old Spice. I crushed myself as close as I could get to him. He chuckled.

Without letting him go, I wiped my eyes, staring up through tears into the white gaze of Ezra Finfrock.

"They say time heals. I doubt that. Time kicks dirt over open sores. They fester, and grow. When opportunity arrives, you do your best, that's the trick. Desperation will create an opportunist in the best of character, Tessa." He rocked me in his arms. "My dear girl."

The End

ABOUT THE AUTHOR

Marie Whittaker is an award-winning essayist and author of urban fantasy, alternative history, children's books, supernatural thrillers, and horror stories. She has enjoyed professions as a truck driver, bartender, and raft guide, and now works as Associate Publisher for WordFire Press. Writing as Amity Green, her debut novel, *Scales*, was released in 2013. A Colorado native, Marie resides in Manitou Springs where she writes and renovates her historic Victorian home. When not writing, she hikes, gardens, and dotes on her family and fur babies.

Join Marie's readers group at mariewhittaker.com.
Follow Marie on Twitter @amitygreenbooks
Follow Marie on Facebook

MARIE WHITTAKER WRITING AS
AMITY GREEN

The Fate and Fire Series
Scales
Phantom Limb Itch
Soul Count (coming soon)

Also by Amity Green
The Witcher Chime: A Haunting

More books here...

www.mariewhittaker.com

www.ingramcontent.com/pod-product-compliance
Lightning Source LLC
Chambersburg PA
CBHW050558260626
47157CB00002B/619